Also by Diana Palmer

Trilby
Lawman
Lacy
Heart of Winter
Outsider
Night Fever
Before Sunrise
Lawless
Diamond Spur
Desperado
The Texas Ranger
Lord of the Desert
The Cowboy and the Lady
Most Wanted
Fit for a King
Paper Rose
Rage of Passion
Once in Paris
After the Music
Roomful of Roses
Champagne Girl
Passion Flower
Diamond Girl
Friends and Lovers
Cattleman's Choice
Lady Love
The Rawhide Man

Coming in March
Man of the Hour
**Two classic novels from bestselling author Diana Palmer
in one great read!**

DIANA PALMER

HQN™

HQN™

ISBN-13: 978-0-373-77255-1
ISBN-10:   0-373-77255-6

LONG, TALL TEXAN LEGACY

Copyright © 2007 by Harlequin Books S.A.

The publisher acknowledges the copyright holder
of the individual works as follows:

THE FOUNDING FATHER
Copyright © 2003 by Diana Palmer

JUSTIN
Copyright © 1988 by Diana Palmer

www.HQNBooks.com

Printed in U.S.A.

Contents

The Founding Father

It took a lot to make Big John Jacobs nervous. He was tall, rawboned, with deep-set green eyes the color of bottle glass, and thick dark brown hair. His lean, rough face had scars left over from the War Between the States. He carried scars both inside and out. He was originally from Georgia, but he'd come to Texas just after the war. Now he lived in one of the wildest parts of southeast Texas on a ranch he'd inherited from his late uncle. He was building up the ranch frugally, heading cattle drives to Kansas and buying livestock with the proceeds. What he had was very little to show for fifteen years of hard work, but he was strong and had a good business head. He'd tripled his uncle's land holdings and bought new bulls from back East to breed with his mangy longhorns. His mother would have been proud.

He noted the deep cut on his left hand, a scar from a knife fight with one of a band of Comanches who'd raided his property for horses. John and his hired help had fought them to a standstill and put them on the run. His ranch was isolated and he had good breeding stock. Over the years he'd had to fight roaming Comanche raiders and renegades from over the Mexican border, as well as carpetbaggers. If it hadn't been for the military presence just after the war ended, courtesy of the Union Army, lawlessness would have been even worse.

John had more reason than most to hate Union officers. But in the part of Texas where his ranch was located, to the southeast of San Antonio, the peace had been kept during Reconstruction by a local commandant who was a gentleman. John had admired the Union officer, who'd caught and prosecuted a thief who stole two horses from the ranch. They were good horses, with excellent bloodlines, which John had purchased from a Kentucky Thoroughbred farm. The officer, who rode a Kentucky Thoroughbred of his own, understood the attachment a rancher felt to his blood stock. John had rarely been more grateful to another human being. Like John himself, the officer was fearless.

Fearless. John laughed at his own apprehension over

what he was about to do. He didn't mind risking his life to save his ranch. But this was no fight with guns or knives. It was a much more civilized sort of warfare. In order to win this battle, John was going to have to venture into a world he'd never seen close up. He wasn't comfortable with high society folk. He hoped he wasn't going to embarrass himself.

He removed his dress hat and ran a big hand through his sweaty brown hair. He'd had Juana cut it before he'd left the 3J Ranch. He hoped it was conservative enough to impress old man Terrance Colby. The railroad magnate was vacationing in Sutherland Springs, not far from the 3J. The popular resort boasted over one hundred separate springs in a small area. John had ridden out there to speak to Colby, without a single idea of how he was going to go about it. He had figured the details would work themselves out if he made the trip.

He was uneasy in company. He'd had to pawn his grandfather's watch to buy the used suit and hat he was wearing. It was a gamble he was taking, a big one. Cattle were no good to anyone if they couldn't be gotten to market. Driving cattle to the railheads in Kansas was becoming ever more dangerous. In some areas, fear of Texas tick fever had caused armed blockades of farmers to deter Texas cattle from entry. If he was going to get his cattle to market, there had to be a more direct route.

He needed a railroad spur close by. Colby owned a railroad. He'd just announced his intentions of expanding it to connect with San Antonio. It would be no great burden to extend a line down through Wilson County to the Jacobs' ranch. There were other ranchers in the area who also wanted the spur.

Old man Colby had a daughter, Camellia Ellen, who was unmarried and apparently unmarriageable. Local gossip said that the old man had no use for his unattractive daughter and would be happy to be rid of her. She got in the way of his mistresses. So Big John Jacobs had come a courting, to get himself a railroad…

It started raining just as he got to town. He cursed his foul luck, his green eyes blazing as he noted the mud his horse's hooves was throwing up and splattering onto his boots and the hem of the one good pair of pants he owned. He'd be untidy, and he couldn't afford to be. Terrance Colby was a New York aristocrat who, from what John had heard, was always impeccably dressed. He was staying at the best hotel the little resort of Sutherland Springs could boast, which was none too luxurious. Rumor was that Colby had come here on a hunting trip and was taking the waters while he was in the area.

John swung down out of the saddle half a block from the hotel Colby was staying at, hoping to have a chance to brush the mud off himself. Just as he got onto the boardwalk, a carriage drew up nearby. A young woman of no particular note climbed down out of it, caught the hem of her dress under her laced shoe, and fell face-first into a mud puddle.

Unforgivably, John laughed. He couldn't help it. The woman's companion gave him a glare, but the look he gave the woman was much more expressive.

"For God's sake, woman, can't you take two steps without tripping over your own garments?" the man asked in a high-pitched British accented voice. "Do get up. Now that we've dropped you off in town, I must go. I've an engagement for which you've already made me late. I'll call on your father later. Driver, carry on!"

The driver gave the woman and Big John a speaking look, but he did as he was instructed. John took note of the stranger, and hoped to meet him again one day.

He moved to the woman's side, and offered her an arm.

"No, no," she protested, managing to get to her feet alone. "You're much too nicely dressed to let me splatter you. Do go on, sir. I'm simply clumsy, there's no cure to be had for it, I'm afraid." She adjusted her oversized hat atop the dark bun of her hair and looked at him with miserable blue eyes in a pleasant but not very attractive face. She was slight and thin, and not the sort of woman to whom he'd ever been attracted.

"Your companion has no manners," he remarked.

"Thank you for your concern."

He tipped his hat. "It was no trouble. I wouldn't have minded being splattered. As you can see, I've already sampled the local mud."

She laughed and her animated face took on a fey quality, of which she was unaware. "Good day."

"Good day."

She moved away and he started into the barbershop to put himself to rights.

"John!" a man called from nearby. "Thought that was you," a heavyset man with a badge panted as he came up to join him. It was Deputy Marshal James Graham, who often stopped by John's ranch when he was in the area looking for fugitives.

They shook hands. "What are you doing in Sutherland Springs?" John asked him.

"I'm looking for a couple of renegades," he said. "They were hiding in Indian Territory, but I heard from a cousin of one of them that they were headed this way, trying to outrun the army. You watch your back."

"You watch yours," he retorted, opening his jacket to display the Colt .45 he always wore in a holster on a gunbelt slung across his narrow hips.

The marshal chuckled. "I heard that. Noticed you were trying to help that poor young woman out of a fix."

"Yes, poor little thing," he commented. "Nothing to look at, and of little interest to a man. Two left feet into the bargain. But it was no trouble to be kind to her. Her companion gave her no more help than the rough edge of his tongue."

"That was Sir Sydney Blythe, a hunting companion of the railroad magnate, Colby. They say the girl has a crush on him, but he has no use for her."

"Hardly surprising. He might have ended in the mud puddle," he added on a chuckle. "She's not the sort to inspire passion."

"You might be surprised. My wife is no looker, but can she cook! Looks wear out. Cooking lasts forever. You remember that. See you around."

"You, too." John went on into the barbershop unaware of a mud-covered female standing behind the corner, trying to deal with wiping some of the mud from her heavy skirt.

She glared at the barbershop with fierce blue eyes. So he was that sort of a man, was he, pitying the poor little scrawny hen with the clumsy feet. She'd thought he was different, but he was just the same as other men. None of them looked twice at a woman unless she had a beautiful face or body.

She walked past the barbershop toward her hotel, seething with fury. She hoped that she might one day have the chance to meet that gentleman again when she was properly dressed and in her own element. It would be a shock for him, she felt certain.

A short while later John walked toward the Sutherland Springs Hotel with a confidence he didn't really feel. He was grateful for the marshal's conversation, which helped calm him. He wondered if Colby's daughter was also enamoured of the atrocious Sir Sydney, as well as that poor scrawny hen who'd been out riding with him? He wasn't certain how he would have to go about wooing such a misfit, although he had it in mind.

At thirty-five, John was more learned than many of his contemporaries, having been brought up by an educated mother who taught him Latin while they worked in the fields. Since then, he'd been educated in other ways while trying to keep himself clothed and fed. His married sister, the only other survivor of his family, had tried to get him to come and work with her husband in North Carolina on their farm, but he hadn't wanted to settle in the East. He was a man with a dream. And if a man could make himself a fortune with nothing more than hard work and self-denial, he was ready to be that man.

It seemed vaguely dishonest to take a bride for monetary reasons, and it cut to the quick to pretend an affection he didn't feel to get a rich bride. If there was an honest way to do this, he was going to find it. His one certainty was that if he married a railroad tycoon's daughter, he had a far better chance of getting a railroad to lay tracks to his ranch than if he simply asked for help. These days, nobody rushed to help a penniless rancher. Least of all a rich Northerner.

John walked into the hotel bristling with assumed self-confidence and the same faint arrogance he'd seen rich men use to get their way.

"My name is John Jacobs," he told the clerk formally. "Mr. Colby is expecting me."

That was a bald lie, but a bold one. If it worked, he could cut through a lot of time-wasting protocol.

"Uh, he is? I mean, of course, sir," the young man faltered. "Mr. Colby is in the presidential suite. It's on the second floor, at the end of the hall. You may go right up. Mr. Colby and his daughter are receiving this morning."

Receiving. Go right up. John nodded, dazed. It was easier than he'd dreamed to see one of the country's richest men!

He nodded politely at the clerk and turned to the staircase.

The suite was easy to find. He knocked on the door confidently, inwardly gritting his teeth to gear himself up for the meeting. He had no idea what he was going to give as an excuse for coming here. He didn't know what Ellen Colby looked like. Could he perhaps say that he'd seen her from afar and had fallen madly in love with her at once? That would certainly ruin his chances with her father, who would be convinced that he only wanted Ellen's money.

While he was thinking up excuses, a maid opened the door and stood back to let him inside. Belatedly he swept off his hat, hoping his forehead wasn't sweating as profusely as it felt.

"Your name, sir?" the middle-aged woman asked politely.

"John Jacobs," he told her. "I'm a local landowner," he added.

She nodded. "Please wait here."

She disappeared into another room behind a closed door. Seconds passed, while John looked around him uncomfortably, reminded by the opulence of the suite how far removed he was from the upper class.

The door opened. "Please go in, sir," the maid said respectfully, and even smiled at him.

Elated, he went into the room and stared into a pair of the coldest pale blue eyes he'd ever seen, in a face that seemed unremarkable compared to the very expensive lacy white dress worn by its owner. She had a beautiful figure, regardless of her lack of beauty. Her hair was thick and a rich dark brown, swept up into a high bun that left a roll of it all around her head. She was very poised, very elegant and totally hostile. With a start, John recognized her. She was the mud puddle swimmer from the hotel entrance.

He must not laugh, he must not...! But a faint grin split his chiseled lips and his green eyes danced on her indignant features. Here was his excuse, so unexpected!

"I came to inquire about your health," he said, his voice deep and lazy. "The weather is cold, and the mud puddle was very large...."

"I am..." She was blushing, now apparently flattered by his visit. "I am very well. Thank you!"

"What mud puddle?" came a crisp voice from the doorway. A man, shorter than John, with balding hair and dark blue eyes, dressed in an expensive suit, came into the room. "I'm Terrance Colby. Who are you?"

"John Jacobs," he introduced himself. He wasn't certain how to go on. "I own a ranch outside town..." he began.

"Oh, you're here about quail hunting," Colby said immediately. He smiled, to John's astonishment, and went forward to shake hands. "But I'm afraid you're a few minutes too late. I've already procured an invitation to the Four Aces Ranch to hunt antelope and quail. You know it, I expect?"

"Certainly I do, sir," John replied. And he did. That ranch was the sort John wanted desperately to own one day, a huge property with purebred cattle and horses, known all over the country—in fact, all over the world! "I'm sure you'll find the accommodations superior."

The older man eyed him curiously. "Thank you for the offer."

John nodded. "My pleasure, sir. But I had another purpose in coming. A passerby mentioned that the young lady here was staying at this hotel. She, uh, had a bad fall on her way inside. I assisted her. I only wanted to assure myself that she was uninjured. Her companion was less than helpful," he added with honest irritation.

"Sir Sydney drove off and left me there," the woman said angrily with flashing eyes.

Colby gave her an unsympathetic glance. "If you will be clumsy and throw yourself into mud puddles, Ellen, you can expect to be ignored by any normal man."

Ellen! This unfortunate little hen was the very heiress John had come to town to woo, and he was having more good fortune than he'd dreamed! Lady Luck was tossing offerings into his path with every word he spoke.

He smiled at Ellen Colby with deliberate interest. "On the contrary, sir, I find her enchanting," he murmured.

Colby looked at him as if he expected men with nets to storm the room.

Ellen gave him a harsh glare. She might have been flattered by the visit, but she knew a line when she heard one. Too many men had sought access to her father through her. Here was another, when she'd hoped he might like her for herself. But when had that ever happened? Disappointed, she drew herself up to her full height. "Please excuse me. I am in the middle of important work." She lifted her chin and added deliberately, "My father's dog is having her bath."

She turned and stalked toward a door between rooms, while John threw back his head and laughed with genuine glee.

Colby had to chuckle, himself, at his daughter's audacity. She never raised her voice, as a rule, and he'd long since come to think of her as a doormat. But this man pricked her temper and made her eyes flash.

"An interesting reaction," he told John. "She is never rude, and I cannot remember a time when she raised her voice."

John grinned. "A gentleman likes to think that he has made an impression, sir," he said respectfully. "Your daughter is far more interesting with a temper than without one. To me, at least."

"You have a ranch, you said?" Colby asked.

John nodded. "A small one, but growing. I have begun to cross breeds to good effect. I have a longhorn seed bull and a small herd of Hereford cattle. I hope to raise a better sort of beef to suit Eastern tastes and ship it to market in Chicago."

The older man sized up his guest, from the worn, but still useful, shoes and suit and the well-worn gunbelt and pistol worn unobtrusively under the open jacket.

"You have a Southern accent," Colby said.

John nodded again. "I am a Georgian, by birth."

Colby actually winced.

John laughed without humor. "You know, then, what Sherman and his men did to my state."

"Slavery is against everything I believe in," Colby said. His face grew hard. "Sherman's conduct was justified."

John had to bite his tongue to keep back a sharp reply. He could feel the heat of the fire, hear his mother and sister screaming as they fell in the maelstrom of crackling flames....

"You owned slaves?" Colby persisted curtly.

John gritted his teeth. "Sir, my mother and sisters and I worked on a farm outside Atlanta," he said, almost choking on memories despite the years between himself and the memory. "Only rich planters could afford slaves. My people were Irish immigrants. You might recall the signs placed at the front gates of estates in the North, which read, No Colored Or Irish Need Apply."

Colby swallowed hard. He had, indeed, seen those signs.

John seemed to grow another inch. "To answer your question, had I been a rich planter, I would have hired my labor, not bought it, for I do not feel that one man of any color has the right to own another." His green eyes flashed. "There were many other small landowners and sharecroppers like my family who paid the price for the greed and luxury of plantation owners. Sherman's army did not discriminate between the two."

"Excuse me," Colby said at once. "One of my laundresses back home had been a slave. Her arms were livid with scars from a mistress who cut her when she burned a dress she was told to iron."

"I have seen similar scars," John replied, without adding that one of the co-owners of his ranch had such unsightly scars, as well as his wife and even their eldest daughter.

"Your mother and sisters live with you?" Colby asked.

John didn't reply for a few seconds. "No, sir. Except for a married sister in North Carolina, my people are all dead."

Colby nodded, his eyes narrow and assessing. "But, then, you have done well for yourself in Texas, have you not?" He smiled.

John forced himself to return the smile and forget the insults. "I will do better, sir," he said with unshakeable confidence. "Far better."

Colby chuckled. "You remind me of myself, when I was a young man. I left home to make my fortune, and had the good sense to look toward trains as the means."

John twirled his hat in his big hands. He wanted to approach Colby about his spur, which would give him the opportunity to ship his cattle without having to take the risk of driving them north to railheads in Kansas. But that would be pushing his luck. Colby might feel that John was overstepping his place in society and being "uppity." He couldn't risk alienating Colby.

He shifted his weight. "I should go," he said absently. "I had no intention of taking up so much of your time, sir. I wanted only to offer you the freedom of my ranch for hunting, and to inquire about the health of your daughter after her unfortunate accident."

"Unfortunate accident." Colby shook his head. "She is the clumsiest woman I have ever known," he said coldly, "and I have found not one single gentleman who lasted more than a day as a suitor."

"But she is charming," John countered gallantly, his eyes dancing. "She has a sense of humor, the ability to laugh at herself, and despite her companion's rudeness, she behaved with dignity."

Colby was listening intently. "You find her... attractive?"

"Sir, she is the most attractive woman I have ever met," John replied without choosing his words.

Colby laughed and shook his head. "You want something," he mused. "But I'm damned if I don't find you a breath of fresh air, sir. You have style and dash."

John grinned at him. "Thank you, sir."

"I may take you up on that invitation at a later date, young man. In the meantime, I have accepted the other offer. But you could do me a favor, if you're inclined."

"Anything within my power, sir," John assured him.

"Since you find my daughter so alluring, I would like you to keep an eye on her during my absence."

"Sir, there would not be adequate chaperones at my ranch," John began quickly, seeing disaster ahead if the old man or his daughter got a glimpse of the true state of affairs at the Jacobs' ranch.

"Oh, for heaven's sake, man, I'm not proposing having her live with you in sin!" Colby burst out. "She will stay here at the hotel, and I have told her not to venture out of town. I meant only that I would like you to check on her from time to time, to make sure that she is safe. She will be on her own, except for the maid we have retained here."

"I see." John let out the breath he'd been holding. "In

that case, I would be delighted. But what of her companion, Sir Sydney?" he added.

"Sir Sydney will be with me, to my cost," Colby groaned. "The man is an utter pain, but he has a tract of land that I need very badly for a new roundhouse near Chicago," he confessed. "So I must humor him, to some extent. I assure you, my daughter will not mourn his absence. She only went to drive with him at my request. She finds him repulsive."

So did John, but he didn't want to rock the boat.

"I'm glad you came, young man." Colby offered his hand, and John shook it.

"So am I, sir," he replied. "If you don't mind, I would like to take my leave of your daughter."

"Be my guest."

"Thank you."

John walked toward the open door that contained a maid, Miss Ellen Colby and a very mad wet dog of uncertain age and pedigree. It was a shaggy dog, black and white, with very long ears. It was barking pitifully and shaking soapy water everywhere.

"Oh, Miss Colby, this doggy don't want no bath," the maid wailed as she tried to right her cap.

"Never you mind, Lizzie, we're going to bathe her or die in the attempt." Ellen blew back a strand of loose hair, holding the dog down with both hands while the maid laved water on it with a cup.

"A watering trough might be a better proposition, Miss Colby," John drawled from the doorway.

His voice shocked her. She jerked her head in his direction and loosened the hold she had on the dog. In the few seconds that followed, the animal gave a yelp of pure joy, leaped out of the pan, off the table, and scattered the rugs as it clawed its way to the freedom of the parlor.

"Oh, my goodness!" Ellen yelled. "Catch her, Lizzie, before she gets to the bedroom! She'll go right up on Papa's bed, like she usually does!"

"Yes, ma'am!"

The maid ran for all she was worth. Ellen Colby put her soapy hands on her hips and glared daggers at the tall green-eyed man in the doorway.

"Now see what you've done!" Ellen raged at John.

"Me?" John's eyebrows arched. "I assure you, I meant only to say goodbye."

"You diverted my attention at a critical moment!"

He smiled slowly, liking the way her blue eyes flashed in anger. He liked the thickness of her hair. It looked very long. He wondered if she let it down at bedtime.

That thought disturbed him. He straightened. "If your entire social life consists of bathing the dog, miss, you are missing out."

"I have a social life!"

"Falling into mud puddles?"

She grabbed up the soaking brush they'd used on the dog and considered heaving it.

John threw back his head and laughed uproariously.

"Do be quiet!" she muttered.

"You have hidden fires," he commented with delight. "Your father has asked me to keep an eye on you, Miss Colby, while he's off on his hunting trip. I find the prospect delightful."

"I can think of nothing I would enjoy less!"

"I'm quite a good companion," he assured her. "I know where birds' nests are and where flowers grow, and I can even sing and play the guitar if asked."

She hesitated, wet splotches all over her lacy dress and soap in her upswept hair. She looked at him with open curiosity. "You are wearing a gun," she pointed out. "Do you shoot people with it?"

"Only the worst sort of people," he told her. "And I have yet to shoot a woman."

"I am reassured."

"I have a cattle ranch not too far a ride from here," he continued. "In the past, I have had infrequently to help defend my cattle from Comanche raiding parties."

"Indians!"

He laughed at her expression. "Yes. Indians. They

have long since gone to live in the Indian Territory. But there are still rustlers and raiders from across the Mexican border, as well as deserting soldiers and layabouts from town hoping to steal my cattle and make a quick profit by selling them to the army."

"How do you stop them?"

"With vigilance," he said simply. "I have men who work for me on shares."

"Shares?" She frowned. "Not for wages?"

He could have bitten his tongue. He hadn't meant to let that slip out.

She knew that he'd let his guard down. She found him mysterious and charming and shrewd. But he had attractions. He was the first man she'd met who made her want to know more about him.

"I might take you for a ride in my buggy," he mused.

"I might go," she replied.

He chuckled, liking her pert response. She wasn't much to look at, truly, but she had qualities he'd yet to find in other women.

He turned to go. "I won't take the dog along," he said.

"Papa's dog goes with me everywhere," she lied, wanting to be contrary.

He glanced at her over his shoulder. "You were alone in the mud puddle, as I recall."

She glared at him.

He gave her a long, curious scrutiny. He smiled slowly. "We can discuss it at a later date. I will see you again in a day or two." He lifted his hat respectfully. "Good day, Miss Colby."

"Good day, Mr....?" It only then occurred to her that she didn't even know his name.

"John," he replied. "John Jackson Jacobs. But most people just call me 'Big John.'"

"You are rather large," she had to agree.

He grinned. "And you are rather small. But I like your spirit, Miss Colby. I like it a lot."

She sighed and her eyes began to glow faintly as they met his green ones.

He winked at her and she blushed scarlet. But before he could say anything, the maid passed him with the struggling wet dog.

"Excuse me, sir, this parcel is quite maddeningly wet," the maid grumbled as she headed toward the bowl on the table.

"So I see. Good day, ladies." He tipped his hat again, and he was gone in a jingle of spurs.

Ellen Colby looked after him with curiosity and an odd feeling of loss. Strange that a man she'd only just met could be so familiar to her, and that she could feel such joy in his presence.

Her life had been a lonely one, a life of service, helping to act as a hostess for her father and care for her grandmother. But with her grandmother off traveling, Ellen was now more of a hindrance than a help to her family, and it was no secret that her father wanted badly to see her married and off his hands.

But chance would be a fine thing, she thought. She turned back to the dog with faint sadness, wishing she were prettier.

Chapter Two

John rode back to his ranch, past the newfangled barbed wire which contained his prize longhorn bull, past the second fence that held his Hereford bull and his small herd of Hereford cows with their spring calves, to the cabin where he and his foremen's families lived together. He had hundreds of head of beef steers, but they ranged widely, free of fences, identified only by his 3J brand, burned into their thick coats. The calves had been branded in the spring.

Mary Brown was at the door, watching him approach. It was early June, and hot in south Texas. Her sweaty black hair was contained under a kerchief, and her brown eyes smiled at him. "Me and Juana washed your old clothes, Mister John," she said. "Isaac and Luis went fishing with the boys down to the river for supper, and the girls are making bread."

"Good," he said. "Do I have anything dry and pressed to put on?" he added.

Mary nodded her head. "Such as it is, Mister John. A few more holes, and no amount of sewing is gonna save you a red face in company."

"I'm working on that, Mary," he told her, chuckling. He bent to lift her youngest son, Joe, a toddler, up into his arms. "You get to growing fast, young feller, you got to help me herd cattle."

The little boy gurgled at him. John grinned at him and set him back down.

Isaac came in the back door just then, with a string of fish. "You back?" He grinned. "Any luck?"

"A lot, all of it unexpected," he told the tall, lithe black man. He glanced at Luis Rodriguez, his head vaquero, who was short and stout and also carrying a string of fish. He took Isaac's and handed both to the young boys. "You boys go clean these fish for Mary, you hear?"

"Yes, Papa," the taller black boy said. His shorter Latino companion grinned and followed him out the door.

"We have another calf missing, *señor*," Luis said irritably. "Isaac and I only came to bring the boys and the fish to the house." He pulled out his pistol and checked it. "We will go and track the calf."

"I'll go with you," John said. "Give me a minute to change."

He carried his clothing to the single room that had a makeshift door and got out of his best clothes, leaving them hanging over a handmade chair he'd provided for Mary. He whipped his gunbelt back around his lean hips and checked his pistol. Rustlers were the bane of any rancher, but in these hard times, when a single calf meant the difference between keeping his land or losing it, he couldn't afford to let it slide.

He went back out to the men, grim-faced. "Let's do some tracking."

They found the calf, butchered. Signs around it told them it wasn't rustlers, but a couple of Indians—Comanches, in fact, judging from the broken arrow shaft and footprints they found nearby.

"Damn the luck!" John growled. "What are Comanches doing this far south? And if they're hungry, why can't they hunt rabbits or quail?"

"They all prefer buffalo, *señor*, but the herds have long gone, and game is even scarce here. That is why we had to fish for supper."

"They could go the hell back to the Indian Territory, couldn't they, instead of riding around here, harassing us poor people!" John pursed his lips thoughtfully, remembering what he'd heard in Sutherland Springs. "I wonder," he mused aloud, "if these could be the two renegades from Indian Territory being chased by the army?"

"What?" Isaac asked.

"Nothing," John said, clapping him on the shoulder affectionately. "Just thinking to myself. Let's get back to work."

The next day, he put on his good suit and went back to the Springs to check on Ellen Colby. He expected to find her reclining in her suite, or playing with her father's dog. What he did find was vaguely shocking.

Far from being in her room, Ellen was on the sidewalk with one arm around a frightened young black boy who'd apparently been knocked down by an angry man.

"…he got in my way. He's got no business walking on the sidewalk anyway. He should be in the street. He should be dead. They should all be dead! We lost everything because of them, and then they got protected by the very army that burned down our homes! You get away from him, lady, he's not going anywhere until I teach him a lesson!"

She stuck out her chin. "I have no intention of moving, sir. If you strike him, you must strike me, also!"

John moved up onto the sidewalk. He didn't look at Ellen. His eyes were on the angry man, and they didn't waver. He didn't say a word. He simply flipped back the lapel of his jacket to disclose the holstered pistol he was carrying.

"Another one!" the angry man railed. "You damned Yankees should get the hell out of Texas and go back up north where you belong!"

"I'm from Georgia," John drawled. "But this is where I belong now."

The man was taken aback. He straightened and glared at John, his fists clenched. "You'd draw on a fellow Southerner?" he exclaimed.

"I'm partial to brown skin," John told him with a honeyed drawl. His tall, lithe figure bent just enough to make an older man nearby catch his breath. "But you do what you think you have to," he added deliberately.

"There," Ellen Colby said haughtily, helping the young man to his feet. "See what you get when you act out of ignoble motives?" she lashed at the threatening man. "A child is a child, regardless of his heritage, sir!"

"That is no child," the man said. "It is an abomination...."

"I beg to disagree." The voice came from a newcomer,

wearing a star on his shirt, just making his way through the small crowd. It was Deputy Marshal James Graham, well known locally because he was impartially fair. "Is there a problem, madam?" he asked Ellen, tipping his hat to her.

"That man kicked this young man off the sidewalk and attacked him," Ellen said, glaring daggers at the antagonist. "I interfered and Mr. Jacobs came along in time to prevent any further violence."

"Are you all right, son?" the marshal asked the young boy, who was openmouthed at his unexpected defense.

"Uh, yes, sir. I ain't hurt," he stammered.

Ellen Colby took a coin from her purse and placed it in the young man's hand. "You go get yourself a stick of peppermint," she told him.

He looked at the coin and grinned. "Thank you kindly, miss, but I'll buy my mama a sack of flour instead. Thank you, too," he told the marshal and John Jacobs, before he cut his losses and rushed down the sidewalk.

Graham turned to the man who'd started the trouble. "I don't like troublemakers," he said in a voice curt with command. "If I see you again, in a similar situation, I'll lock you up. That's a promise."

The man spat onto the ground and gave all three of the boy's defenders a cold glare before he turned and stomped off in the opposite direction.

"I'm obliged to both of you," Ellen Colby told them.

John shrugged. "It was no bother."

The deputy marshal chuckled. "A Georgian defending a black boy." He shook his head. "I am astonished."

John laughed. "I have a former slave family working with me," he explained. His face tautened. "If you could see the scars they carry, even the children, you might understand my position even better."

The deputy nodded. "I do understand. If you have any further trouble," he told Ellen, "I am at your service." He tipped his hat and went back to his horse.

"You are a man of parts, Mr. Jacobs," Ellen told John, her blue eyes soft and approving. "Thank you for your help."

He shrugged. "I was thinking of Isaac's oldest boy who died in Georgia," he confessed, moving closer as the crowd melted away. "Isaac is my wrangler," he added. "His first son was beaten to death by an overseer just before the end of the war."

She stood staring up into his lean, hard face with utter curiosity. "I understood that all Southerners hated colored people."

"Most of us common Southerners were in the fields working right beside them," John said coldly. "We were little more than slaves ourselves, while the rich lived in luxury and turned a blind eye to the abuse."

"I had no idea," she said hesitantly.

"Very few northern people do," he said flatly. "Yet there was a county in Georgia that flew the Union flag all through the war, and every attempt by the confederacy to press-gang them into the army was met with open resistance. They ran away and the army got tired of going back to get them again and again." He chuckled at her surprise. "I will tell you all about it over tea, if you like."

She blushed. "I would like that very much, Mr. Jacobs."

He offered his arm. She placed her small hand in the crook of his elbow and let him escort her into the hotel's immaculate dining room. He wondered if he should have told Graham about the Comanche tracks he'd found on his place. He made a note to mention it to the man when he next saw him.

Ellen liked the lithe, rawboned man who sat across from her sipping tea and eating tea cakes as if he were born to high society. But she knew that he wasn't. He still had rough edges, but even those were endearing. She couldn't forget the image she had of him, standing in front of the frightened boy, daring the attacker to try again. He was brave. She admired courage.

"Did you really come to see my father to inquire about my welfare?" she asked after they'd discussed the war.

He looked up at her, surprised by her boldness. He put his teacup down. "No," he said honestly.

She laughed self-consciously. "Forgive me, but I knew that wasn't the real reason. I appreciate your honesty."

He leaned back in his chair and studied her without pretense. His green gaze slid over her plain face, down to the faint thrust of her breasts under the green and white striped bodice of her dress and up to the wealth of dark hair piled atop her head. "Lies come hard to me," he told her. "Shall I be completely honest about my motives and risk alienating you?"

She smiled. "Please do. I have lost count of the men who pretended to admire me only as a means to my father's wealth. I much prefer an open approach."

"I inherited a very small holding from my uncle, who died some time ago." He toyed with the teacup. "I have worked for wages in the past, to buy more land and cattle. But just recently I've started to experiment with crossing breeds. I am raising a new sort of beef steer with which I hope to tempt the eastern population's hunger for range-fed beef." His eyes lifted to hers. "It's a long, slow process to drive cattle to a railhead up in Kansas, fraught with danger and risk, more now than ever since the fear of Texas fever in cattle has caused so much resistance to be placed in the path of the cattle drives. My finances are so tight now that the loss of a single calf is a major setback to me."

She was interested. "You have a plan."

He smiled. "I have a plan. I want to bring a railroad to this area of south Texas. More precisely, I want a spur to run to my ranch, so that I can ship cattle to Chicago without having to drive them to Kansas first."

Her eyes brightened. "Then you had no real purpose of inviting my father to hunt quail on your ranch."

"Miss Colby," he said heavily, "my two foremen and their families live with me in a one-room cabin. It looks all right at a distance, but close up, it's very primitive. It is a pretend mansion. As I am a pretend aristocrat." He gestured at his suit coat. "I used the last of my ready cash to disguise myself and I came into town because I had heard that your father was here, and that he had a marriageable daughter." His expression became self-mocking when she blinked. "But I'm not enough of a scoundrel to pretend an affection I do not feel." He studied her quietly, toying with a spoon beside his cup and saucer. "So let me make you a business proposition. Marry me and let your father give us a railroad spur as a wedding present."

She gulped, swallowed a mouthful of hot tea, sat back and expelled a shocked breath. "Sir, you are blunt!"

"Ma'am, I am honest," he replied. He leaned forward quickly and fixed her with his green eyes. "Listen to me. I have little more than land and prospects. But I have a good head for business, and I know cattle. Given the opportunity, I will build an empire such as Texas has never seen. I have good help, and I've learned much about raising cattle from them. Marry me."

"And…what would I obtain from such a liaison?" she stammered.

"Freedom."

"Excuse me?"

"Your father cares for you, I think, but he treats you as a liability. That gentleman," he spat the word, "who was escorting you stood idly by when you fell in a mud puddle and didn't even offer a hand. You are undervalued."

She laughed nervously. "And I would not be, if I married a poor stranger and went to live in the wilds where rustlers raid?"

He grinned. "You could wear pants and learn to ride a horse and herd cattle," he said, tempting her. "I would even teach you to brand cattle and shoot a gun."

Her whole demeanor changed. She just stared at him for a minute. "I have spent my entire life under the care of my mother's mother, having lost my own mother when I was only a child. My grandmother Greene believes that a lady should never soil her hands in any way. She insists on absolute decorum in all situations. She would not hear of my learning to ride a horse or shoot a gun because such things are only for men. I have lived in a cage all my life." Her blue eyes began to gleam. "I should love to be a tomboy!"

He laughed. "Then marry me."

She hesitated once again. "Sir, I know very little of men. Having been sheltered in all ways, I am uneasy with the thought of…with having a stranger…with being…"

He held up a hand. "I offer you a marriage of friends. In truth, anything more would require a miracle, as there is no privacy where I live. We are all under the single roof. And," he added, "my foremen and their families are black and Mexican, not white." He watched for her reactions. "So, as you can see, there is a further difficulty in regard to public opinion hereabouts."

She clasped her hands before her on the table. "I would like to think about it a little. Not because of any prejudice," she added quickly, and smiled. "But because I would like to know you a little better. I have a friend who married in haste at the age of fifteen. She is now twenty-four, as I am. She has seven living children and her husband treats her like property. It is not a condition which I envy her."

"I understand," he said.

The oddest thing, was that she thought he really did understand. He was a complex man. She had a sudden vision of him years down the road, in an elegant suit, in an elegant setting. He had potential. She'd never met anyone like him.

She sighed. "But my father must not know the entire truth," she cautioned. "He has prejudices, and he would not willingly let me go to a man he considered a social inferior."

His thin lips pursed amusedly. "Then I'll do my utmost to convince him that I am actually the illegitimate grandson of an Irish earl."

She leaned forward. "Are there Irish earls?"

He shrugged. "I have no idea. But, then, he probably has no idea, either." His eyes twinkled.

She laughed delightedly. It changed her face, her eyes, her whole look. She was pretty when she laughed.

"There is one more complication," he said in a half-serious tone.

"Which is?"

His smile was outrageous. "We have lots of mud puddles at the ranch."

"Oh, you!" she exclaimed, reaching for the teapot.

"If you throw it, the morning papers will have a more interesting front page."

"Will it? And what would you do?" she challenged brightly.

"I am uncivilized," he informed her. "I would put

you across my knee and paddle your backside, after which I would toss you over my shoulder and carry you home with me."

"How very exciting!" she exclaimed. "I have never done anything especially outrageous. I think I might like being the object of a scandal!"

He beamed. "Tempting," he proclaimed. "But I have great plans and no desire to start tongues wagging. Yet."

"Very well. I'll restrain my less civilized impulses for the time being."

He lifted his teacup and toasted her. "To unholy alliances," he teased.

She lifted hers as well. "And madcap plots!"

They clicked teacups together and drank deeply.

It was unseemingly for them to be seen going out of town alone, so Ellen was prevented from visiting John's ranch. But he took her to church on Sunday—a new habit that he felt obliged to acquire—and promenading along the sidewalk after a leisurely lunch in the hotel.

The following week, John was a frequent visitor. He and Ellen became friends with an elegant Scottish gentleman and his wife who were staying at the hotel and taking the waters, while they toured the American West.

"It is a grand country," the Scotsman, Robert Maxwell, told Ellen and John. "Edith and I have been longing to ride out into the country, but we are told that it is dangerous."

"It is," John assured him grimly. "My partners and I have been tracking rustlers all week," he added, to Ellen's surprise, because he hadn't told her. "There are dangerous men in these parts, and we have rustlers from across the border, also."

"Do you have Red Indians?" Maxwell exclaimed. His eyes twinkled. "I would like to meet one."

"They're all in the Indian Territory now, and no, you wouldn't like to meet one," John said. "The Comanches who used to live hereabouts didn't encourage foreign visitors, and they had a well-deserved reputation for opposing any people who tried to invade their land."

"Their land?" the Scotsman queried, curiously.

"Their land," John said firmly. "They roamed this country long before the first white man set foot here. They intermarried with the Mexican population...."

Maxwell seemed very confused, as he interrupted, "Surely there were no people here at all when you arrived," he said.

"Perhaps they don't know it back East, but Texas was part of Mexico just a few decades back," John informed him. "That's why we went to war with Mexico, because Texas wanted independence from it. Our brave boys died in the Alamo in San Antonio, and at Goliad and San

Jacinto, to bring Texas into the union. But the Mexican boys fought to keep from losing their territory, is how they saw it. They considered us invaders."

Ellen was watching John covertly, with quiet admiration.

"Ah, now I understand," the Scot chuckled. "It's like us and England. We've been fighting centuries to govern ourselves, like the Irish. But the British are stubborn folk."

"So are Texans," John chuckled.

"I don't suppose you'd go riding with us, young man?" Maxwell asked him wistfully. "We should love to see a little of the area, and I see that you wear a great pistol at your hip. I assume you can shoot any two-legged threats to our safety."

John glanced at Ellen and saw such appreciation in her blue eyes that he lost his train of thought for a few seconds.

Finally he blinked and darted his green gaze back to the foreigners, hoping his heartbeat wasn't audible.

"I think I'd like that," John replied, "as long as Ellen comes with us."

"Your young lady," the Scotswoman, Nell Maxwell, added with a gentle, indulgent smile.

"Yes," John said, his eyes going back to Ellen's involuntarily. "My young lady."

Ellen blushed red and lowered her eyes, which caused the foreign couple to laugh charmingly. She was so excited that she forgot her father's admonition that she was not to leave the hotel and go out of town. In fact, when she recalled it, she simply ignored it.

They rented a surrey and John helped Ellen into the back seat before he climbed up nimbly beside her. He noted that it was the best surrey the stable had, with fringe hanging all the way around, and the horses' livery was silver and black leather.

"I suppose this is nothing special for you," John murmured to her, looking keenly at the horses' adornments, "but it's something of a treat for me."

Ellen smoothed the skirt of her nice blue suit with its black piping. "It's a treat for me, too," she confessed. "I had very much wanted to drive out in the country, but my father only thinks of hunting, not sightseeing, and he dislikes my company."

"I like your company very much," John said in a deep, soft tone.

She looked up at him, surprised by the warmth in his deep voice. She was lost in the sudden intensity of his green eyes under the wide brim of his dress hat. She felt her whole world shift in the slow delight it provoked.

He smiled, feeling as if he could fly all of a sudden.

Impulsively his big, lean hand caught hers on the seat between them and curled her small fingers into it.

She caught her breath, entranced.

"Are you two young people comfortable?" Maxwell asked.

"Quite comfortable, thank you, sir," John replied, and he looked at Ellen with possession.

"So am I, thank you," Ellen managed through her tight throat.

"We'll away, then," Maxwell said with a grin at his wife, and he flicked the reins.

The surrey bounded forward, the horses obviously well chosen for their task, because the ride was as smooth as silk.

"Which way shall we go?" Maxwell asked.

"Just follow the road you're on," John told him. "I know this way best. It runs past my own land up to Quail Run, the next little town along the road. I can show you the ruins of a log cabin where a white woman and her Comanche husband held off a company of soldiers a few years back. He was a renegade. She was a widow with a young son, and expecting another when her husband was killed by a robber. Soon after, the Comanche was part of a war party that encountered a company of soldiers trailing them. He was wounded and she found him and nursed him back to health. It was winter.

She couldn't hunt or fish, or chop wood, and she had no family at all. He undertook her support. They both ran from the soldiers, up into the Indian Territory. She's there now, people say. Nobody knows where he is."

"What a fascinating story!" Maxwell exclaimed. "Is it true?"

"From what I hear, it is," John replied.

"What a courageous young woman," Ellen murmured.

"To have contact with a Red Indian, she would have to be," Mrs. Maxwell replied. "I have heard many people speak of Indians. None of what they say is good."

"I think all people are good and bad," Ellen ventured. "I have never thought heritage should decide which is which."

John chuckled and squeezed her hand. "We think alike."

The Maxwells exchanged a complicated look and laughed, too.

The log cabin was pointed out. It was nothing much to look at. There was a well tucked into high grass and briar bushes, and a single tree in what must once have been the front yard.

"What sort of tree is that?" Mrs. Maxwell asked. "What an odd shape."

"It's a chinaberry tree," John recalled. "We have them in Georgia, where I'm from. My sisters and I used to throw the green berries that grow on them back and forth, playing." He became somber.

"You have family back in Georgia?" Ellen asked pointedly, softly.

He sighed. "I have a married sister in North Carolina. No one else."

Ellen knew there was more to it than just that, and she had a feeling the war had cost him more than his home. She stroked the back of his callused hand gently. "Mama died of typhoid when I was just five. So except for Papa and Grandmother, I have no one, either."

He caught his breath. He hadn't thought about her circumstances, her family, her background. All he'd known was that she was rich. He began to see her with different eyes.

"I'm sorry, about your family," she said quietly.

He sighed. He didn't look at her. Memories tore at his heart. He looked out beyond the horses drawing the surrey at the yellow sand of the dirt road, leading to the slightly rolling land ahead. The familiar *clop-clop* of the horses' hooves and the faint creak of leather and wood and the swishing sound of the rolling wheels seemed very loud in the silence that followed. The dust came up into the carriage, but they were all used to it, since dirt roads were somewhat universal. The boards that made the seats of the surrey were hard on the backside during a long trip, but not less comfortable than the saddle of a horse, John supposed.

"Do you ride at all?" he asked Ellen.

"I was never allowed to," she confessed. "My grandmother thought it wasn't ladylike."

"I ride to the hounds," Mrs. Maxwell said, eavesdropping, and turned to face them with a grin. "My father himself put me on my first horse when I was no more than a girl. I rode sidesaddle, of course, but I could outdistance any man I met on a horse. Well, except for Robert," she conceded, with an affectionate look at her husband. "We raced and I lost. Then and there, I determined that I needed to marry him."

"And she did," he added with a chuckle, darting a look over his broad shoulder. "Her father told me I must keep her occupied to keep her happy, so I turned the stables over to her."

"Quite a revolution of sorts in our part of the country, I must add," Mrs. Maxwell confessed. "But the lads finally learned who had the whip hand, and now they do what I say."

"We have the finest stable around," Maxwell agreed. "We haven't lost a race yet."

"When I have more horses, you must come and

teach my partners how to train them," John told Mrs. Maxwell.

"And didn't I tell you that people would not be stuffy and arrogant here in Texas?" she asked her husband.

"I must agree, they are not."

"Well, two of them, at least," John murmured dryly. "There," he said suddenly, pointing out across a grassy pasture. "That is my land."

All three heads turned. In the distance was the big cabin, surrounded by pecan and oak trees and not very visible. But around it were red-and-white-coated cattle, grazing in between barbed wire fences.

"It is fenced!" Maxwell exclaimed.

"Fencing is what keeps the outlaws out and my cattle in," John said, used to defending his fences. "Many people dislike this new barbed wire, but it is the most economical way to contain my herds. And I don't have a great deal of capital to work with."

"You are an honest man," Maxwell said. "You did not have to admit such a thing to a stranger."

"It is because you are a stranger that I can do it," John said amusedly. "I would never admit to being poor around my own countrymen. A man has his pride. However, I intend to be the richest landowner hereabouts in a few years. So you must plan to come back to Texas. I can promise you will be very welcome as houseguests."

"If I am able, I will," Maxwell agreed. "So we must keep in touch."

"Indeed we must. We will trade addresses before you leave town. But for now," John added, "make a left turn at this next crossroads, and I will show you a mill, where we take our corn to be ground into meal."

"We have mills at home, but I should like to see yours," Mrs. Maxwell enthused.

"And so you shall," John promised.

Chapter Three

Two hours later, tired and thirsty, the tourists returned to the livery stable to return the horses and surrey.

"It has been a pleasure," John told the Maxwells, shaking hands.

"And for me, as well," Ellen added.

The older couple smiled indulgently. "We leave for New York in the morning," Maxwell said regretfully, "and then we sail to Scotland. It has been a pleasure to meet you both, although I wish we could have done so sooner."

"Yes," Mrs. Maxwell said solemnly. "How sad to make friends just as we must say goodbye to them."

"We will keep in touch," John said.

"Indeed we will. You must leave your address for us

at the desk, and we will leave ours for you," Maxwell told John. "When you have made your fortune, I hope very much to return with my wife to visit you both."

Ellen flushed, because she had a sudden vivid picture of herself with John and several children on a grand estate. John was seeing the same picture. He grinned broadly. "We will look forward to it," he said to them both.

The Maxwells went up to their rooms and John stopped with Ellen at the foot of the stairs, because it would have been unseemly for a gentleman to accompany a lady all the way to her bedroom.

He took her hand in his and held it firmly. "I enjoyed today," he said. "Even in company, you are unique."

"As you are." She smiled up at him from a radiant face surrounded by wisps of loose dark hair that had escaped her bun and the hatpins that held on her wide-brimmed hat.

"We must make sure that we build a proper empire," he teased, "so that the Maxwells can come back to visit."

"I shall do my utmost to assist you," she replied with teasing eyes.

He chuckled. "I have no doubt of that."

"I will see you tomorrow?" she fished.

"Indeed you will. It will be in the afternoon, though," he added regretfully. "I must help move cattle into a new pasture first. It is very dry and we must shift them closer to water."

"Good evening, then," she said gently.

"Good evening." He lifted her hand to his lips in a gesture he'd learned in polite company during his travels.

It had a giddy effect on Ellen. She blushed and laughed nervously and almost stumbled over her own feet going up the staircase.

"Oh, dear," she said, righting herself.

"Not to worry," John assured her, hat in hand, green eyes brimming with mirth. "See?" He looked around his feet and back up at her. "No mud puddles!"

She gave him an exasperated, but amused, look, and went quickly up the staircase. When she made the landing, he was still there, watching.

John and Ellen saw each other daily for a week, during which they grew closer. Ellen waited for John in the hotel dining room late the next Friday afternoon, but to her dismay, it was not John who walked directly to her table. It was her father, home unexpectedly early. Nor was he smiling.

He pulled out a chair and sat down, motioning imperiously to a waiter, from whom he ordered coffee and nothing else.

"You are home early," Ellen stammered.

"I am home to prevent a scandal!" he replied curtly. "I've had word from an acquaintance of Sir Sydney's that you were seen flagrantly defying my instructions that you should stay in this hotel during my absence! You have been riding, in the country, alone, with Mr. Jacobs! How dare you create a scandal here!"

The Ellen of only a week ago would have bowed her head meekly and agreed never to disobey him again. But her association with John Jacobs had already stiffened her backbone. He had offered her a new life, a free life, away from the endless social conventions and rules of conduct that kept her father so occupied.

She lifted her eyebrows with hauteur. "And what business of Sir Sydney's friend is my behavior?" she wanted to know.

Her father's eyes widened in surprise. "I beg your pardon?"

"I have no intention of being coupled with Sir Sydney in any way whatsoever," she informed him. "In fact, the man is repulsive and ill-mannered."

It was a rare hint of rebellion, one of just a few he had ever seen in Ellen. He just stared at her, confused and amused, all at once.

"It would seem that your acquaintance with Mr. Jacobs is corrupting you."

"I intend to be further corrupted," she replied coolly. "He has asked me to marry him."

"Child, that is out of the question," he said sharply.

She held up a dainty hand. "I am no child," she informed him, blue eyes flashing. "I am a woman grown. Most of my friends are married with families of their own. I am a spinster, an encumbrance to hear you tell it, of a sort whom men do not rush to escort. I am neither pretty nor accomplished…"

"You are quite wealthy," he inserted bluntly. "Which is, no doubt, why Mr. Jacobs finds you so attractive."

In fact, it was a railroad spur, not money, that John wanted, but she wasn't ready to tell her father that. Let him think what he liked. She knew that John Jacobs found her attractive. It gave her confidence to stand up to her parent for the first time in memory.

"You may disinherit me whenever you like," she said easily, sipping coffee with a steady hand. Her eyes twinkled. "I promise you, it will make no difference to him. He is the sort of man who builds empires from nothing more than hard work and determination. In time, his fortune will rival yours, I daresay."

Terrance Colby was listening now, not blustering. "You are considering his proposal."

She nodded, smiling. "He has painted me a delightful picture of muddy roads, kitchen gardens, heavy labor, cooking over open fires and branding cattle." She chuckled. "In fact, he has offered to let me help him brand cattle in the fall when his second crop of calves drop."

Terrance caught his breath. He waited to speak until the waiter brought his coffee. He glowered after the retreating figure. "I should have asked for a teacup of whiskey instead," he muttered to himself. His eyes went back to his daughter's face. "Brand cattle?"

She nodded. "Ride horses, shoot a gun…he offered to teach me no end of disgusting and socially unacceptable forms of recreation."

He sat back with an expulsion of breath. "I could have him arrested."

"For what?" she replied.

He was disconcerted by the question. "I haven't decided yet. Corrupting a minor," he ventured.

"I am far beyond the age of consent, Father," she reminded him. She sipped coffee again. "You may disinherit me at will. I will not even need the elegant wardrobes you have purchased for me. I will wear dungarees and high-heeled boots."

His look of horror was now all-consuming. "You will not! Remember your place, Ellen!"

Her eyes narrowed. "My place is what I say it is. I am not property, to be sold or bartered for material gain!"

He was formulating a reply when the sound of heavy footfalls disturbed him into looking up. John Jacobs was standing just to his side, wearing his working gear, including that sinister revolver slung low in a holster slanted across his lean hips.

"Ah," Colby said curtly. "The villain of the piece!"

"I am no villain," John replied tersely. He glanced at Ellen with budding feelings of protectiveness. She looked flushed and angry. "Certainly, I have never given Ellen such pain as that I see now on her face." He looked back at Colby with a cold glare.

Colby began to be impressed. This steely young man was not impressed by either his wealth or position when Ellen was distressed.

"Do you intend to call me out?" he asked John.

The younger man glanced again at Ellen. "It would be high folly to kill the father of my prospective bride," he said finally. "Of course, I don't have to kill you," he added, pursing his lips and giving Colby's shoulder a quiet scrutiny. "I could simply wing you."

Colby's gaze went to that worn pistol butt. "Do you know how to shoot that hog leg?"

"I could give you references," John drawled. "Or a demonstration, if you prefer."

Colby actually laughed. "I imagine you could. Stop bristling like an angry dog and sit down, Mr. Jacobs. I have ridden hard to get here, thinking my daughter was about to be seduced by a bounder. And I find only an honest suitor who would fight even her own father to protect her. I am quite impressed. Do sit down," he emphasized. "That gentleman by the window looks fit to jump through it. He has not taken his eyes off your gun since you approached me!"

John's hard face broke into a sheepish grin. He pulled out a chair and sat down close to Ellen, his green eyes soft now and possessive as they sketched her flushed, happy face. He smiled at her, tenderly.

Colby ordered coffee for John as well and then sat back to study the determined young man.

"She said you wish to teach her to shoot a gun and brand cattle," Colby began.

"If she wants to, yes," John replied. "I assume you would object…?"

Colby chuckled. "My grandmother shot a gun and once chased a would-be robber down the streets of a North Carolina town with it. She was a local legend."

"You never told me!" Ellen exclaimed.

He grimaced. "Your mother was very straitlaced, Ellen, like your grandmother Greene," he said. "She wanted no image of my unconventional mother to tempt you into indiscretion." He pursed his lips and chuckled. "Apparently blood will out, as they say." He looked at her with kind eyes. "You have been pampered all your life. Nothing that money could buy has ever been beyond your pocket. It will not be such a life with this man," he indicated John. "Not for a few years, at least," he added with a chuckle. "You remind me of myself, Mr. Jacobs. I did not inherit my wealth. I worked as a farm laborer in my youth," he added, shocking his daughter. "I mucked out stables and slopped hogs for a rich man in our small North Carolina town. There were eight of us children, and no money to be handed down. When I was twelve, I jumped on a freight train and was arrested in New York when I was found in a stock car. I was taken to the manager's office where the owner of the railroad had chanced to venture on a matter of business. I was rude and arrogant, but he must have seen something in me that impressed him. He had a wife, but no children. He took me home with him, had his wife clean me up and dress me properly, and I became his adoptive child. When he died, he left the business to me. By then, I was more than capable of running it."

"Father!" Ellen exclaimed. "You never spoke of your parents. I had no idea…!"

"My parents died of typhoid soon after I left the farm," he confessed. "My brothers and sisters were taken in by cousins. When I made my own fortune, I made sure that they were provided for."

"You wanted a son," she said sorrowfully, "to inherit what you had. And all you got was me."

"Your mother died giving birth to a stillborn son," he confessed. "You were told that she died of a fever, which is partially correct. I felt that you were too young for the whole truth. And your maternal grandmother was horrified when I thought to tell you. Grandmother Greene is very correct and formal." He sighed. "When she knows what you have done, I expect she will be here on the next train to save you, along with however many grandsons she can convince to accompany her."

She nodded slowly, feeling nervous. "She is formidable."

"I wouldn't mind a son, but I do like little girls," John said with a warm smile. "I won't mind if we have daughters."

She flushed, embarrassed.

"Let us speak first of marriage, if you please," Colby said with a wry smile. "What would you like for a wedding present, Mr. Jacobs?"

John was overwhelmed. He hesitated.

"*We* would like a spur line run down to *our* ranch," Ellen said for him, with a wicked grin. "So that we don't have to drive our cattle all the way to Kansas to get them shipped to Chicago. We are going to raise extraordinary beef."

John sighed. "Indeed we are," he nodded, watching her with delight.

"That may take some little time," Colby mused. "What would you like in the meantime?"

"A sidesaddle rig for Ellen, so that she can be comfortable in the saddle," John said surprisingly.

"I do not want a sidesaddle," she informed him curtly. "I intend to ride astride, as I have seen other women do since I came here."

"I have never seen a woman ride in such a manner!" Colby exploded.

"She's thinking of Tess Wallace," John confessed. "She's the wife of old man Tick Wallace, who owns the stagecoach line here. She drives the team and even rides shotgun sometimes. He's twenty years older than she is, but nobody doubts what they feel for each other. She's crazy for him."

"An unconventional woman," Colby muttered.

"As I intend to become. You may give me away at the wedding, and it must be a small, intimate one, and very soon," she added. "I do not wish my husband embarrassed by a gathering of snobby aristocrats."

Her father's jaw dropped. "But the suddenness of the wedding…!"

"I am sorry, Father, but it will be my wedding, and I feel I have a right to ask for what I wish," Ellen said stubbornly. "I have done nothing wrong, so I have nothing to fear. Besides," she added logically, "none of our friends live here, or are in attendance here at the Springs."

Her father sighed. "As you wish, my dear," he said finally, and his real affection for her was evident in the smile he gave her.

John was tremendously impressed, not only by her show of spirit, but by her consideration for him. He was getting quite a bargain, he thought. Then he stopped to ask himself what she was getting, save for a hard life that would age her prematurely, maybe even kill her. He began to frown.

"It will be a harder life than you realize now," John said abruptly, and with a scowl. "We have no conveniences at all…."

"I am not afraid of hard work," Ellen interrupted.

John and Colby exchanged concerned glances. They both knew deprivation intimately. Ellen had never been without a maid or the most luxurious accommodations in her entire life.

"I'll spare you as much as I can," John said after a minute. "But most empires operate sparsely at first."

"I will learn to cook," Ellen said with a chuckle.

"Can you clean a game hen?" her father wanted to know.

She didn't waver. "I can learn."

"Can you haul water from the river and hoe in a

garden?" her father persisted. "Because I have no doubt that you will have to do it."

"There will be men to do the lifting," John promised him. "And we will take excellent care of her, sir."

Her father hesitated, but Ellen's face was stiff with determination. She wasn't backing down an inch.

"Very well," he said on a heavy breath. "But if it becomes too much for you, I want to know," he added firmly. "You must promise that, or I cannot sanction your wedding."

"I promise," she said at once, knowing that she would never go to him for help.

He relaxed a little. "Then I will give you a wedding present that will not make your prospective bridegroom chafe too much," he continued. "I'll open an account for you both at the mercantile store. You will need dry goods to furnish your home."

"Oh, Father, thank you!" Ellen exclaimed.

John chuckled. "Thank you, indeed. Ellen will be grateful, but I'll consider it a loan."

"Of course, my boy," Colby replied complacently.

John knew the man didn't believe him. But he was capable of building an empire, even if he was the only one at the table who knew it at that moment. He reached over to shake hands with the older man.

"Within ten years," he told Colby, "we will entertain you in the style to which you are accustomed."

Colby nodded, but he still had reservations. He only hoped he wasn't doing Ellen a disservice. And he still had to explain this to her maternal grandmother, who was going to have a heart attack when she knew what he'd let Ellen do.

But all he said to the couple was, "We shall see."

They were married by a justice of the peace, with Terrance Colby and the minister's wife as witnesses. Colby had found a logical reason for the haste of the wedding, pleading his forthcoming trip home and Ellen's refusal to leave Sutherland Springs. The minister, an easygoing, romantic man, was willing to defy convention for a good cause. Colby congratulated John, kissed Ellen, and led them to a buckboard which he'd already had filled with enough provisions to last a month. He'd even included a treadle sewing machine, cloth for dresses and the sewing notions that went with them. Nor had he forgotten Ellen's precious knitting needles and wool yarn, with which she whiled away quiet evenings.

"Father, thank you very much!" Ellen exclaimed when she saw the rig.

"Thank you very much, indeed," John added with a handshake. "I shall take excellent care of her," he promised.

"I'm sure you'll do your best," Colby replied, but he was worried, and it showed.

Ellen kissed him. "You must not be concerned for me," she said firmly, her blue eyes full of censure. "You think I am a lily, but I mean to prove to you that I am like a cactus flower, able to bloom in the most unlikely places."

He kissed her cheek. "If you ever need me…"

"I do know where to send a telegram," she interrupted, and chuckled. "Have a safe trip home."

"I will have your trunks sent out before I leave town," he added.

John helped Ellen into the buckboard in the lacy white dress and veil she'd worn for her wedding, and he climbed up beside her in the only good suit he owned. They were an odd couple, he thought. And considering the shock she was likely to get when she saw where she must live, it would only get worse. He felt guilty for what he was doing. He prayed that the ends would justify the means. He had promised little, and she had asked for nothing. But many couples had started with even less and made a go of their marriages. He meant to keep Ellen happy, whatever it took.

Ellen Jacob's first glimpse of her future home would have been enough to discourage many a young woman from getting out of the buckboard. The shade trees shaded a large, rough log cabin with only one door and a single window and a chimney. Nearby were cactus plants and brush. But there were tiny pink climbing roses in full bloom, and John confessed that he'd brought the bushes here from Georgia planted in a syrup can. The roses delighted her, and made the wilderness look less wild.

Outside the cabin stood a Mexican couple and a black couple, surrounded by children of all ages. They stared and looked very nervous as John helped Ellen down out of the buckboard.

She had rarely interacted with people of color, except as servants in the homes she had visited most of her life. It was new, and rather exciting, to live among them.

"I am Ellen Colby," she introduced herself, and then colored. "I do beg your pardon! I am Ellen Jacobs!"

She laughed, and then they laughed as well.

"We're pleased to meet you, *señora,*" the Mexican man said, holding his broad sombrero in front of him. He grinned as he introduced himself and his small family. "I am Luis Rodriguez. This is my family—my wife Juana, my son Alvaro and my daughters Juanita, Elena and Lupita." They all nodded and smiled.

"And I am Mary Brown," the black woman said gently. "My husband is Isaac. These are my boys, Ben, the oldest, and Joe, the youngest, and my little girl Libby, who is the middle child. We are glad to have you here."

"I am glad to be here," Ellen said.

"But right now, you need to get into some comfortable clothing, Mrs. Jacobs," Mary said. "Come along in. You men go to work and leave us to our own chores," she said, shooing them off.

"Mary, I can't work in these!" John exclaimed defensively.

She reached into a box and pulled out a freshly ironed shirt and patched pants. "You go off behind a tree and put those on, and I'll do my best to chase the moths out of this box so's I can put your suit in it. And mind you don't get red mud in this shirt!"

"Yes, ma'am," he said with a sheepish grin. "See you later, Ellen."

Mary shut the door on him, grinning widely at Ellen. "He is a good man," she told Ellen in all seriousness as she produced the best dress she had and offered it to Ellen.

"No," Ellen said gently, smiling. "I thank you very much for the offer of your dress, but I not only brought a cotton dress of my own—I have brought bolts of fabric and a sewing machine."

There were looks of unadulterated pleasure on all the feminine faces. "New...fabric?" Mary asked haltingly.

"Sewing machine?" her daughter exclaimed.

"In the buckboard," Ellen assured them with a grin.

They vanished like summer mist, out the door. Ellen followed behind them, still laughing at their delight. She'd done the right thing, it seemed—rather, her father had. She might have thought of it first if she'd had the opportunity.

The women and girls went wild over the material, tearing it out of its brown paper wrapping without even bothering to cut the string that held it.

"Alvaro, you and Ben get this sewing machine and Mrs. Jacobs's suitcase into the house right this minute! Girls, bring the notions and the fabric! I'll get the coffee and sugar, but Ben will have to come back for the lard bucket and the flour sack."

"Yes, ma'am," they echoed, and burst out laughing.

Three hours later, Ellen was wearing a simple navy skirt with an indigo blouse, fastened high at the neck. She had on lace-up shoes, but she could see that she was going to have to have boots if she was to be any help to John. The cabin was very small, and all of the families would sleep inside, because there were varmints out at night. And not just crawly ones or four-legged ones, she suspected. Mary had told her about the Comanches John and Luis and Isaac had been hunting when a calf was taken. She noted that a loaded shotgun was kept in a corner of the room, and she had no doubt that either of her companions could wield it if necessary. But she would ask John to teach her to shoot it, as well.

"You will have very pretty dresses from this material," Mary sighed as she touched the colored cottons of many prints and designs.

"*We* will have many pretty dresses," Ellen said, busily filling a bobbin for the sewing machine. She looked up at stunned expressions. "Surely you did not think I could use this much fabric by myself? There is enough here for all of us, I should imagine. And it will take less for the girls," she added, with a warm smile at them.

Mary actually turned away, and Ellen was horrified that she'd hurt the other woman's feelings. She jumped up from the makeshift chair John had cobbled together from tree limbs. "Mary, I'm sorry, I…!"

Mary turned back to her, tears running down her cheeks. "It's just, I haven't had a dress of my own, a new dress, in my whole life. Only hand-me-downs from my mistress, and they had to be torn up or used up first."

Ellen didn't know what to say. Her face was shocked.

Mary wiped away the tears. She looked at the other woman curiously. "You don't know about slaves, do you, Mrs. Ellen?"

"I know enough to be very sorry that some people

think they can own other people," she replied carefully. "My family never did."

Mary forced a smile. "Mr. John brought us out here after the war. We been lucky. Two of our kids are lost forever, you know," she added matter-of-factly. "They got sold just before the war. And one of them got beat to death."

Ellen's eyes closed. She shuddered. It was overwhelming. Tears ran down her cheeks.

"Oh, now, Mrs., don't you…don't you do that!" Mary gathered her close and rocked her. "Don't you cry. Wherever my babies gone, they free now, don't you see. Alive or dead, they free."

The tears ran even harder.

"It was just as bad for Juana," Mary said through her own tears. "Two of her little boys got shot. This man got drunk and thought they was Indians. He just killed them right there in the road where they was playing, and he didn't even look back. He rode off laughing. Luis told the *federales,* but they couldn't find the man. That was years ago, before Mr. John's uncle hired Luis to work here, but Juana never forgot them little boys."

Ellen drew back and pulled a handkerchief out of her sleeve. She wiped Mary's eyes and smiled sadly. "We live in a bad world."

Mary smiled. "It's gonna get better," she said. "You wait and see."

"Better," Juana echoed, nodding, smiling. *"Mas bueno."*

"Mas...bueno?" Ellen repeated.

Juana chuckled. *"¡Vaya! ¡Muy bien!* Very good!"

Mary smiled. "You just spoke your first words of Spanish!"

"Perhaps you can teach me to speak Spanish," Ellen said to Juana.

"Señora, it will be my pleasure!" the woman answered, and smiled beautifully.

"I expect to learn a great deal, and very soon," Ellen replied.

That was an understatement. During her first week of residence, she became an integral part of John's extended family. She learned quite a few words of Spanish, including some range language that shocked John when she repeated it to him with a wicked grin.

"You stop that," he chastised. "Your father will have me shot if he hears you!"

She only chuckled, helping Mary put bread on the table. She was learning to make bread that didn't bounce, but it was early days yet. "My father thinks I will be begging him to come and get me within two weeks. He is in for a surprise!"

"I got the surprise," John had to admit, smiling at her.

"You fit right in that first day." He looked from her to the other women, all wearing new dresses that they'd pieced on Ellen's sewing machine. He shook his head. "You three ought to open a dress shop in town."

Ellen glanced at Mary and Juana with pursed lips and twinkling eyes. "You know, that's not really such a bad idea, John," she said after a minute. "It would make us a little extra money. We could buy more barbed wire and we might even be able to afford a milk cow!"

John started to speak, but Mary and Juana jumped right in, and before he ate the first piece of bread, the women were already making plans.

Chapter Four

Ellen had John drive her into town the following Saturday, to the dry goods store. She spoke with Mr. Alton, the owner.

"I know there must be a market for inexpensive dresses in town, Mr. Alton," she said, bright-eyed. "You order them and keep them in stock, but the ones you buy are very expensive, and most ranch women can't afford them. Suppose I could supply you with simple cotton dresses, ready-made, at half the price of the ones you special order for customers?"

He lifted both eyebrows. "But, Mrs. Jacobs, your father is a wealthy man…!"

"My husband is not," she replied simply. "I must help

him as I can." She smiled. "I have a knack for sewing, Mr. Alton, and I think I do quite good work. I also have two helpers who are learning how to use the machine. Would you let me try?"

He hesitated, adding up figures in his head. "All right," he said finally. "You bring me about six dresses, two each of small, medium and large ones, and we will see how they sell."

She grinned. "Done!" She went to the bolts of fabric he kept. "You must allow me credit, so that I can buy the material to make them with, and I will pay you back from my first orders."

He hesitated again. Then he laughed. She was very shrewd. But, he noticed that the dress she was wearing was quite well-made. His women customers had complained about the lack of variety and simplicity in his ready-made dresses, which were mostly for evening and not everyday.

"I will give you credit," he said after a minute. He shook his head as he went to cut the cloth she wanted. "You are a shrewd businesswoman, Mrs. Jacobs," he said. "I'll have to watch myself, or I may end up working for you!"

Which amused her no end.

John was dubious about his wife's enterprise, but Ellen knew what she was doing. Within three weeks, she and the women had earned enough money with their dressmaking to buy not one, but two Jersey milk cows with nursing calves. These John was careful to keep separate from his Hereford bull. But besides the milk, they made butter and buttermilk, which they took into town with their dresses and sold to the local restaurant.

"I told you it would work," Ellen said to John one afternoon when she'd walked out to the makeshift corral where he and the men were branding new calves.

He smiled down at her, wiping sweat from his face with the sleeve of his shirt. "You are a wonder," he murmured with pride. "We're almost finished here. Want to learn to ride?"

"Yes!" she exclaimed. But she looked down at her cotton dress with a sigh. "But not in this, I fear."

John's eyes twinkled. "Come with me."

He led her to the back of the cabin, where he pulled out a sack he'd hidden there. He offered it to her.

She opened it and looked inside. There was a man's cotton shirt, a pair of boots, and a pair of dungarees in it. She unfolded the dungarees and held them up to herself. "They'll just fit!" she exclaimed.

"I had Mr. Alton at the dry goods store measure one of your dresses for the size. He said they should fit even after shrinkage when you wash them."

"Oh, John, thank you!" she exclaimed. She stood on tiptoe and kissed him on the cheek.

He chuckled. "Get them on, then, and I'll teach you to mount a horse. I've got a nice old one that Luis brought with him. He's gentle."

"I won't be a minute!" she promised, darting back into the cabin.

John was at the corral when she came back out. She'd borrowed one of John's old hats and it covered most of her face as well as her bundled-up hair. She looked like a young boy in the rig, and he chuckled.

"Do I look ridiculous?" she worried.

"You look fine," he said diplomatically, his eyes twinkling. "Come along and meet Jorge."

He brought forward a gentle-looking old chestnut horse who lowered his head and nudged at her hand when she extended it. She stroked his forehead and smiled.

"Hello, old fellow," she said softly. "We're going to be great friends, aren't we?"

John pulled the horse around by its bridle and taught Ellen how to mount like a cowboy. Then, holding the reins, he led her around the yard, scattering their new flock of chickens along the way.

"They won't lay if we frighten them," Ellen worried.

He looked up at her with a grin. "How did you know that?"

"Mary taught me."

"She and Juana are teaching you a lot of new skills," he mused. "I liked the biscuits this morning, by the way."

Her heart skipped. "How did you know that I made them?"

"Because you watched every bite I took."

"Oh, dear."

He only laughed. "I am constantly amazed by you," he confessed as they turned away from the cabin and went toward the path that led through the brush to a large oak tree. "Honestly, I never thought you'd be able to live in such deprivation. Especially after...Ellen?"

He'd heard a faint scraping sound, followed by a thud. When he turned around, Ellen was sitting up in the dirt, looking stunned.

He threw the reins over the horse's head and ran to where she was sitting, his heart in his throat. "Ellen, are you hurt?!"

She glared up at him. "Did you not notice the tree limb, John?" she asked with a meaningful glance in its direction.

"Obviously not," he murmured sheepishly. "Did you?" he added.

She burst out laughing. "Only when it hit me."

He chuckled as he reached down and lifted her up into his arms. It was the first time she'd been picked up

in her adult life, and she gasped, locking her hands be-
hind his neck so that she didn't fall.

His green eyes met her blue ones at point blank range.
The laughter vanished as suddenly as it had come. He
studied her pert little nose, her high cheekbones, her
pretty bow of a mouth. She was looking, too, her gaze
faintly possessive as she noted the hard, strong lines of
his face and the faint scars she found there. His eyes were
very green at the proximity, and his mouth looked hard
and firm. He had high cheekbones, too, and a broad
forehead. His hair was thick under the wide-brimmed
hat he wore, and black. His ears were, like his nose, of
imposing size. The hands supporting her were big, too,
like his booted feet.

"I have never been carried since I was a child," she
said in a hushed, fascinated tone.

"Well, I don't usually make a practice of carrying
women, either," he confessed. His chiseled lips split in
a smile. "You don't weigh much."

"I am far too busy becoming an entrepreneur to gain
weight," she confessed.

"A what?"

She explained the word.

"You finished school, I reckon," he guessed.

She nodded. "I wanted to go to college, but Father
does not think a woman should be overeducated."

"Bull," John said inelegantly. "My mother educated herself and even learned Latin, which she taught me. If we have daughters, they'll go to college."

She beamed, thinking of children. "I should like to have children."

He pursed his lips and lifted an eyebrow. His smile was sheer wickedness.

She laughed and buried her face in his throat, embarrassed. But he didn't draw back. His arms contracted around her and she felt his breath catch as he enveloped her soft breasts against the hard wall of his chest.

She felt unsettled. Her arms tightened around his strong neck and she shivered. She had never been held so close to a man's body. It was disconcerting. It was...delightful.

His cheek slid against hers so that he could find her soft lips with his mouth. He kissed her slowly, gently, with aching respect. When he pulled back, her lips followed. With a rough groan, he kissed her again. This time, there was less respect and more blatant hunger in the mouth that ravished hers.

She moaned softly, which brought him to his senses immediately. He drew back, his green eyes glittering with feeling. He wasn't breathing steadily anymore. Neither was she.

"We would have to climb a tree to find much privacy,

and even then, the boys would probably be sitting in the branches," he said in a hunted tone.

She understood what he meant and flushed. But she laughed, too, because it was very obvious that he found her as attractive as she found him. She smiled into his eyes.

"One day, we will have a house as big as a barn, with doors that lock!" she assured him.

He chuckled softly. "Yes. But for now, we must be patient." He put her back on her feet with a long sigh. "Not that I feel patient," he added rakishly.

She laughed. "Nor I." She looked up at him demurely. "I suppose you have kissed a great many girls."

"Not so many," he replied. "And none as unique as you." His eyes were intent on her flushed face. "I made the best bargain of my life when I enticed you into marriage, Ellen Colby."

"Thank you," she said, stumbling over the words.

He pushed back a lock of disheveled dark hair that had escaped from under her hat. "It never occurred to me that a city woman, an aristocrat, would be able to survive living like this. I have felt guilty any number of times when I watched you carry water to the house, and wash clothes as the other women do. I know that you had maids to do such hard labor when you lived at home."

"I am young and very strong," she pointed out. "Besides, I have never found a man whom I respected enough to marry, until now. I believe you will make an empire here, in these wilds. But even if I didn't believe it, I would still be proud to take your name. You are unique, also."

His eyes narrowed. He bent again and kissed her eyelids shut, with breathless tenderness. "I will work hard to be worthy of your trust, Ellen. I will try never to disappoint you."

She smiled. "And you will promise never to run me under oak limbs again?" she teased.

"You imp!" He laughed uproariously, hugging her to him like a big brother. "You scamp! What joy you bring to my days."

"And you to mine," she replied, hugging him back.

"Daddy! Mr. John and Mrs. Ellen are spooning right here in the middle of the road!" one of Isaac and Mary's boys yelled.

"Scatter, you varmints, I'm kissing my wife!" John called in mock-rage.

There was amused laughter and the sound of brush rustling.

"So much for the illusion of privacy," Ellen said, pulling back from him with a wistful sigh. "Shall we get back to the business at hand? Where's my horse?"

John spied him in the brush, munching on some small green growth of grass he had found there. "He's found something nice to eat, I'll wager," he said.

"I'll fetch him," Ellen laughed, and started into the brush.

"Ellen, stop!"

John's voice, full of authority and fear, halted her with one foot in the act of rising. She stopped and stood very still. He was cursing, using words Ellen had never heard in her life. "Isaac!" he tacked onto the end, "fetch my shotgun! Hurry!"

Ellen closed her eyes. She didn't have to look down to know why he was so upset. She could hear a rustling sound, like crackling leaves, like softly frying bacon. She had never seen a rattlesnake, but during her visit to Texas with her father, she had heard plenty about them from local people. Apparently they liked to lie in wait and strike out at unsuspecting people who came near them. They could cause death with a bite, or extreme pain and sickness. Ellen was mortally afraid of snakes, in any event. But John would save her. She knew he would.

There were running feet. Crashing brush. The sound of something being thrown and caught, and then the unmistakable sound of a hammer being pulled back.

"Stand very still, darling," John told her huskily. "Don't move…a muscle!"

She swallowed, her eyes still closed. She held her breath. There was a horrifying report, like the sound of thunder and lightning striking, near her feet. Flying dirt hit her dungarees. She heard furious thrashing and opened her eyes. For the first time, she looked down. A huge rattlesnake lay dismembered nearby, still writhing in the hot sun.

"Ellen, it didn't strike you?" John asked at once, wrapping her up in the arm that wasn't supporting the shotgun. "You're all right?"

"I am, thanks to you," she whispered, almost collapsing against him. "What a scare!"

"For both of us," he said curtly. He bent and kissed the breath out of her, still shaken from the experience. "Don't ever march into the brush without looking first!"

She smiled under his lips. "You could have caught the brush on fire with that language," she murmured reproachfully. "Indeed, I think the snake was shocked to death by it!"

He laughed, and kissed her harder. She kissed him back, only belatedly aware of running feet and exclamations when the snake was spotted.

He linked his big hand into her small one. "Luis, bring the horse, if you please. I think we've had enough riding practice for one day!"

"*Si, señor,*" Juan agreed with a chuckle.

* * *

That evening around the campfire all the talk was of the close call Ellen had with the snake.

"You're on your way to being a living legend," John told her as they roasted the victim of his shotgun over the darting orange and yellow tongues of flame. "Not to mention the provider of this delicious delicacy. Roasted rattler."

Ellen, game as ever, was soon nibbling on her own chunk of it. "It tastes surprisingly like chicken," she remarked.

John glowered at her. "It does not."

She grinned at him, and his heart soared. He grinned back.

"If you want another such treat, you will have to teach me how to shoot a gun," she proposed. "I am never walking into a rattler's mouth again, not even to provide you with supper!"

"Fair deal," he responded, while the others laughed uproariously.

In the days that followed, Ellen learned with hard work and sore muscles the rudiments of staying on a horse through the long days of watching over John's growing herd of cattle.

She also learned how not to shoot a shotgun. Her first

acquaintance with the heavy double-barreled gun was a calamity. Having shouldered it too lightly, the report slammed the butt back into her shoulder and gave her a large, uncomfortable bruise. They had to wait until it healed before she could try again. The one good thing was that it made churning butter almost impossible, and she grinned as she watched Mary shoulder that chore.

"You hurt your shoulder on purpose," Mary chided with laughing dark eyes. "So you wouldn't have to push this dasher up and down in the churn."

"You can always get Isaac to teach you how to shoot, and use the same excuse," Ellen pointed out.

Mary grinned. "Not me. I am not going near a shotgun, not even to get out of such chores!"

Juana agreed wholeheartedly. "Too much bang!"

"I'll amen that," Mary agreed.

"I like it," Ellen mused. She liked even more knowing that John was afraid for her, that he cared about her. He'd even called her "darling" when he'd shot the snake. He wasn't a man to use endearments normally, which made the verbal slip even more pleasurable. She'd been walking around in a fog of pleasure ever since the rattler almost bit her. She was in love. She hoped that he was feeling something similar, but he'd been much too busy with work to hang around her, except at night. And then there was a very large audience. She sighed, thinking that privacy must be the most valuable commodity on earth. Although she was growing every day fonder of her companions, she often wished them a hundred miles away, so that she had even an hour alone with her husband. But patience was golden, she reminded herself. She must wait and hope for that to happen. Right now, survival itself was a struggle.

So was the shotgun. Her shoulder was well enough for a second try a week later. Two new complications, unbeknownst to Ellen, had just presented themselves. There were new mud puddles in the front yard, and her father had come to town and rented a buggy to ride out to visit his only child.

Ellen aimed the shotgun at a tree. The resulting kick made the barrel fly up. A wild turkey, which had been sitting on a limb, suddenly fell to the ground in a limp heap. And Ellen went backward right into the deepest mud puddle the saturated yard could boast.

At that particular moment, her father pulled up in front of the cabin.

Her father looked from Ellen to the turkey to the mud puddle to John. "I see that you are teaching my daughter to bathe and hunt at the same time," he remarked.

Ellen scrambled to her feet, wiping her hair back with

a muddy hand. She was so disheveled, and so dirty, that it was hard for her immaculate father to find her face at all.

He grimaced. "Ellen, darling, I think it might not be a bad idea if you came home with me," he began uneasily.

She tossed her head, slinging mud onto John, who was standing next to her looking concerned. "I'm only just learning to shoot, Father," she remarked proudly. "No one is proficient at first. Isn't that so, John?"

"Uh, yes," John replied, but without his usual confidence.

Her father looked from one to the other and then to the turkey. "I suppose buying meat from the market in town is too expensive?" he asked.

"I like variety. We had rattlesnake last week, in fact," Ellen informed him. "It was delicious."

Her father shook his head. "Your grandmother is going to have heart failure if I tell her what I've seen here. And young man, this house of yours…!" He spread an expansive hand helplessly.

"The sooner we get *our* spur line," Ellen told her father, "the quicker we will have a real house instead of merely a cabin."

John nodded hopefully.

Terrance Colby sighed heavily. "I'll see what I can do," he promised.

They both smiled. "Will you stay for dinner?" Ellen invited, glancing behind her. She grinned. "We're having turkey!"

Her father declined, unwilling to share the sad surroundings that his daughter seemed to find so exciting. There were three families living in that one cabin, he noted, and he wasn't certain that he was democratic enough to appreciate such close quarters. It didn't take a mind reader to note that Ellen and John had no privacy. That might be an advantage, he mused, if Ellen decided to come home. There would be no complications. But she seemed happy as a lark, and unless he was badly mistaken, that young man John Jacobs was delighted with her company. His wife's mother was not going to be happy when he got up enough nerve to tell her what had happened to Ellen. She was just on her way home from a vacation in Italy. Perhaps the ship would be blown off course and she would not get home for several months, he mused. Otherwise, Ellen was going to have a very unhappy visitor in the near future.

He did make time to see John's growing herd of cattle, and he noticed that the young man had a fine lot of very healthy steers. He'd already seen how enterprising Ellen was with her dressmaking and dairy sales. Now he saw a way to help John become quickly self-sufficient.

* * *

Word came the following week that Ellen's father was busy buying up right of way for the spur that would run to John's ranch. Not only that, he had become a customer for John's yearling steers, which he planned to feed to the laborers who were already hard at work on another stretch of his railroad. The only difficulty was that John was going to have to drive the steers north to San Antonio for Terrance Colby. Colby would be there waiting for him in a week. That wasn't a long cattle drive, certainly not as far as Kansas, but south Texas was still untamed and dangerous country. It would be risky. But John knew it would be worth the risk if he could deliver the beef.

So John and his men left, reluctantly on John's part, to drive the steers north. He and his fellow cowhands went around to all the other ranches, gathering up their steers, making sure they appropriated only the cattle that bore their 3J brand for the drive.

"I don't want to go," John told Ellen as they stood together, briefly alone, at the corral. "But I must protect our investment. There will be six of us to drive the herd, and we are all armed and well able to handle any trouble. Isaac and the older boys are going with me, but Luis will stay here to look after the livestock and all of you."

She sighed, smoothing her arms over the sleeves of

his shirt, enjoying the feel of the smooth muscles under it. "I do not like the idea of you going away. But I know that it is necessary, so I'll be brave."

"I don't like leaving you, either," he said bluntly. He bent and kissed her hungrily. "When I return, perhaps we can afford a single night away from here," he whispered roughly. "I am going mad to have you in my arms without a potential audience!"

"As I am," she choked, kissing him back hungrily.

He lifted her clear of the ground in his embrace, flying as they kissed without restraint. Finally, he forced himself to put her back down and he stepped away. There was a ruddy flush on his high cheekbones, and his green eyes were fierce. Her face was equally flushed, but her eyes were soft and dreamy, and her mouth was swollen.

She smiled up at him bravely, despite her concern. "Don't get shot."

He grimaced. "I'll do my best. You stay within sight of the cabin and Luis, even when you're milking those infernal cows. And don't go to town without him."

She didn't mention that it would be suicide to take Luis away from guarding the cattle, even for that long. She and the women would have to work something out, so that they could sell their dresses and butter and milk in town. But she would spare him the worry.

"We'll be very careful," she promised.

He sighed, his hand resting on the worn butt of his .45 caliber pistol. "We'll be back as soon as humanly possible. Your father…"

"If he comes to town, I'll go there to wait for you," she promised, a lie, because she'd never leave Mary and Juana by themselves, even with Luis and a shotgun around.

"Possibly that's what you should do, anyway," he murmured thoughtfully.

"I can't leave here now," she replied. "There's too much at stake. I'll help take care of our ranch. You take care of our profit margin."

He chuckled, surprised out of his worries. "I'll be back before you miss me too much," he said, bending to kiss her again, briefly. "Stay close to the cabin."

"I will. Have a safe trip."

He swung into the saddle, shouting for Isaac and the boys. The women watched them ride away. The cattle had already been pooled in a nearby valley, and the drovers were ready to get underway. As Ellen watched her tall husband ride away, she realized why he'd wanted his railroad spur so badly. Not only was it dangerous to drive cattle a long way to a railhead, but the potential risk to the men and animals was great. Not only was there a constant threat from thieves, there were floods and thunderstorms that could decimate herds. She prayed that John and Isaac and the men going with them would be safe. It was just as well that Luis was staying at the ranch to help safeguard the breeding bulls and cows, and the calves that were too young for market. Not that she was going to shirk her own responsibilities, Ellen thought stubbornly. Nobody was stealing anything around here while she could get her hands on a gun!

The threat came unexpectedly just two days after John and the others had left south Texas for San Antonio on the cattle drive.

Ellen had just carried a bucketful of milk to the kitchen when she peered out the open, glassless window at two figures on horseback, watching the cabin. She called softly to Juana and Mary.

Juana crossed herself. "It is Comanches!" she exclaimed. "They come to raid the cattle!"

"Well, they're not raiding them today," Ellen said angrily. "I'll have to ride out and get Luis and the boys," she said. "There's nothing else for it, and I'll have to go bareback. I'll never have time to saddle a horse with them sitting out there."

"It is too dangerous," Juana exclaimed. "You can hardly ride a saddled horse, and those men are Comanches. They are the finest riders of any men, even my Luis. You will never outrun them!"

Ellen muttered under her breath. They had so few cattle that even the loss of one or two could mean the difference between bankruptcy and survival. Well, she decided, there was only one thing to do. She grabbed up the shotgun, loaded it, and started out the back door, still in her dress and apron.

"No!" Mary almost screamed. "Are you crazy? Do you know what they do to white women?!"

Ellen didn't say a word. She kept walking, her steps firm and sure.

She heard frantic calls behind her, but she didn't listen. She and John had a ranch. These were her cattle as much as his. She wasn't about to let any thieves come and carry off her precious livestock!

The two Comanches saw her coming and gaped. They didn't speak. They sat on their horses with their eyes fixed, wide, at the young woman lugging a shotgun toward them.

One of them said something to the other one, who laughed and nodded.

She stopped right in front of them, lifted the shotgun, sighted along it and cocked it.

"This is my ranch," she said in a firm, stubborn tone. "You aren't stealing my cattle!"

There was pure admiration in their eyes. They didn't reach for the rifles lying across their buckskinned laps. They didn't try to ride her down. They simply watched her.

The younger of the two Indians had long pigtails and a lean, handsome face. His eyes, she noted curiously, were light.

"We have not come to steal cattle," the young one said in passable English. "We have come to ask Big John for work."

"Work?" she stammered.

He nodded. "We felt guilty that we butchered one of his calves. We had come far and were very hungry. We will work to pay for the calf. We hear from the Mexican people that he is also fair," he added surprisingly. "We know that he looks only at a man's work. He does not consider himself better than men of other colors. This is very strange. We do not understand it. Your people have just fought a terrible war because you wanted to own other people who had dark skin. Yet Big John lives with these people. Even with the Mexicans. He treats them as family."

"Yes," she said. She slowly uncocked the shotgun and lowered it to her side. "That is true."

The younger one smiled at her. "We know more about horses than even his vaquero, who knows much," he said without conceit. "We will work hard. When we pay back the cost of the calf, he can pay us what he thinks is fair."

She chuckled. "It's not really a big cabin, and it has three families living in it," she began.

They laughed. "We can make a teepee," the older one said, his English only a little less accented than the younger one's.

"I say," she exclaimed, "can you teach me to shoot a bow?!"

The younger one threw back his head and laughed uproariously. "Even his woman is brave," he told the older one. "Now do you believe me? This man is not as others with white skin."

"I believe you."

"Come along, then," Ellen said, turning. "I'll introduce you to…Luis! Put that gun down!" she exclaimed angrily when she saw the smaller man coming toward them with two pistols leveled. "These are our two new horse wranglers," she began. She stopped. "What are your names?" she asked.

"I am called Thunder," the young one said. "He is Red Wing."

"I am Ellen Jacobs," she said, "and that is Luis. Say hello, Luis."

The Mexican lowered his pistols and reholstered them with a blank stare at Ellen.

"Say hello," she repeated.

"Hello," he obliged, and he nodded.

The Comanches nodded back. They rode up to the cabin and dismounted. The women in the cabin peered out nervously.

"Luis will show you where to put your horses," Ellen told them. "We have a lean-to. Someday, we will have a barn!"

"Need bigger teepee first," Red Wing murmured, eyeing the cabin. "Bad place to live. Can't move house when floor get dirty."

"Yes, well, it's warm," Ellen said helplessly.

The young Comanche, Thunder, turned to look at her. "You are brave," he said with narrow light eyes. "Like my woman."

"She doesn't live with you?" she asked hesitantly.

He smiled gently. "She is stubborn, and wants to live in a cabin far away," he replied. "But I will bring her back here one day." He nodded and followed after Luis with his friend.

Juana and Mary came out of the cabin with worried expressions. "You going to let Indians live with us?" Juana exclaimed. "They kill us all!"

"No, they won't," Ellen assured them. "You'll see. They're going to be an asset!"

The Comanches did know more about horses than even Luis did, and they were handy around the place. They hunted game, taught Luis how to tan hides, and set about building a teepee out behind the cabin.

"Very nice," Ellen remarked when it was finished. "It's much roomier than the cabin."

"Easy to keep clean," Red Wing agreed. "Floor get dirty, move teepee."

She laughed. He smiled, going off to help Thunder with a new corral Juan was building.

John rode back in with Isaac and stopped short at the sight of a towering teepee next to the cabin he'd left two weeks earlier.

His hand went to his pistol as he thought of terrible possibilities that would explain its presence.

But Ellen came running out of the cabin, followed by Mary and Juana, laughing and waving.

John kicked his foot out of the stirrup of his new saddle and held his arm down to welcome Ellen as she leaped up into his arms. He kissed her hungrily, feeling as if he'd come home for the first time in his life.

He didn't realize how long that kiss lasted until he felt eyes all around him. He lifted his head to find two tall Comanches standing shoulder to shoulder with Juan and the younger boys and girls of the group, along with Juana and Mary.

"Bad habit," Thunder remarked disapprovingly.

"Bound to upset horse," Red Wing agreed, nodding.

"What the hell…!" John exclaimed.

"They're our new horse wranglers," Ellen said quickly. "That's Thunder, and that's Red Wing."

"They taught us how to make parfleche bags," Juana's eldest daughter exclaimed, showing one with beautiful beadwork.

"And how to make bows and arrows!" the next youngest of Isaac's sons seconded, showing his.

"And quivers," Luis said, resigned to being fired for what John would surely consider bad judgment in letting two Comanches near the women. He stood with his sombrero against his chest. "You may fire me if you wish."

"If you fire me, I'm going with them," Isaac's second son replied, pointing toward the Indians.

John shook his head, laughing uproariously. "I expect there'll be a lynch mob out here any day now," he sighed.

Everybody grinned.

Ellen beamed up at him. "Well, they certainly do know how to train horses, John," she said.

"Your woman meet us with loaded shotgun," Red Wing informed him. "She has strong spirit."

"And great heart," Thunder added. "She says we can work for you. We stay?"

John sighed. "By all means. All we need now is an Eskimo," he murmured to Ellen under his breath.

She looped her arms around his neck and kissed him. "Babies would be nice," she whispered.

He went scarlet, and everyone laughed.

"I got enough for the steers to buy a new bull," John told her. "Saddles for the horses we have, and four new horses," he added. "They're coming in with the rest of the drovers. I rode ahead to make sure you were all right."

She cuddled close to him as they stood out behind the cabin in a rare moment alone. "We had no trouble at all.

Well, except for the Comanches, but they turned out to be friends anyway."

"You could have blown me over when I saw that tee-pee," he confessed. "We've had some hard battles with Comanches in the past, over stolen livestock. And I know for a fact that two Comanches ate one of my calves…"

"They explained that," she told him contentedly. "They were hungry, but they didn't want to steal. They came here to work out the cost of the calf, and then to stay on, if you'll keep them. I think they decided that it's better to join a strong foe than oppose him. That was the reason they gave me, at least."

"Well, I must admit, these two Comanches are un-usual."

"The younger one has light eyes."

"I noticed." He didn't add what he was certain of—that these two Comanches were the fugitives that the de-puty marshal in Sutherland Springs had been looking for. Fortunately for them, James Graham had headed up beyond San Antonio to pursue them, acting on what now seemed to be a very bad tip.

She lifted her head and looked up at him. "They rode up and just sat there. I loaded my shotgun and went out to see what they wanted."

"You could have been killed," he pointed out.

"It's what you would have done, in my place," she reminded him, smiling gently. "I'm not afraid of much. And I've learned from you that appearances can be deceptive."

"You take chances."

"So do you."

He sighed. "You're learning bad habits from me."

She smiled and snuggled close. "Red Wing is going to make us a teepee of our own very soon." She kissed him, and was kissed back hungrily.

"Yesterday not be soon enough for that teepee," came a droll accented voice from nearby.

Red Wing was on the receiving end of two pairs of glaring eyes. He shrugged and walked off noiselessly, chuckling to himself.

John laughed. "Amen," he murmured.

"John, there's just one other little thing," Ellen murmured as she stood close to him.

"What now? You hired a gunslinger to feed the chickens?"

"I don't know any gunslingers. Be serious."

"All right. What?"

"My grandmother sent me a telegram. She's coming out here to save me from a life of misery and poverty."

He lifted his head. "Really!"

She drew in a soft breath. "I suppose she'll faint dead away when she sees this place, but I'm not going to be dragged back East by her or an army. I belong here."

"Yes, you do," John replied. "Although you certainly deserve better than this, Ellen," he said softly. He touched her disheveled hair. "I promise you, it's only going to get better."

She smiled. "I know that. We're going to have an empire, all our own."

"You bet we are."

"Built with our own two hands," she murmured, reaching up to kiss him, "and the help of our friends. All we need is each other."

"Need teepee worse," came Red Wing's voice again.

"Listen here," John began.

"Your horse got colic," the elder of the Comanches stood his ground. "What you feed him?"

"He ate corn," John said belligerently. "I gave him a feed bucket full!"

The older man scoffed. "No wonder he got colic. I fix."

"Corn is good for horses, and I know what to do for colic!"

"Sure. Not feed horse corn. Feed him grass. We build teepee tomorrow."

John still had his mouth open when the older man stalked off again.

"Indian ponies only eat grass," Ellen informed him brightly. "They think grain is bad for horses."

"You've learned a lot," he remarked.

"More than you might realize," she said dryly. She reached up to John's ear. "These two Comanches are running from the army. But I don't think they did anything bad, and I told Mr. Alton that I saw two Comanches heading north at a dead run. He told the…"

"…deputy marshal," he finished for her, exasperated.

"When you get to know them, you'll think they're good people, too," she assured him. "Besides, they're teaching me things I can't learn anywhere else. I can track a deer," she counted off her new skills, "weave a mat, make a bed out of pine straw, do beadwork, shoot a bow and arrow, and tan a hide."

"Good Lord, woman!" he exclaimed, impressed.

She grinned. "And I'm going to learn to hunt just as soon as you take me out with my shotgun."

He sighed. This was going to become difficult if any of her people stopped by to check on her. He didn't want to alienate them, but this couldn't continue.

"Ellen, what do you think about schooling?" he asked gently.

She blinked. "Excuse me?"

"Well, do any of the children know how to read and write?"

She hadn't considered that. "I haven't asked, but I don't expect they can. It was not legal for slaves to be taught such things, and I know that Juana can't even read Spanish, although it is her native tongue."

"The world we build will need educated people," he said thoughtfully. "It must start with the children, with this new generation. Don't you agree?"

"Yes," she said, warming quickly to the idea. "Educated people will no longer have to work at menial jobs, where they are at the mercy of others."

"That is exactly what I think. So, why don't you start giving the children a little book learning, in the evenings, after supper?" he suggested.

She smiled brightly. "You know, that's a very good idea. But, I have no experience as a teacher."

"All you will need are some elementary books and determination," he said. "I believe there is a retired schoolteacher in Victoria, living near the blacksmith. Shall I take you to see him?"

She beamed. "Would you?"

"Indeed I would. We'll go up there tomorrow," he replied, watching her consider the idea. If nothing else, it would spare her the astonished surprise of her people if they ever came to visit and found Ellen in dungarees and muddy boots skinning out a deer.

He drove her to Victoria the next morning in the small, dilapidated buggy he'd managed to afford from his cattle sales, hitched to one of the good horses he'd also acquired. Fortunately it took to pulling a buggy right away. Some horses didn't, and people died in accidents when they panicked and ran away.

The schoolteacher was long retired, but he taught Ellen the fundamentals she would need to educate small children. He also had a basic reader, a grammar book and a spelling book, which he gave to Ellen with his blessing. She clutched them like priceless treasure all the way back down the dusty road to the 3J Ranch.

"Do you think the Brown and the Rodriguez families will let me teach the children?" she wondered, a little worried after the fact. "They might not believe in education."

"Luis and Isaac can't even sign a paper," he told her. "They have to make an 'x' on a piece of paper and have me witness it. If they ever leave the ranch, they need to know how to read and write so that nobody will take advantage of them."

She looked at him with even more admiration than usual. He was very handsome to her, very capable and strong. She counted her blessings every single day that he'd thought her marriageable.

"You really care for them, don't you?" she asked softly.

"When the Union Army came through Atlanta, they burned everything in sight," he recalled, his face hardening. "Not just the big plantations where slaves were kept.

They burned poor white people's houses, because they thought we all had slaves down south." He laughed coldly. "Sharecroppers don't own anything. Even the house we lived in belonged to the plantation owner. They set it ablaze and my sister and mother were trapped inside. They burned to death while my other sister and I stood outside and watched." He touched his lean cheek, where the old scars were still noticeable. "I tried to kill the cavalry officer responsible, but his men saved him. They gave me these," he touched his cheek. "I never kept slaves. I hid Isaac and Mary in the root cellar when they ran away from the overseer. I couldn't save their oldest son, but Mary was pregnant. She and Isaac saved me from the Union Army," he said with a sigh. "They pleaded for my life. Shocked the cavalry into sparing me and my oldest sister. Isaac helped me bury my mother and my younger sister." He looked down at her soft, compassionate expression. "My sister went to North Carolina to live with a cousin, but I wanted to go to my uncle in Texas. Isaac and Mary had no place else to go, so they traveled with me. They said they wanted to start over, but they didn't fool me. They came with me to save me from the Union Army if I got in trouble. Those two never forget a debt. I owe them everything. My life. That's why they're partners with me."

"And how did you meet Luis and Juana?" she asked.

"Luis was the only cowboy my uncle had who wasn't

robbing him blind. Luis told me what the others had done, and I fired the lot. I took care of my uncle, with their help, and rounded up stray calves to start my herd." He chuckled. "The cabin was the only structure on the place. It got real crowded when Isaac and Mary moved in with me. Juana and Luis were going to live in the brush, but I insisted that we could all manage. We have. But it hasn't been easy."

"And now the Comanches are building teepees for us," she told him. "They've been hunting constantly to get enough skins. We're going to have privacy for the very first time. I mean…" She flushed at her own forwardness.

He reached for her small hand and held it tight. His eyes burned into hers. "I want nothing more in the world than to be alone with you, Camellia Ellen Jacobs," he said huskily. "The finest thing I ever did in my life was have the good sense to marry you!"

"Do you really think so?" she asked happily. "I am no beauty…"

"You have a heart as big as all outdoors and the courage of a wolf. I wouldn't trade you for a debutante."

She beamed, leaning against his broad shoulder. "And I would not trade you for the grandest gentleman who ever lived. Although I expect you will make a fine gentleman, when we have made our fortune."

He kissed her forehead tenderly. "You are my fortune," he said huskily.

"You mean, because my father is giving us a railroad spur for a wedding present," she said, confused.

He shook his head. "Because you are my most prized treasure," he whispered, and bent to kiss her mouth tenderly.

She kissed him back, shyly. "I had never kissed anyone until you came along," she whispered.

He chuckled. "You improve with practice!"

"John!" she chided.

He only laughed, letting her go to pay attention to the road. "We must get on down the road. It looks like rain." He gave her a roguish glance. "We would not want you to tumble into a mud puddle, Mrs. Jacobs."

"Are you ever going to forget that?" she moaned.

"In twenty years or so, perhaps," he said. "But I cannot promise. That is one of my most delightful memories. You were so game, and Sir Sydney was such a boor!"

"Indeed he was. I hope he marries for money and discovers that she has none."

"Evil girl," he teased.

She laughed. "Well, you will never be able to accuse ME of marrying you for your money," she said contentedly. "In twenty years or so," she added, repeating his own phrase, "you will be exceedingly rich. I just know it."

"I hope to break even, at least, and be able to pay my debts," he said. "But I would love to have a ranch as big as a state, Ellen, and the money to breed fine cattle, and even fine horses." He glanced at her. "Now that we have two extra horse wranglers, we can start building up our herd."

She only smiled. She was glad that she'd stood up to the Comanches. She wondered if they'd ever have wanted to work for them if she'd run away and hid.

The teepee the Comanches built for the couple was remarkably warm and clean. No sooner was it up than Ellen built a small cooking fire near its center and put on a black iron pot of stew to cook. Red Wing had already taught her how to turn the pole in the center to work the flap for letting smoke out while she cooked. She also learned that she was born to be a rancher's wife. Every chore came easily to her. She wasn't afraid of hard work, and she fell more in love with her roguish, unconventional husband every day. She did still worry about her grandmother coming down to rescue her. She had no intention of being carted off back East, where she would have to dress and act with decorum.

She sat the children down in the cabin one evening after she and the other women and older girls had cleared away the precious iron cookware and swished the tin plates and few utensils in a basin of soapy water and wiped them with a dishrag.

"What are we going to do?" one of Juana's daughters asked.

Ellen produced the books that the retired Victoria schoolteacher had given her, handling them like treasure.

"I'm going to teach you children to read and write," she told them.

Mary and Juana stood quietly by, so still that Ellen was made uneasy.

"Is it all right?" she asked the adults, concerned, because she'd worried that they might think education superfluous.

"Nobody ever taught me to write my name," Mary said. "Nor Isaac, either. We can only make an x. Could you teach me to write? And read?"

"Me, too!" Juana exclaimed.

Their husbands looked as if they might bite their tongues off trying not to ask if they could learn, too, but they managed.

"You can all gather around and we'll let the older folk help show the young ones how to do it," she said, managing a way to spare the pride of the men in the process of teaching them as well.

"Yes, we can show them, *señora*," Luis said brightly.

"Sure we can," Isaac added with a big grin.

"Gather around, then." She opened the book with a huge smile and began the first lesson.

She looked down at the dungarees she was wearing with boots that John had bought her. She had on one of his big checked long-sleeved shirts, with the sleeves rolled up, and her hair was caught in a ponytail down her back. She checked the stew in her black cooking pot and wiped sweat from her brow with a weary hand. The Comanches had gathered pine straw from under the short-leafed pines in the thicket to make beds, which Ellen covered with quilts she and the other women had made in their precious free time. It wasn't a mansion, but she and John would have privacy for the first time that night. She thought of the prospect with joy and a certain amount of trepidation. Like most young women of her generation, her upbringing had been very strict and moral. She knew almost nothing of what happened between married people in the dark. What she didn't know made her nervous.

The sudden noise outside penetrated her thoughts. She heard voices, one raised and strident, and she ran out of the teepee and to the cabin to discover a well-dressed, elderly woman with two young men in immaculate suits exchanging heated words with Juana, who couldn't follow a thing they were saying. Mary was out with the others collecting more wood for the fireplace in the small cabin.

"Do you understand me?" the old woman was shouting. "I am looking for Ellen Colby!"

"Grandmother!" Ellen exclaimed when she recognized the woman.

Her grandmother Amelia Greene was standing beside the buggy beside two tall young men whom Ellen recognized as her cousins.

Amelia turned stiffly, her whole expression one of utter disapproval when she saw the way her granddaughter was dressed.

"Camellia Ellen Colby!" she exclaimed. "What has become of you!"

"Now, Grandmother," Ellen said gently, "you can't expect a pioneer wife to dress and act as a lady in a drawing room."

The older woman was not convinced. She was bristling with indignation. "You will get your things together and come home with me right away!" she demanded. "I am not leaving you here in the dirt with these peasants!"

Ellen's demeanor changed at once from one of welcome and uneasiness to one of pure outrage. She stuck both hands on her slender hips and glared at her grandmother.

"How dare you call my friends peasants!" she exclaimed furiously. She went to stand beside Juana. "Juana's husband Luis, and Mary's husband Isaac, are our partners in this ranching enterprise. They are no one's servants!"

Mary came to stand beside her as well, and the children gathered around them. While the old woman and her companions were getting over that shock, John came striding up, with his gunbelt on, accompanied by Luis and Isaac and the two Comanche men.

Amelia Greene screeched loudly and jumped behind the tallest of her grandchildren.

"How much you want for old woman?" Red Wing asked deliberately, pointing at Amelia.

Amelia looked near to fainting.

Ellen laughed helplessly. "He's not serious," she assured her grandmother.

"I should hope not!" the tallest of her cousins muttered, glaring at him. "The very idea! Why do you allow Indians here?"

"These are our horse wranglers," Ellen said pointedly. "Red Wing and Thunder. And those are our partners, Luis Rodriguez and Isaac Brown. Gentlemen, my grandmother, Amelia Greene of New York City."

Nobody spoke.

John came forward to slide his arm around Ellen's waist. He was furious at the way her relatives were treating the people nearby.

"Hospitality is almost a religion to us out here in Texas," John drawled, although his green eyes were flashing like green diamonds. "But as you may notice, we have no facilities to accommodate visitors yet."

"You cannot expect that we would want to stay?" the shorter cousin asked indignantly. "Come, Grandmother, let us go back to town. Ellen is lost to us. Surely you can see that?"

Ellen glared at him. "Five years from now, cousin, you will not recognize this place. A lot of hard work is going to turn it into a showplace...."

"Of mongrels!" her grandmother said haughtily.

"I'm sorry you feel that way, but I find your company equally taxing," Ellen shot back. "Now will you all please leave? I have chores, as do the others. Unlike you, I do not sit in the parlor waiting for other people to fetch and carry at my instructions."

The old woman glowered. "Very well, then, live out here in the wilds with savages! I only came to try and save you from a life of drudgery!"

"Pickles and bread," Ellen retorted haughtily. "You came hoping to entice me back into household slavery.

Until I escaped you and came west with my father, I was your unpaid maidservant for most of my life."

"What else are you fit for?" her grandmother demanded. "You have no looks, no talent, no…!"

"She is lovely," John interrupted. "Gentle and kind and brave. She is no one's servant here, and she has freedom of a sort you will never know."

The old woman's eyes were poisonously intent. "She will die of hard work here, for certain!"

"On her own land, making her own empire," John replied tersely. "The road is that way," he added, pointing.

She tossed her head and sashayed back to the buggy, to be helped in by her grandsons, one of whom gave Ellen a wicked grin before he climbed in and took the reins.

"Drive on," Amelia said curtly. "We have no kinfolk here!"

"Truer words were never spoken," Ellen said sweetly. "Do have a safe trip back to town. Except for cattle thieves from Mexico and the bordering counties of Texas, and bank robbers, there should be nothing dangerous in your path. But I would drive very fast, if I were you!"

There were muttered, excited exchanges of conversation in the buggy before the tallest grandson used the buggy whip and the small vehicle raced forward down the dusty dirt road in the general direction of town.

"You wicked girl!" John exclaimed on a burst of laughter, hugging her close.

"So much for my rescuers," she murmured contentedly, hugging him back. "Now we can get back to work!"

That night, Ellen and John spent their first night alone, without prying eyes or ears, in the teepee the Comanches had provided for them.

"I am a little nervous," she confessed when John had put out the small fire and they were together in the darkness.

"That will not last," he promised, drawing her close. "We are both young, and we have all the years ahead to become more accustomed to each other. All you must remember is that I care more for you than for any woman I have ever known. You are my most prized treasure. I love you. I will spend my life trying to make you happy."

"John!" She pressed close to him and raised her face. "I will do the same. I adore you!"

He bent and kissed her softly, and then not so softly. Tender caresses gave way to stormy, devouring kisses. They sank to the makeshift mattress and there, locked tight in each others' arms, they gave way to the smoldering passion that had grown between them for long weeks. At first she was inhibited, but he was skillful and slow and tender. Very soon, her passion rose to meet his. The sharpness of passion was new between them, and as it grew, they became playful together. They laughed, and then the laughing stopped as they tasted the first sweet sting of mutual delight in the soft, enveloping darkness.

When Ellen finally fell asleep in John's arms, she thought that there had never been a happier bride in the history of Texas.

Chapter Six

Ellen's grandmother and cousins went back East. Her father came regularly to visit them in their teepee, finding it touching and amusing at once that they were happy with so little. He even offered to loan them enough to build a bigger cabin, but they refused politely. All they wanted, Ellen reminded him, was a spur of the railroad.

That, too, was finally finished. John loaded his beef cattle into the cattle cars bound for the stockyards of the Midwest. The residents of the ranch settled into hard work and camaraderie, and all their efforts eventually resulted in increasing prosperity.

The first thing they did with their newfound funds was to add to the cattle herd. The second was to build individual cabins for the Rodriguez and Brown clans, replacing the teepees the Comanches had built for them. The Comanches, offered a handsome log cabin of their own, declined abruptly, although politely. They could never understand the white man's interest in a stationary house that had to be cleaned constantly, when it was so much easier to move the teepee to a clean spot! However, John and Ellen continued to live in their own teepee for the time being, as well, to save money.

A barn was the next project. As in all young communities, a barbecue and a quilting bee were arranged along with a barnraising. All the strong young men of the area turned out and the resulting barn and corral were quick fruit of their efforts. Other ranches were springing up around the 3J Ranch, although not as large and certainly not with the number of cattle and horses that John's now boasted.

The railroad spur, when it came, brought instant prosperity to the area it served. It grew and prospered even as some smaller towns in the area became ghost towns. Local citizens decided that they needed a name for their small town, which had actually grown up around the ranch itself even before the railroad came. They decided to call it Jacobsville, for John Jacobs, despite his protests. His hard work and lack of prejudice had made him good friends and dangerous enemies in the surrounding area.

But when cattle were rustled and houses robbed, his was never among them. Bandits from over the border made a wide route around the ranch.

As the cattle herd grew and its refinement continued, the demand for Jacobs's beef grew as well. John bought other properties to go along with his own, along with barbed wire to fence in his ranges. He hired on new men as well, black drovers as well as Mexican and white. There was even a Chinese drover who had heard of the Jacobs ranch far away in Arizona and had come to it looking for a job. Each new addition to the ranch workforce was placed under the orders of either Luis or Isaac, and the number of outbuildings and line camps grew steadily.

Ellen worked right alongside the other women, adding new women to her dressmaking enterprise, until she had enough workers and enough stock to open a dress shop in their new town of Jacobsville. Mary and Juana took turns as proprietors while Ellen confined herself to sewing chair and sofa covers for the furniture in the new white clapboard house John had built her. She and her handsome husband grew closer by the day, but one thing was still missing from her happiness. Their marriage was entering into its second year with no hope of a child.

John never spoke of it, but Ellen knew he wanted children. So did she. It was a curious thing that their passion for each other was ever growing, but bore no fruit. Still, they had a good marriage and Ellen was happier than she ever dreamed of being.

In the second year of their marriage, his sister Jeanette came west on the train with her husband and four children to visit. Only then did Ellen learn the extent of the tragedy that had sent John west in the first place. The attack by the Union troops had mistakenly been aimed at the sharecroppers' cabin John and his mother and sisters occupied, instead of the house where the owner's vicious overseer lived. The house had caught fire and John's mother and elder sister had burned to death. John had not been able to save them. The attack had been meant for the overseer who had beaten Isaac and Mary's son to death, along with many other slaves. John was told, afterward, but his grief was so sweeping that he hardly understood what was said to him. His sister made sure that he did know. The cavalry officer had apologized to her, and given her money for the trip to North Carolina, unbeknownst to John. His sister obviously adored him, and he was a doting uncle to her children.

She understood John's dark moods better after that, the times when he wanted to be alone, when he went hunting and never brought any wild game home with him. Ellen and Jeanette became close almost at once, and wrote to each other regularly even when Jeanette and her family went home to North Carolina.

Deputy Marshal James Graham had come by unexpectedly and mentioned to John that he hadn't been able to find the two Comanche fugitives who were supposed to have shot a white man over a horse. It turned out that the white man had cheated the Comanches and had later been accused of cheating several army officers in horse trading deals. He was arrested, tried and sent to prison. So, Graham told John, the Comanches weren't in trouble anymore. Just in case John ever came across them.

Thunder and Red Wing, told of the white man's arrest, worked a few months longer for John and then headed north with their wages. Ellen was sad to see them go, but Thunder had promised that they would meet again one day.

The Maxwells came to visit often from Scotland, staying in the beautiful white Victorian house John later built for his beloved wife. They gave the couple the benefit of their extensive experience of horses, and John branched out into raising Thoroughbreds. Eventually a Thoroughbred of the lineage from his ranch would win the Triple Crown.

Years passed with each year bringing new prosperity to the 3J Ranch. One May morning, Ellen unexpectedly fainted at a church social. John carried her to the office of their new doctor, who had moved in just down the boardwalk from the new restaurant and hotel.

The doctor examined her and, when John had been invited into the examination room, grinned at him. "You are to be a father, young man," he said. "Congratulations!"

John looked at Ellen as if she'd just solved the great mystery of life. He lifted her clear of the floor and kissed her with aching tenderness. His happiness was complete, now.

Almost immediately, he began to worry about labor. He remembered when Luis's and Isaac's wives had given birth, and he turned pale.

The doctor patted him on the back. "You'll survive the birth of your children, Mr. Jacobs, we all do. Yes, even me. I have had to deliver mine. Something, I daresay, you will be spared!"

John laughed with relief, thanked the doctor for his perception, and kissed Ellen again.

She bore him three sons and two daughters in the years that followed, although only two of their children, their son Bass and their daughter Rose Ellen, lived to adulthood. The family grew and prospered in Jacobsville. Later, the entire county, Jacobs, was named for John as well. He diversified his holdings into mining and real estate and banking. He was the first in south Texas to try new techniques in cattle ranching and to use mechanization to improve his land.

The Brown family produced six children in all. Their youngest, Caleb, would move to Chicago and become a famous trial lawyer. His son would be elected to the United States Senate.

The Rodriguez family produced ten children. One of their sons became a Texas Ranger, beginning a family tradition that lived on through subsequent generations.

John Jacobs founded the first bank in Jacobs County, along with the first dry goods store. He worked hard at breeding good cattle, but he made his fortune in the terrible blizzard of 1885-86 in which so many cattlemen lost their shirts. He endowed a college and an orphanage, and, always active in local politics, he was elected to the U.S. Senate at the age of fifty. He and Ellen never parted for fifty years.

His son, Bass Jacobs, married twice. By his young second wife, he had a son, Bass, Jr., and a daughter, Violet Ellen. Bass Jacobs, Jr., was the last of the Jacobs family to own land in Jacobs County. The 3J Ranch was sold after his death. His son, Ty, born in 1955, eventually moved to Arizona and married and settled there. His daughter, Shelby, born in 1961, stayed in Jacobsville and married a local man, Justin Ballenger. They produced three sons. One of them was named John Jackson Jacobs Ballenger, so that the founding father of Shelby's family name would live on in memory.

A bronze statue of Big John Jacobs, mounted on one of the Arabian stallions his ranch became famous for, was erected in the town square of Jacobsville just after the first world war.

Portraits of the Rodriguez family and the Brown family are prominently displayed in the Jacobs County Museum, alongside a portrait of Camellia Ellen Jacobs, dressed in an elegant blue gown, but with a shotgun in a fringed sheath at her feet and a twinkle in her blue eyes. All three portraits, which had belonged to Bass Jacobs, Jr., were donated to the museum by Shelby Jacobs Ballenger. In a glass case nearby are a bow and arrow in a beaded rawhide quiver, in which also resides a black-and-white photograph of a Comanche warrior with a blond woman and five children, two of whom are also blond. But that is another story…

Justin

Chapter One

It was a warm morning, and the weatherman had already promised temperatures into the eighties for the afternoon. But the weather didn't seem to slow down the bidders, and the auctioneer standing on the elegant porch of the tall white mansion kept his monotone steady even though he had to periodically wipe streams of sweat from his heavily jowled face.

As he watched the estate auction, Justin Ballenger's black eyes narrowed under the brim of his expensive creamy Stetson. He wasn't buying. Not today. But he had a personal interest in this particular auction. The Jacobs's home was being sold, lock, stock, and barrel, and he should have felt a sense of triumph at seeing old Bass

Jacobs's legacy go down the drain. Oddly enough, he didn't. He felt vaguely disturbed by the whole proceeding. It was like watching predators pick a helpless victim to the bone.

He kept searching the crowd for Shelby Jacobs, but she was nowhere in sight. Possibly she and her brother, Tyler, were in the house, helping to sort the furniture and other antique offerings.

A movement to his left caught his eye. Abby Ballenger, his sister-in-law of six weeks, stood beside him.

"I didn't expect to see you here," she remarked, smiling up at him. She'd lived with him and Calhoun, her almost-stepbrothers, since the tragic deaths of their father and her mother. Their parents were to have been married, so the brothers took Abby in and looked after her. And just weeks before, she and Calhoun had married.

"I never miss an auction," he replied. He looked toward the auctioneer. "I haven't seen the Jacobses."

"Ty's in Arizona." Abby sighed, and she didn't miss the sudden glare of Justin's dark eyes. "He didn't go without a fight, either, but there was some kind of emergency on that ranch he's helping to manage."

"Shelby's alone?" The words were almost wrenched from him.

"Afraid so." Abby glanced up at him and away, barely

suppressing a smile. "She's at the apartment she's rented in town." Abby smoothed a fold of her gray skirt. "It's above the law office where she works…"

Justin's hard, dark face went even tauter. The smoking cigarette in his hand was forgotten as he turned to Abby, his whipcord-lean body towering over her. "That isn't an apartment, for God's sake, it's an old storeroom!"

"Barry Holman is letting her convert it," Abby said, her guileless pale eyes the picture of innocence under her dark hair. "She doesn't have much choice, Justin. With the house being sold, where else can she afford to live on what she makes? Everything had to go, you know. Tyler and Shelby thought they could at least hold onto the house and property, but it took every last dime to meet their father's debts."

Justin muttered something under his breath, glaring toward the big, elegant house that somehow embodied everything he'd hated about the Jacobs family for the past six years, since Shelby had broken their engagement and betrayed him.

"Aren't you glad?" Abby baited him gently. "You hate her, after all. It should please you to see her brought to her knees in public."

He didn't say another word. He turned abruptly, his expression as uncompromising as stone, and strode to where his black Thunderbird was parked. Abby smiled secretively. She'd thought that he'd react, if she could make him see how badly this was going to hurt Shelby. All these long years he'd avoided any contact with the Jacobs family, any mention of them at home. But in recent months, the strain was beginning to tell on him. Abby knew almost certainly that he still felt something for the woman who'd jilted him, and she knew Shelby felt something for Justin, too. Abby, deliriously happy in her own marriage, wanted the rest of the world to be as happy as she was. Perhaps by nudging Justin in the right direction, she might make two miserable people happy.

Justin had only found out about the estate sale that morning, when Calhoun mentioned it at the office at their joint feedlot operation. It had been in the papers, but Justin had been out of town looking at cattle and he hadn't seen the notice.

He wasn't surprised that Shelby was staying away from the auction. She'd been born in that house. She'd lived in it all her life. Shelby's grandfather, in fact, had founded the small Texas town of Jacobsville. They were old money, and the ragged little Ballenger boys from the run-down cattle ranch down the road weren't the kind of friends Mrs. Bass Jacobs had wanted for her children, Tyler and Shelby. But she'd died, and Mr. Jacobs had been friendly toward the Ballengers, especially when

Justin and Calhoun had opened their feedlot. And when the old man found out that Shelby intended to marry Justin Ballenger, he'd told Justin he couldn't be more pleased.

Justin tried never to think about the night Bass Jacobs and young Tom Wheelor had come to see him. Now it all came back. Bass Jacobs had been upset. He told Justin outright that Shelby was in love with Tom and not only in love, the couple had been sleeping together all through the farce of Shelby's "engagement" to Justin. He was ashamed of her, Bass lamented. The engagement was Shelby's way of bringing her reluctant suitor into line, and now that Justin had served his purpose, Shelby didn't need him anymore. Sadly, he handed Justin Shelby's engagement ring and Tom Wheelor had mumbled a red-faced apology. Bass had even cried. Perhaps his shame had prompted his next move, because he'd promised on the spot to give Justin the financial backing he needed to make the new feedlot a success. There was only one condition—that Shelby never know where the money came from. Then he'd left.

Never one to believe ill of anyone without hard evidence, Justin phoned Shelby while Bass was still starting his car. But she didn't deny what Justin had been told. In fact, she confirmed all of it, even the part about having slept with Wheelor. She'd only wanted to make

Tom jealous so he'd propose, she told Justin. She hoped he hadn't been too upset with her, but then, she'd always had everything she wanted, and Justin wasn't rich enough to cater to her tastes just yet. But Tom was...

Justin had believed her. And because she'd pushed him away the one time he'd tried to make love to her, her confession rang with the truth. He'd gone on a legendary bender afterward. And for the past six years, no other woman had ever gotten close enough to make a dent in his heart. He'd been impervious to all the offers, and there had been some. He wasn't a handsome man. His dark face was too craggy, his features too irregular, his unsmiling countenance too forbidding. But he had wealth and power, and that drew women to him. He was too bitter, though, to accept that kind of attention. Shelby had hurt him as no one else in his life ever had, and for years all he'd lived for was the thought of vengeance.

But now that he saw her brought to her knees financially, it was unsatisfying. All he could think of was that she was going to be hurt and she had no family, no friends to comfort her.

The apartment above the law office where she worked was tiny, and it didn't sit well with him that it was in such proximity to her bachelor boss. He knew Holman by reputation, and rumor had it that he liked pretty women. Shelby, with her long black hair, slender figure and green, sparkling eyes, would more than qualify. She was twenty-seven now, hardly a girl, but she didn't look much older than she had when she and Justin became engaged. She had an innocence about her, still, that made Justin grind his teeth. It was false; she'd even admitted it.

He paused at the door to the apartment, his hand raised to knock. There was a muffled noise from inside. Not laughter. Tears?

His jaw tautened and he knocked roughly.

The noise ceased abruptly. There was a scraping sound, like a chair being moved, and soft footsteps that echoed the quick, hard beat of his heart.

The door opened. Shelby stood there, in clinging faded jeans and a blue checked shirt, her long dark hair disheveled and curling down her back, her green eyes red-rimmed and wet.

"Did you come to gloat, Justin?" she asked with quiet bitterness.

"It gives me no pleasure to see you humbled," he replied, his chin lifted, his black eyes narrow. "Abby said you were alone."

She sighed, dropping her eyes to his dusty, worn boots. "I've been alone for a long time. I've learned to live with it." She shifted restlessly. "Are there a lot of people at the auction?"

"The yard's full," he said. He took off his hat and held it in one hand while the other raked his thick, straight black hair.

She looked up, her eyes lingering helplessly on the hard lines of his craggy face, on the chiseled mouth she'd kissed so hungrily six years ago. She'd been so desperately in love with him then. But he'd become something out of her slight experience the night they became engaged, and his ardor had frightened her. She'd fought away from him, and the memory of how it had been with him, just before the fear became tangible, was formidable. She'd wanted so much more than they'd shared, but she had more reason than most women to fear intimacy. But Justin didn't know that and she'd been too shy to explain her actions.

She turned away with a groan of anguish. "If you can bear my company, I'll fix you a glass of iced tea."

He hesitated, but only for an instant. "I could use that," he said quietly. "It's hot as hell out there."

He followed her inside, absently closing the door behind him. But he stopped dead when he saw what she was having to contend with. He stiffened and almost cursed out loud.

There were only two rooms in the makeshift apartment. They were bare except for a worn sofa and chair, a scratched coffee table and a small television set. Her clothes were apparently being kept in a closet, because there was no evidence of a dresser. The kitchen boasted a toaster oven and a hot plate and a tiny refrigerator. This, when she was used to servants and silk robes, silver services and Chippendale furniture.

"My God," he breathed.

Her back stiffened, but she didn't turn when she heard the pity in his deep voice. "I don't need sympathy, thank you," she said tightly. "It wasn't my fault that we lost the place, it was my father's. It was his to lose. I can make my own way in the world."

"Not like this, damn it!" He slammed his hat down on the coffee table and took the pitcher of tea out of her hands, moving it aside. His lean, work-roughened hands held her wrists and he stared down at her with determination. "I won't stand by and watch you try to survive in a rattrap like this. Barry Holman and his charity be damned!"

Shelby was shocked, not only by what he was saying, but by the way he looked. "It's not a rattrap," she faltered.

"Compared to what you were used to, it is," he returned doggedly. His chest rose and fell on an angry sigh. "You can stay with me for the time being."

She blushed beet red. "In your house, alone with you?"

He lifted his chin. "In my house," he agreed. "*Not* in my bed. You won't have to pay me for a roof over your head. I do remember with vivid clarity that you don't like my hands on you."

She could have gone through the floor at the bitter mockery in the words. She couldn't meet those black eyes or challenge the flat statement without embarrassing them both. Anyway, it was so long ago. It didn't matter now.

She looked at his shirt instead, at the thick mat of black hair under the white silk. He'd let her touch him there, once. The night of their engagement, he'd unbuttoned it and given her hands free license to do what they liked. He'd kissed her as if he'd die to kiss her, but he'd frightened her half out of her mind when the kisses went a little too far.

Until that night, he'd never tried to touch her, or gone further than brief, light kisses. His holding back had first disturbed her and then made her curious. Surely Justin was as experienced as his brother, Calhoun. But perhaps he'd had hang-ups about the distance between their social standing. Justin had been barely middle class at the time, and Shelby's family was wealthy. It hadn't mattered to her, but she could see that it might have bothered Justin. And especially after she jilted him, because of her father's treacherous insistence.

She'd gotten even with her father, though. He'd planned for her to marry Tom Wheelor, in a cold-blooded merger of property, and Justin had gotten in the way. But Shelby had refused Tom Wheelor's advances and she'd never let him touch her. She'd told Bass Jacobs she wouldn't marry his wealthy young friend. The old man hadn't capitulated then, but just before his death, when he realized how desperately Shelby loved Justin, he'd felt bad about what he'd done. He hadn't told her that his guilt had driven him to stake Justin's feedlot, but he'd apologized.

She looked up then, searching Justin's dark eyes quietly, remembering. It had been hard, going on without him. Her dreams of loving him and bearing his sons had died long ago, but it was still a pleasure beyond bearing just to look at him. And his hands on her wrists made her body glow, tingle with forbidden longings, like the warm threat of his powerful, cologne-scented body. If only her father hadn't interfered. Inevitably, she'd have been able to explain her fears to Justin, to ask him to be gentle, to go slow. But it was too late now.

"I know you don't want me anymore, Justin," she said gently. "I even understand why. You don't need to feel responsible for me. I'll be all right. I can take care of myself."

He breathed slowly, trying to keep himself under control. The feel of her silky skin was giving him some problems. Unwillingly, his thumbs began to caress her wrists.

"I know that," he said. "But you don't belong here."

"I can't afford a better apartment just yet," she said. "But I'll get a raise when I've been working for two months, and then maybe I can get the room that Abby had at Mrs. Simpson's."

"You can get it now," he said tersely. "I'll loan you the money."

She lowered her eyes. "No. It wouldn't look right."

"Only you and I would know."

She bit her lower lip. She couldn't tell him that she hated the thought of being in this place, so near Barry Holman, who was a nice boss but a hopeless womanizer. She hesitated.

Before she could say yes or no, there was a knock on the door. Justin let her go reluctantly and watched her move toward the door.

Barry Holman stood there, in jeans and a sweatshirt, blond and blue-eyed and hopeful. "Hi, Shelby," he said pleasantly. "I thought you might need some help moving…in." His voice trailed away as he saw Justin standing behind her.

"Not really," Justin said with a cold smile. "She's on her

way over to Mrs. Simpson's to take on Abby's old room. I'm helping her move, although I knew she appreciated the offer of this—" he looked around distastefully "—apartment."

Barry Holman swallowed. He'd known Justin for a long time, and he was just about convinced that the rumors he'd heard were true. Justin might not want Shelby himself, but he was damned visible if anybody else made a pass at her.

"Well," he said, still smiling, "I'd better get back downstairs then. I had some calls to make. Good to see you again, Justin. See you early Monday morning, Shelby."

"Thanks anyway, Mr. Holman," she said. "I don't want to seem ungrateful, but Mrs. Simpson offers meals as well, and it's peaceful there." She smiled. "I'm not used to town living, and Mrs. Simpson has the room free right now…"

"No hard feelings, you go right ahead." Barry grinned. "So long."

Justin glared after him. "Lover boy," he muttered. "Just what you need."

She turned, her eyes soft on his face. "I'm twenty-seven," she said. "I want to marry and have children eventually. Mr. Holman is very nice, and he doesn't have any bad habits."

"Except that he'll sleep with anything that wears skirts," he replied tersely. He didn't like thinking about Shelby having another man's children. His black eyes searched over her body. Yes, she was getting older, not that she looked it. In eight or ten years, children might be a risk for her. His expression hardened.

"He's never said anything improper to me." She faltered, confused by the way he was looking at her.

"Give him time." He drew in a slow breath. "I said I'll loan you enough to get the room at Mrs. Simpson's. If you're hell-bent on independence, you can pay me back at your convenience."

She had to swallow her pride, and it hurt to let him help her when she knew how bitter he was about the past. But he was a caring man, and she was a stray person in the world. Justin's heart was too big to allow him to turn his back on her, even after what he thought she'd done to him. Quick, hot tears sprang to her green eyes as she remembered what she'd been forced to say to him, the way she'd hurt him.

"I'm so sorry," she said unexpectedly, biting her lip as she turned away.

The words, and the emotion behind them, surprised him. Surely she didn't have any regrets this late. Or was she just putting on an act to get his sympathy? He couldn't trust her.

She got herself back together and brushed at the loose hair at her neck as she poured the tea into two glasses filled with ice. "I'll let you lend me the money, if you really don't mind," she said, handing him his glass without looking up. "I don't like the idea of living alone."

"Neither do I, Shelby, but it's something you get used to after a while," he said quietly. He sipped his tea, but he couldn't pry his eyes away from her soft oval face. "What is it like, having to work for a living?"

She didn't react to the mockery in the words. She smiled. "I like it," she said surprisingly, and lifted her eyes to his. "I had things to do, you know, when we had money. I belonged to a lot of volunteer groups and charities. But law offices cater to unhappy people. When I can help them feel a little better, it makes me forget my own problems."

His black brows drew together as he sipped the cool, sweet amber liquid. The glass was cold under his lean fingers.

She searched his black eyes. "You don't believe me, do you, Justin?" she asked perceptively. "You saw me as a socialite; a reasonably attractive woman with money and a cultured background. But that was an illusion. You never really knew me."

"I wanted you, though," he replied, watching her. "But you never wanted me, honey. Not physically, at any rate."

"You rushed me!" she burst out, coloring as she remembered that night.

"Rushed you! Up until that night, I hadn't even kissed you intimately, for God's sake!" His black eyes glittered at her as he remembered her rejection and his own sick certainty that she didn't love him. "I'd kept you on a pedestal until then. And all the time, you were sleeping with that boy millionaire!"

She threw up her hands. "I never slept with Tom Wheelor!"

"You said you did," he reminded her with a cold smile. "You swore it, in fact."

She closed her eyes on a wave of bitter regret. "Yes, I said it," she agreed wearily, and turned away. "I'd almost forgotten."

"And all the post mortems accomplish nothing, do they?" he asked. He put down the glass and pulled out a cigarette, lighting it without removing his eyes from her stiff expression. "It doesn't matter anymore. Let's go. I'll run over to Mrs. Simpson's and you can see about the room."

Shelby knew that he'd never give an inch. He hadn't forgotten anything and he still despised her. She felt as if the world was sitting on her thin shoulders as she got her purse and followed him to the door. She didn't look at him as they left.

Justin tucked a wad of bills into Shelby's purse when he stopped the Thunderbird on the side of the road near Mrs. Simpson's house. She tried to protest, but he simply smoked his cigarette and ignored her.

"I told you earlier that the money was between you and me," he said quietly, his dark eyes challenging as he cut the engine. He turned in the bucket seat, his long legs stretched out as he touched the power-window switch on the console panel. It was a rural road, and sparsely traveled. He had stopped under a spreading oak tree. He hooked his elbow on the open window to study Shelby narrowly. "I meant it. If you want to look on it as a loan, that's up to you."

She chewed on her lower lip. "I'll be able to pay you back one day," she said doggedly, even though she knew better. With what she made, it was going to be a struggle to eat and pay the rent. New clothes might become impossible.

"I'm not worried about it."

"Yes, but I am." She looked up, all her misgivings in her green eyes. "Oh, Justin, what am I going to do?" she moaned. "I'm alone for the first time in my life. Ty's in Arizona, I have no family…" She got a grip on herself, averting her eyes. "It's just panic," she said tightly. "Just fear. I'll get used to it. I'm sorry I said that."

He didn't speak. He'd never seen Shelby helpless. She'd always been poised and calm. It was new and faintly disturbing to see her frightened.

"If things get too rough," he replied quietly, "you can move in with me."

She laughed hollowly. "That would do our reputations a world of good."

He blew out a cloud of smoke. "If gossip bothers you all that much, we can get married." He said it carelessly, but his eyes were sharp on her face.

She knew she wasn't breathing. She looked at him as the old wounds opened with a vengeance. "Why?" she asked.

He didn't want to answer her. He didn't want to admit,

even to himself, that he was still vulnerable. He shrugged. "You need a place to stay. I'm tired of living alone. Since Abby and Calhoun moved out, the damned house is like a mausoleum."

"You feel sorry for me," she accused.

He took another draw from the cigarette. "Maybe I do. So what? Right now you don't have many options. Either you borrow from me to afford Mrs. Simpson's boarding house, or you marry me." He studied the tip of the cigarette. "Of course, you can always go back to that converted storeroom over Barry Holman's office and show him that you're available—"

"You stop that," she muttered. She shifted restlessly. "Mr. Holman isn't that kind of man. And you have no reason to feel possessive about me."

"Haven't I?" His black eyes searched hers. "But I am, just the same. And I remember your saying the same thing about me. We were engaged once, Shelby. That kind of involvement doesn't go away."

"Some involvement," she said with a tired sigh. "I never could decide why you wanted to marry me."

"You were a feather in my cap," he said coldly, lying through his teeth. "A rich sophisticate. I was just a country boy with stars in my eyes, and you took me for a hell of a ride, lady. Now it's my turn. I've got money and you haven't." His dark eyes narrowed. "And don't think I want to marry you out of some lingering passion."

He hadn't forgotten. It was in his eyes, his whole look. He'd marry her and make her hunger for a love he'd never felt, couldn't feel for her. He held her in contempt because he thought she'd slept with Tom Wheelor, and that was the biggest joke of all. She was still a virgin, and wouldn't it throw a stick into his spokes to find that out the hard way?

"No." She sighed, belatedly answering his question. "I'm not stupid enough to think you still want me, after what I did to your pride." She lifted her eyes to study the proud, arrogant set of his dark head, his eyes shadowed by the Stetson he always wore. "I used to think you cared for me a little, even though you never said you did."

That was the truth. She'd never really been sure why he wanted to marry her. Except for that one night, he hadn't been wild to try to get her into bed, and he'd never seemed emotionally involved, either. But she'd been so in love with him that she had not realized how relatively uninvolved he'd seemed until after their engagement had been broken.

He ignored her remarks. "If you want security, I can give it to you," he said quietly. "I've got money now, although I'll never be in the same class as your father was. He had millions."

She closed her eyes on a wave of shame. She had her father and her own naïveté to thank for Justin's bitterness. But Justin wanted revenge and she'd be a fool to deliver herself on a silver platter to him. "No, Justin. I can't marry you," she said after a minute. Her hand reached for the door handle. "It was a crazy idea!" She averted her face so that all he could see of it was her profile.

He put his hand over hers briefly, holding it, and then withdrew his fingers almost as quickly. His expression hardened. "It's a big house," he said. "With Calhoun and Abby living down the road, there's only Lopez and Maria living with me. You wouldn't need to work if you didn't want to, and you'd have security."

He was offering her heaven, except that it was impersonal on his part. More than anything else, he felt sorry for her. But under the pity was a darker need; she could feel it. Something in him wanted revenge for her rejection six years ago. His pride wanted restitution. Well, didn't she owe him that, she wondered bitterly, after what her father had cost him? And she'd be near him. She'd have meals with him. She could sit with him in the evenings while he watched television. She could sleep under the same roof. Her hungry heart wanted that, so badly. Too badly.

"I don't guess you'd…I don't suppose you'd ever want

a…" She couldn't even say it. *A child*, she was thinking, although God only knew how she'd manage to deal with what had to happen to produce one.

"I won't want a divorce," he said, misunderstanding her thoughts. His eyes narrowed. "I'm not exactly Mr. America, in case you haven't noticed. And I don't want a woman I have to buy, unless it's on my terms."

That sounded suspiciously like a dig at her, because she'd refused him for what he thought was a lack of money. Her eyes lifted to his. "Do you still hate me, Justin?" she asked; she needed to know.

He stared at her without speaking for a long moment, quietly smoking his cigarette. "I'm not sure what I feel."

That reply was honest enough, even if it wasn't a declaration of undying love. There were so many wounds between them, so much bitterness. It was probably an insane thing to do, but she couldn't resist the temptation.

She stared at his cigarette instead of at him. "I'll marry you, then, if you mean it."

He didn't move, but something inside him went wild at the words. She couldn't know how many nights he'd spent aching for just the sight of her, how desperately he wanted her near him. But he could never trust her again, and that was the hell of it. She was just a stray person, he told himself. Just someone who needed help. He had to think of her that way, and not want the moon. She might even play up to him out of gratitude, so he'd have to be on his guard every minute. But, oh, God, he wanted her so!

"Then we don't need to see Mrs. Simpson until we've had time to make plans." He started the car, pulled out onto the road and turned the Thunderbird toward the feedlot and his house. His hands had a perceptible tremor. He gripped the steering wheel hard to keep Shelby from seeing how her answer affected him.

If Maria and Lopez were shocked to see Shelby with Justin, they didn't say anything. Lopez vanished into the kitchen while Maria fussed over Shelby, bringing coffee and pastries into the living room where Justin sprawled in his armchair and Shelby perched nervously on the edge of the sofa.

"Thank you, Maria," Shelby said with a warm smile.

The Mexican woman smiled back. "It is my pleasure, *señorita*. I will be in the kitchen if you need me, *señor*," she added to Justin before she went out, discreetly closing the door behind her.

Shelby noticed that Justin didn't comment on Maria's obvious conclusions. Perhaps Maria thought he might want to wrestle her down onto the sofa, but Shelby knew better. Justin had done that once, and only once. And she'd been so frightened that she'd reacted stupidly.

She'd never forgiven herself for that. Justin had proba-
bly thought she found his ardor distasteful, and that was
the last thing it had been.

She sighed, lowering her eyes to his black boots. They
weren't working boots; they were the ones he wore when
he dressed up. He had such big feet and hands. She
smiled, remembering how it had been when they'd first
started dating. They'd been like children, fascinated with
each other's company, both of them a little shy and re-
served. It had never gone beyond kisses except the night
they got engaged.

"I said, do you want some coffee?" Justin repeated
pointedly, holding the silver coffeepot over a cup he'd just
filled.

"Oh. Yes, thank you." She took it black, and appar-
ently he remembered her preference, because he didn't
offer her any cream or sugar. He poured his own cup full,
put a dash of cream in it and sat back with the china cup
and saucer balanced on his crossed knee.

Shelby glanced at him and wondered how she could
contemplate living under the same roof with him. He
was so unapproachable. Obviously he wanted revenge.
She'd be a fool to give him that much rope to hang her
with.

On the other hand, if she was living with him, she had
a better chance than ever of changing his mind about

her. All she really had to do to prove her innocence was to get him into bed. But that was the whole problem. She was scared to death of intimacy.

"Why the blush?" he asked, watching her.

She cleared her throat. "It's warm in here," she said.

"Is it?" He laughed mirthlessly and sipped his coffee. "In case you wondered, you'll have your own room. I won't expect any repayment for giving you a home."

The blush went scarlet. She had to fight not to fling her cup at him. "You're making me sound like a charity case."

"I'll bet that rankles," he agreed. "But Tyler can't help you and hold down a job at the same time. And you'll never make it on what Holman pays you, with all due respect to him. Secretaries in small towns don't make much."

"I'm not mercenary," she said defensively.

"Sure," he replied. He sipped his coffee without another word.

"Listen, Justin, it was all my father's idea, that fake engagement to Tom Wheelor—"

"Your father would never have done that to me," he interrupted coldly, and his eyes went black, threatening as he leaned forward. "Don't try to use him for a scapegoat just because he's dead. He was one of the best friends I had."

That's what you think, she mused bitterly. Obviously it wasn't going to do any good to talk to him. Just because her father had put on a show of liking him was no reason to put the man on a pedestal. God only knew why Justin had such respect for a man who'd caused him years of bitter humiliation.

"You'll never trust me again, will you?" she asked softly.

He studied her lovely face, her pale green eyes staring at him, her gaze burning into his soul. "No," he replied with the honesty that was as much a part of him as his craggy face and thick black hair. "There's too much water under the bridge. But if you think I'm nursing a broken heart, don't. I found you out just a little too soon. My pride suffered, but you never touched my heart."

"I don't imagine any woman ever got close enough to do that," she said, her voice soft. She traced the rim of the china cup. "Abby told me once that you haven't dated anyone for a long time."

"I'm thirty-seven years old," he reminded her. "I sowed my wild oats years ago, even before I started going with you." He finished his coffee and put the cup down. His black eyes met hers in a direct gaze. "And we both know that you've sown yours, and who with."

"You don't know me at all, Justin," she said. "You never did. You said I was a status symbol to you, and looking back, I guess I was, at that." She laughed bitterly. "You used to take me around to your friends to show me off, and I felt like one of those purebred horses Ty used to take to the steeplechase."

He stared at her over his smoking cigarette. "I took you around because you were pretty and sweet, and I liked being with you," he said heavily. "That was a lot of garbage about wanting you for a status symbol."

She leaned back wearily. "Thank you for telling me," she said. "But I guess it doesn't matter now, does it?" She finished her coffee and put the cup down. "Are we going to have a church wedding?" she asked.

"Aren't we a little old for that kind of ceremony?" he asked.

"I can see you're still eating live rattlesnakes to keep your venom potent," she said without flinching. "I want a church wedding."

He dusted the long ash from his cigarette into an ashtray. "It would be quicker to go to a justice of the peace."

"I'm not pregnant," she reminded him, averting her self-conscious face. "There's no great rush, is there?"

She was tying him up in knots. He glared at her. "All right, have your church wedding. You can stay at Mrs. Simpson's until we're married, just to keep everything discreet." His dark eyes narrowed as he got up and crushed out his cigarette. "There's just one thing. Don't you come down that aisle in a white dress. If you dare, I'll walk out the front door of the church and keep going."

She lifted her chin. "Don't you know what every woman in the congregation will think?"

The soft accusation in her green eyes made him feel guilty. He was still hurt by Shelby's affair with Tom Wheelor. He'd wanted to sting her, but he hadn't counted on the wounded look in her eyes.

"You can wear something cream-colored," he muttered reluctantly.

Her lower lip trembled. "Take me to bed." Her eyes dared him, even though she went scarlet and shuddered at her own boldness. "If you think I'm lying about being innocent, I can prove I'm telling the truth!"

His black eyes cut back to hers, unblinking. "You know as well as I do that it takes a doctor to establish virginity. Even an experienced man can't tell."

Her face colored. She could have told him that in her case, it would be more than normally evident, and that her doctor could so easily settle all his doubts. She started to, despite her embarrassment at discussing such an intimate subject, but before she could open her mouth, there was a quick knock at the door and Lopez came in with a message for Justin.

"I've got some cattle out in the road," he told Shelby.

"Come on. I'll run you over to Mrs. Simpson's first. You can call Abby and make plans for the wedding. She'll be glad to help with the invitations and such."

She didn't even argue. She was too drained. They were going to be married, but he was going to see to it that she was publicly disgraced, like an adultress being paraded through the streets.

Her teeth ground together as they went out to the car. Well, she'd get around him somehow. She wasn't going to wear anything except a white gown to walk down that aisle. And if he left her standing there, all right. Maybe he didn't even mean what he'd said. She had to keep believing that, for the sake of her pride. He didn't know, and she'd hurt him badly. But, oh, how different things had been six years ago.

Shelby had known the Ballengers all her life. Ty, her brother, and Calhoun, Justin's brother, were friends. That meant that she naturally saw Justin from time to time. At first he'd been cold and very standoffish, but Shelby had thought of him as a challenge. She'd started teasing him gently, flirting shyly. And the change in him had been devastating.

They'd gone to a Halloween party at a mutual friend's, and someone had handed Shelby a guitar. To Justin's amazement, she'd played it easily, trying to slow down enough to adjust to the rather inept efforts of their host, who was learning to play lead guitar.

Without a word, Justin had perched himself on a chair beside her and held out his hand. Their host, with a grin that Shelby hadn't understood at the time, gave the instrument to Justin. He nodded to Shelby, tapped out the meter with his booted foot and launched into a rendition of *San Antonio Rose* that brought the house down.

After the first shock wore off, Shelby's long, graceful fingers caught up the rhythm and seconded him to perfection. He looked into her eyes as they wound to a finish, and he smiled. And at that moment, Shelby gave him her heart.

It wasn't a sudden thing, really. She'd known for years how kind he was. He'd just taken Abby in and given her a home when the girl's mother and Mr. Ballenger had died in a tragic car wreck. Justin was always around when someone needed a helping hand, and there wasn't a more generous or harder working man in Jacobsville. He had a temper, too, but he controlled it most of the time, and his men respected him because he didn't ask them to do anything he wasn't willing to do himself. He was the boss, along with Calhoun, but Justin was always the first to arrive and the last to leave when there was a job to be done. He had many admirable qualities, and

Shelby was young and impressionable, and just at the right age to fall hopelessly in love with an older man.

After that night, she seemed to see Justin everywhere. At the restaurant where she had lunch with a friend on Tuesdays and Thursdays, at social events, at charity bazaars, where she went riding on trails that wound near the Ballenger property. It didn't occur to her to wonder why such a reclusive, hard-working man suddenly had so much free time and spent it at places she was known to frequent. She was in love, and every second spent with Justin fed her hungry heart.

She hadn't thought he was interested in her at first. They had a lot in common, despite their very different backgrounds, and he seemed to enjoy talking to her.

Then, very suddenly, everything changed. They were walking down the trail, near where they'd tied their horses, and Justin had suddenly stopped walking to lean against a tree. He didn't say a word, but the expression in his eyes spoke volumes. He had a smoking cigarette in one hand, but he held out the other one to Shelby.

Shelby didn't know what to expect when she took it. Her heart was hammering and she looked at his mouth and wanted it obsessively. Perhaps he knew that, but he didn't take advantage of it.

He pulled her closer. Only their hands were touching. Then, his black eyes searching her soft green ones, he bent slowly, giving her all the time in the world to pull back, to hesitate, to show him that she didn't want him.

But she did. She stood very still as his hard lips brushed hers, her eyes open, watching him. He lifted his head and searched her eyes.

He dropped the cigarette and ground it out under his boot while her heart went crazy. His arms slid around her, bringing her against him but not intimately. He bent again and kissed her with tenderness and respect, with soft wonder. She kissed him back the same way, her arms around his shoulders, her mind sinking into layers of pleasure.

He drew back a minute later and let her go without a word. He took her hand in his and they started walking.

"Do you want a big wedding, or will a civil service do?" he asked as easily as if they were discussing the weather.

And just that quickly they were engaged. That night they went back to her house and told her father. Although his first expression was explosive, they didn't see it. He turned away long enough to compose himself, and then he made happy conversation and welcomed Justin into the family. Justin took Shelby home to share the news with Calhoun and Abby, but Abby was spending the night with a girlfriend and Calhoun had flown to Oklahoma to see a man on business.

They'd had the house to themselves. Shelby remembered so vividly how they'd laughed and toasted their future happiness. Then he'd drawn her to him and kissed her in a very different way, and she'd blushed at the intimacy of his tongue probing delicately inside her lips.

"We're going to be married," he'd whispered with open delight at her innocence. "I won't hurt you."

"I know." She buried her face in his white silk shirt. "But it's so new, being like this with you."

"It's new for me, too," he breathed. His chest rose and fell heavily. He moved her hands a little to the side of the buttons on his shirt and pressed them hard against him while he flipped buttons out of buttonholes and then guided her fingers to the thick mat of hair that covered his muscular, suntanned chest.

"Now," he breathed. "Touch me, Shelby."

She was shocked at this new intimacy, but when he bent and took her mouth under his, she forgot the shock and relaxed against him. Her fingers curled, liking the feel of him, the smell of him that lingered like spice in her nostrils.

"Harder," he whispered roughly. He pressed her hands closer and when she looked up, there was an expression in his eyes that she'd never seen in the weeks they'd been going together. Something wild and out of control was visible there. She trembled a little at that glimpse of desire she hadn't expected to find in such a controlled man.

Then his hand went under her nape, lifting her up to his mouth, and he took her lips in brief, biting kisses that had an unexpected, unbelievable effect on her. She moaned helplessly, frightened at the new sensations.

But to Justin, a moan had a totally different meaning. He thought she was as immersed in pleasure as he was, and his mouth grew suddenly invasive, insistent. His hands dropped to Shelby's slender hips and suddenly lifted her against him into an embrace that shocked her senseless.

She knew very little about men and intimacy, but the changed contours of Justin's hard body told her graphically what he was feeling. He groaned into her mouth as he moved against her in blatant arousal.

She struggled, but he was strong and half out of his mind with unbridled passion. He didn't realize that she was trying to get away until she dragged her mouth away from his and pushed at him, begging him to stop.

He lifted his head, breathing roughly, his eyes black with frustration.

"Shelby…" he ground out in agony.

"Let me go!" she moaned. "Please…Justin, don't!"

"I'll stop before we go all the way," he whispered

against her mouth, and bent to kiss her again. Her protests muffled under his warm, drugging mouth, he lifted her off the floor and carried her to the sofa, putting her down gently, full-length, on its soft cushions.

He shuddered with unbearable need, his mouth rough as it pressed against hers. His body slid over her, pushing her into the cushions, heavy and hard and intimate. She felt his sudden loss of control with real fear. She knew what could happen, and that they were engaged. He might not try very hard to stop.

"Justin!"

"I'm not going to take your chastity, Shelby," he breathed into her mouth. His brows drew together in agonized pleasure as his hands slid over her hips. "Oh, God, honey, don't hold back with me. Let me love you. Kiss me back…"

The words died against her soft mouth. He kissed her with growing hunger, his loss of control evident in the urgent movement of his hips against hers, his hands suddenly searching as they moved over her soft breasts. Then his knee moved between her legs and she panicked.

She began to fight him, afraid of the unfamiliar intimacy that was beyond her experience. She pushed at him. All at once, he seemed to feel her resistance. He lifted his head, his eyes blazing with black hunger, and just stared at her for an instant, disoriented. Then when he saw the rejection, felt it in the stiffness of her body, he suddenly tore away from her and got to his feet. By the time she was able to breathe again, he was standing several feet away smoking a cigarette. Several tense minutes passed before he turned around again to pour brandy into two snifters. He gave her one and smiled mockingly at the way she avoided touching him.

He turned away from her to stare out the window while he sipped his brandy. His back was ramrod stiff. "We'll sleep together when we're married," he said. "I hope you know that I don't plan on separate rooms."

"I know." She sipped her own drink with shaking hands, wanting to explain, but his attitude was hardly welcoming. "Justin...I'm a virgin."

"Don't you think I knew that?" he asked tersely. He looked at her and his expression was a cold and totally unreadable mask, hiding emotions she couldn't even guess at. "My God, we're going to be married. Do I have to stop touching you altogether until the ring's on your finger?"

She started to speak and lowered her eyes to her glass. She stiffened. "Perhaps...it might be wiser."

"Considering my lack of control, I suppose you mean." He said it icily, in a tone she'd never heard him use. He drank his brandy and after a while, the anger seemed to go out of him, to Shelby's relief. He didn't apologize, but he went to her and took her hand gently, smiling at her as if nothing at all had happened. They drank brandy, and he taught her a Mexican drinking song as the aftereffects of the evening and the potency of the aged brandy began to work on them. Maria and Lopez had chanced to come home then from a party and Justin had taken Shelby home. Maria had been raging at him in Spanish, and Shelby only found out later that the song he'd been teaching her wasn't one she could ever sing in public.

She'd looked forward to the wedding with joy and also with apprehension. Justin's passion had unsettled her and made her doubt her ability to match him. He was experienced and she wasn't, and she was more afraid than ever of having him make love to her when he was totally out of control.

But there was no cause for alarm, because there was no more heated lovemaking. The most ardent move he made for days afterward was to kiss her cheek or hold hands with her, and all the while, those black eyes wandered over her with the strangest searching expression. She relaxed and began to enjoy his company again, losing her nervousness since he wasn't making any more demands on her.

Then, suddenly, her father had put an end to it. Give

up Justin, he'd demanded, or watch him lose everything
he had. Justin would end up hating her, her father had
said. He'd blame her for making him poor and their mar-
riage wouldn't stand a chance. His pride alone would kill
it.

She'd been very young and unworldly, and her father
was an old hand at getting what he wanted. He'd enlisted
aid from Tom Wheelor, who was motivated by the
thought of a beneficial merger. And she'd done what her
father asked and lied to Justin, admitted to having an af-
fair with Tom, to wanting wealth and position, things
that Justin couldn't give her.

So long ago, she thought. So much pain. She'd only
been protecting Justin, trying to spare him the agony of
losing everything he and his family had worked so long
and so hard to achieve. But in the process, she'd sacri-
ficed her own happiness. She had only herself to blame
for Justin's cold attitude. And not only did she blame her-
self for her betrayal, but she also hadn't been honest
with him about the reasons she'd been afraid to let him
touch her.

Now he was going to marry her out of pity, not out
of love. And, too, there was always his wish for revenge.
She didn't know how she was going to live with him, but
only proximity was going to change his mind about her.
And living with him would be so sweet. Even though

she couldn't be the kind of woman he needed, it was all of heaven to be near him. Maybe one day she'd find the courage to tell him the truth about herself, to make him understand.

All her doubts were back. But she'd given her word to go through with the wedding, and she couldn't back down now. She was going to have to make the best of it, and hope that Justin's thirst for revenge wasn't prompting his decision to marry her.

Abby was enlisted to help Shelby with the wedding preparations. Shelby had always liked the Ballenger brothers' ward. Abby seemed to understand so well what was going on between Justin and his ex-fiancée.

"I don't imagine Justin is making it easy for you," Abby said while they addressed envelopes for the invitations that they'd just picked up from the printer.

Shelby brushed back a strand of dark hair, sighing gently. "He feels sorry for me," she said with a faint smile. "And maybe he's bent on revenge. But I'm afraid that's all he's got to give me."

"He seemed to be coming around pretty well the night we all went to that square dance and Calhoun spent most of it dancing with you," Abby recalled, tongue in cheek. It was easy to laugh about the past now, although she and Justin had been devastated at the time.

Shelby cleared her throat. "Justin had enough to say to me when we danced. Afterward, I guess he gave Calhoun the devil, if his expression was anything to go by. He was mad."

"Mad!" Abby laughed. Her blue-gray eyes searched Shelby's. "He went home and got drunk. Worse," she confessed ruefully, "he got me drunk, too. When Calhoun got back from taking you home, we were sprawled on the sofa together trying to figure out a way to get up and lock him out of the house."

Shelby's eyes glistened with amused light. "Abby!"

"Oh, it gets even better," she added. "Justin taught me this horribly obscene Spanish drinking song…"

Shelby blushed, remembering the first time she'd heard that song. "He taught it to me, too, the night we got engaged, and we were just starting to sing it when Maria came in and was furious."

Abby finished one of the envelopes and put an invitation in it, sealing it absently while she studied Shelby's reflective expression. "Justin never got over you, you know."

Shelby's eyes lifted. "He never got over what I did, you mean. He's so unbending, Abby. And I can't blame him for the way he feels. At the time, I lacerated his pride."

"Why?"

The other woman only smiled. "I thought I was saving him, you see," she said quietly. "My father didn't want a cowboy for a son-in-law. He had a rich man all earmarked for me, a financially advantageous marriage. But I wouldn't play along, and when he found out I'd agreed to marry Justin, he set out to destroy the relationship." She turned a sealed envelope in her hands. "I never realized how ruthless my father could be until then. He threatened to ruin Justin if I didn't go along." She smoothed the envelope as she remembered the bitterness. "I didn't believe him, so I called his bluff. The bank foreclosed on the feedlot and the Ballenger boys almost lost everything."

"It was a long time ago," Abby said, touching her hand gently. "The feedlot is prosperous now. In fact, it was then. Wasn't it?"

"My father promised that if I went along with his proposition, he'd pull a few strings and talk the bank out of putting the place on public auction. Justin told me about the bankruptcy proceedings," she added. "He was devastated. He even talked about calling off the engagement, so I figured I was going to lose him anyway and it might as well be to his advantage. At the time," she added, remembering how distant Justin had been, how standoffish, "I remember thinking that he'd changed his mind about marrying me. I was pretty reserved." She didn't enlarge on that, but she remembered clearly the way Justin had reacted when she'd struggled away from him on the sofa. But surely that hadn't hurt his pride. He must have been pretty experienced.

Abby leaned forward. "What did your father do?"

"He produced Tom Wheelor, my new fiancé, and took him to meet Justin. He told Justin," she continued dully, "that I'd only been dating him to make Tom propose, because Tom was rich and Justin wasn't. He made out that it was all my fault, that I was the culprit. Justin believed him. He believed that I'd deliberately led him on, just to get Tom jealous enough to marry me. And then Dad told Justin that Tom and I were lovers, and Tom confirmed it."

Abby lifted her eyes. "You weren't," she said with certainty.

Shelby smiled. "Bless you for seeing the truth. Of course we weren't. But in order to save Justin's fledgling business, I had to go along with my father's lie. So when Justin called me and asked me for the truth, I told him what I'd been coached to say." She lowered her gaze to the carpet. "I told him that I wanted money, that I'd never wanted him, that it was all a game I'd been playing to amuse myself while I brought Tom in line." Her eyes closed. "I don't think I'll ever be able to forget the silence on the line, or the way he hung up, so quietly. A few weeks later, all the talk of bankruptcy died down, so I guess Dad convinced the bank that the Ballengers were a good risk. Tom Wheelor and I went around together for a while, to convince Justin, and then I went to Europe for six months and did my best to get myself killed on ski jumps all over Switzerland. Eventually I came back, but something in me died because of what my father did. He realized it at last, just before I lost him. He even apologized. But it was much too late."

"If you could just make Justin listen…" Abby sighed.

"He won't. He can't forgive me, Abby. It was like a public execution. Everybody knew that I'd jilted him for a richer man. You know how he hates gossip. That destroyed his pride."

Abby grimaced. "He must have realized that your father didn't approve of him."

"Oh, that was the beauty of it. My father welcomed Justin into the family with open arms and made a production about how proud he was going to be of his new son." She laughed bitterly. "Even when he went to Justin with Tom, my father played his part to perfection. He was almost in tears at the callous way I'd treated poor Justin."

"But why? Just for a merger? Didn't he care about your happiness?"

"My father was an empire builder," she said simply. "He let nothing get in the way of business, especially not the children. Ty never knew," she added. "He'd have been furious if he'd had any inkling, but it was part of the bargain that I couldn't tell Ty, either."

"Haven't you ever told Ty the truth?"

"It didn't seem necessary," Shelby replied. "Ty is a loner. It's hard even for me to talk to him, to get close to him. I think that may be why he's never married. He can't open up to people. Dad was hard on him. Even harder than he was on me. He ridiculed Ty and browbeat him most of our childhood. He grew up tough because he had to be, to survive his home life."

"I never knew. I like Ty," Abby said with a smile. "He's a very special man."

Shelby smiled back. She didn't tell Abby that Ty had been infatuated with her. And on top of losing his entire heritage and having to go to work for someone else, losing his chance with Abby was just the last straw. Ty had left for Arizona and his new job without a voiced regret. Perhaps the change would do him good.

Mrs. Simpson brought in a tray of cake and coffee and the three women sat and talked about the wedding until Abby had to leave. Shelby hadn't told anyone what Justin had said about her dress. But the next day she went into Jacobsville to the small boutique that one of her childhood playmates now owned, and the smart linen suit she bought to be married in was white.

That didn't worry her, because she knew she could prove to Justin that she was more than entitled to the symbolic white dress. Then she went for her premarital examination.

Dr. Sims had been her family doctor for half her life, and the tall, graying man was like family to all his patients. His quiet explanation after the examination, after the blood test was done by his lab, made her feel sick all over. And even though she protested, he was quietly firm about the necessity.

"It's only a very minor bit of surgery," he said. "You'll hardly feel it. And frankly, Shelby, if it isn't done, your wedding night is going to be a nightmare." He explained it in detail, and when he finished, she realized that she didn't have a choice. Justin might swear that he was never going to touch her in bed, but she knew it was unrealistic to assume that they could live together without going too far. And with the minor surgery, some pain could be avoided.

She finally agreed, but she insisted that he do only a partial job, so that there was no doubt she was a virgin. Doctor Sims muttered something about old-fashioned idiocy, but he did as she asked. He murmured something about the difficulty she might still encounter because of her stubbornness and that she might need to come back and see him. She hadn't wanted to argue about it, but it was important for Justin to believe her. This was the only proof she had left. The thing was, she hadn't counted on the prospect of such discomfort, and it began to wear on her mind. Had she done the right thing? She wanted Justin to know, without having to be told, that she was innocent. But that prospect of being hurt was just as frightening as it had been in the past—more so.

The wedding was the social event of the season. Shelby hadn't expected so many people to congregate in the Jacobsville Methodist church to see her get married. Certainly there were more spectators than she'd included on her list.

Abby and Calhoun were sitting in the family pew, holding hands, the tall blond man and the dark-haired woman so much in love that they radiated it all around. Beside them was Shelby's green-eyed, black-haired brother, Tyler, towering above everyone except Calhoun. There were neighbors and friends, and Misty Davies, Abby's friend, on the other side of the church. Justin was nowhere in sight, and Shelby almost panicked as she remembered his threat to leave if she wore a white dress.

But when the wedding march struck up, the minister and Justin were waiting for her at the altar. She had to bite her lower lip hard and grip her bouquet of daisies to keep from shaking as she walked down the aisle.

She and Justin had decided not to have a best man or a matron of honor, or much ceremony except for the actual service. There were plenty of flowers around the altar, and a candelabra with three unlit white candles. The minister was in his robes, and Justin was in a formal black suit, very elegant as he waited for his bride to join him.

When she reached him, and took her place at his side, she looked up. Her green eyes caught his black ones and her expression invited him to do what he'd threatened, to walk out of the church.

It was a tense moment and for one horrible second, he looked as if he were thinking about it. But the moment passed. He lifted his cold eyes to the minister and he repeated what he was told to say without a trace of expression in his deep voice.

He placed a thin gold band on her hand. There had been no engagement ring, and he hadn't mentioned buying one. He'd bought her ring himself, on a trip to town, and he hadn't asked if she wanted him to wear one. Probably he didn't want to.

They replied to the final questions and lit two candles, each holding a flame to the third candle, signifying the unity of two people into one. The minister pronounced them man and wife. He invited Justin to kiss his bride.

Justin turned to Shelby with an expression she couldn't read. He looked down at her for a long moment before he bent his head and brushed a light, cool kiss across her lips. Then he took her arm and propelled her down the aisle and outside into the hall, where they were surrounded seconds later by well-wishers.

There was no time to talk. The reception was held in the fellowship hall of the church, and punch, cake and canapés were consumed while Shelby and Justin were each occupied with guests.

Someone had a camera and asked them to pose for a photograph. They hadn't hired anyone to take pictures of the wedding, an oversight that Shelby was secretly disappointed at. She'd hoped for at least a photograph of them together, but perhaps this one would do.

She stood behind Justin and smiled, feeling his arm draw her to his side. Her eyes lifted to his, but it was hard to hold the smile as those black eyes cut into hers.

The instant the camera was gone, he glared at her. "I said any color except white."

"Yes, Justin, I know you did," she said calmly. "And think how you'd have felt if I'd insisted that you wear a blue dress instead of a black suit to be married in."

He blinked, as if he wasn't quite sure he'd heard right. "A white dress means—" he began indignantly.

"—a first wedding," she finished for him. "This is mine."

His eyes kindled. "You and I both know there's an implied second reason for wearing white, and you aren't entitled to it." He noticed something darken her eyes and his own narrowed. "You told me you could prove it, though, didn't you, Shelby?" He smiled coldly. "I just might let you do that before we're through."

She blushed and averted her eyes. For an instant, she felt cowardly, thinking about how difficult it was going to be if he wasn't gentle, if he treated her like the scarlet woman he thought she was. It didn't bear consideration, and she shivered. "I don't have to prove anything to you."

He laughed, the sound of it like ice shattering. "You can't, can you? It was all bravado, to keep me guessing until we were married."

Her eyes lifted to his. "Justin…"

"Never mind." He pulled out a cigarette and lit it. "I told you, we won't be sharing a bed. I don't care about your chastity."

She felt an aching sadness for what might have been between them and she looked at him, her eyes soft and quietly adoring on his craggy features. He was so beautiful. Not handsome, but beautifully made, for a man, from his lithe, powerful build to his black eyes and thick black hair and olive complexion. He looked exactly the way a man should, she decided.

He glanced down at her, caught in that warm appraisal. His cigarette hovered in midair while he searched her eyes, holding them for so long that her heart went wild in her chest. She let her eyes fall to his chiseled mouth, and she wanted it suddenly with barely contained passion. If only she could be the uninhibited woman she wanted to be, and not such a frightened innocent. Justin intimidated her. He had to be at least as worldly as Calhoun. She'd disappoint him, anyway, but if only she could tell him the truth and ask him to be gentle. She shivered at the thought of telling him something so intimate.

It was a blessing that Ty chose that moment to say his goodbyes, sparing Shelby the embarrassment of having Justin mock her for her weakness.

"I've got to catch a plane back to Arizona," he told his sister as he bent his head to brush her cheek with his lips. "My temporary lady boss is scared stiff of men."

Shelby's eyes brightened. "She's what?"

Ty looked frankly uncomfortable. "She's nervous around men," he said reluctantly. "Damn it, she hides behind me at dances, at meetings…it's embarrassing."

Shelby had to fight down laughter. Her very independent brother didn't like clinging women, but this one seemed to be affecting him very strangely. His temporary boss was the niece of his permanent boss. She lived in Arizona, where she was trying to cope with an indebted dude ranch. Ty's boss in Jacobsville had sent him out to help. He'd hated it at the beginning, and he still seemed to, but maybe the mysterious Arizona lady was getting to him.

"Maybe she feels safe with you?" Shelby asked.

He glowered at her. "Well, it's got to stop. It's like having poison ivy wrap itself around you."

"Is she ugly?" Shelby persisted.

"Kind of plain and unsophisticated," he murmured. "Not too bad, I guess, if you like tomboys. I don't," he added doggedly.

"Why don't you quit?" Justin asked. "You can work for Calhoun and me, we've already offered you a job."

"Yes, I know. I appreciated it, too, considering how strained things were between our families," Ty said honestly. "But this job is kind of a challenge and that part I like."

Justin smiled. "Come and stay when you get homesick."

Ty shook his outstretched hand. "I might, one day. I like kids," he added. "A few nieces and nephews wouldn't bother me."

Justin looked murderous and Shelby went scarlet. Ty frowned, and Justin thanked God that Calhoun and Abby joined them in time to ward off trouble. He didn't want to think about kids. Shelby sure wouldn't want his, not if the way she'd reacted to him the one time he'd been ardent with her was any indication. She was repulsed by him.

"Isn't this a nice wedding?" Calhoun asked Ty, joining the small group with his arm around a laughing Abby. "Doesn't it give you any ideas?"

Ty smiled at Abby. "It does that, all right. It makes me want to get an inoculation, quick," he murmured dryly.

"You'll outgrow that attitude one day," Calhoun assured him. "We all get chopped down at the ankles eventually," he added, and ducked when Abby hit his chest. "Sorry, honey." He chuckled, brushing a lazy kiss against her forehead. "You know I didn't mean it."

"Can we give you a lift to the airport, or did you rent a car?" Abby asked Ty.

"I rented a car, but thanks all the same. Why don't you two walk me out to it?" He kissed Shelby again. "Be happy," he said gently.

"I expect to," she said, and smiled in Justin's direction.

Ty nodded, but he didn't look convinced. When he followed Abby and Calhoun out of the fellowship hall, he was preoccupied and frowning thoughtfully.

The reception seemed to go on forever, and Shelby was grateful when it was finally time to go home. Justin had sent Lopez to fetch Shelby's things from Mrs. Simpson's house early that morning. The guest room had been prepared for Shelby. Maria had questioned that, but only once, because Justin's cold eyes had silenced her. Maria understood more than he realized, anyway. She, like everyone else on the property, knew that despite his bitterness, Justin still had a soft spot for Shelby. She was alone and impoverished, and it didn't surprise anybody that Justin had married her. If he felt the need for a little vengeance in the process, that wasn't unexpected, either.

"Thank God that's over," Justin said wearily when they were alone in the house. He'd tugged off his tie and jacket and unbuttoned the neck of his shirt and rolled up the sleeves. He looked ten years older than he was.

Shelby put her purse on the hall table and took off her high heels, smoothing her stockinged feet on the soft pile of the carpet. It felt good not to be two inches taller.

Justin glanced at her and smiled to himself, but he turned away before she could see it. "Do you want to go out for supper or have it here?"

"I don't care."

"I suppose it would look odd if we went to a restaurant on our wedding night, wouldn't it?" he added, turning to give her a mocking smile.

She glared at him. "Go ahead," she invited. "Spoil the rest of it, too. God forbid that I should enjoy my own wedding day."

He frowned as she turned and started up the staircase. "What the hell are you talking about?"

She didn't look at him. She held onto the railing and stared up at the landing. "You couldn't have made your feelings plainer if you'd worn a sign with all your grievances painted on it in blood. I know you hate me, Justin. You married me out of pity, but part of you still wants to make me pay for what I did to you."

He'd lit a cigarette and he was smoking it, propped against the doorjamb, his face quiet, his black eyes curious. "Dreams die hard, honey, didn't you know?" he asked coldly.

She turned around, her green eyes steady on his. "You weren't the only one who dreamed, Justin," she said. "I cared about you!"

His jaw tautened. "Sure you did. That's why you sold me out for that boy millionaire."

She stroked the banister absently. "Odd that I didn't marry him, isn't it?" she asked casually. "Very odd, wouldn't you say, when I wanted his money badly enough to jilt you."

He lifted the cigarette to his mouth. "He threw you over, I guess, when he found out you wanted the money more than you wanted him."

"I never wanted him, or his money," she said honestly. "I had enough of my own."

He smiled at her. "Did you?" Surely she didn't expect him to believe she was unaware of how much financial trouble her father had been in.

"You won't listen," she muttered. "You never would. I tried to tell you why I broke off the engagement—"

"You told me, all right! You couldn't stand for me to touch you, but I knew that already." His eyes glittered dangerously. "You pushed me away the night we got engaged," he added huskily. "You were shaking like a leaf and your eyes were as big as saucers. You couldn't get away from me quick enough."

Her lips parted on a slow breath. "And you thought it was revulsion, of course?" she asked miserably.

"What else could it have been?" he shot back, his eyes glaring. "I didn't come down in the last rain shower." He turned. "Change your clothes and we'll have supper. I don't know about you, but I'm hungry."

She wished she could tell him the truth. She wanted to, but he was so remote and his detached attitude intimidated her. With a sigh, she turned and went up the staircase numbly, wondering how she was going to live with a man she couldn't even talk to about intimacy.

They had a quiet wedding supper. Maria put everything on the table and she and Lopez went out for the evening, offering quiet congratulations before they left.

Justin leaned back in his chair when he'd finished his steak and salad, watching Shelby pick at hers.

He felt vaguely guilty about their wedding day. But in a way, he was hiding from her. Hiding his real feelings, hiding his apprehension about losing her a second time. It had wrung him out emotionally six years before. He didn't think he could bear it a second time, so he was trying to protect himself from becoming too vulnerable. But her sad little face was getting to him.

"Damn it, Shelby," he ground out, "don't look like that."

She lifted her eyes. There was no life in them anymore. "I'm tired," she said softly. "Do you mind if I go to bed after we eat?"

"Yes, I mind." He threw down his napkin and lit a cigarette. "It's our wedding night."

She laughed bitterly. "So it is. What did you have in mind, some more comments on my scarlet past?"

He frowned slightly. She didn't sound like Shelby. That edge to her voice was disturbing. His eyes narrowed. She'd lost her father, her home, her entire way of life, even her brother. She'd lost everything in recent weeks, and married him because she needed a little security. He'd given her hell, and now she looked as if today was the last straw on the camel's back. He hadn't meant for it to be that way. He didn't want to hurt her.

But he couldn't seem to keep quiet; there were so many wounds.

He sighed heavily. His black eyes searched her wan face, remembering better times, happier times, when he could look at her and get drunk on just the sight of her smile.

"Are you sure you want to keep on working?" he asked quietly, just to change the subject, to get the conversation on an easier level.

She stared down at her plate. "Yes, I'd like to," she said. "I've never really done any work before, except society functions and volunteer work. I like my job."

"And Barry Holman?" he asked, his smile a challenge.

She got up. She was still wearing her white skirt with a pale pink blouse, and she looked feminine and elegant and very desirable. Her long hair waved down to her shoulders, and Justin wanted to get up and catch two handfuls of it and kiss her until she couldn't stand up.

"Mr. Holman is my boss," she said. "Not my lover. I don't have a lover."

He got up, too, moving closer, his eyes narrow and calculating, his body tense with years of frustrated desire. "You're going to have one," he said curtly.

She wouldn't back away. She wouldn't give him the satisfaction of watching her run. She lifted her face proudly, even though her knees felt weak and her heart was racing madly. She was afraid of him because of their past, because he wanted revenge. She was afraid because he thought she was experienced, and even with that minor surgery, she knew that it wasn't going to be the easiest time of her life. Justin was deceptively strong. She knew the power in that lean, hard body, and to be overwhelmed by it in passion was a little scary.

He watched the fear flicker in her eyes, and understood it instantly. "You're off base, honey," he said quietly. "Way off base. I'd never hurt you in bed, not for revenge or any other reason."

Her lower lip trembled on a stifled sob and tears welled in her eyes. She lowered her gaze to his broad chest, missing the faint shock in his face at her reaction. "Maybe you wouldn't be able to help it," she whispered.

"Shelby, are you really afraid of me?" he asked huskily.

Her thin shoulders shifted. "Yes. I'm sorry."

"Were you afraid with him?" he asked. "With Wheelor?"

She opened her mouth to speak and just gave up. What was the use? He wasn't going to listen. She turned away and went toward the staircase.

"Running won't solve anything," he said shortly, watching her go with mingled feelings, the foremost of which was anger.

"Neither will trying to talk to you," she replied. She turned at the bottom of the staircase, her green eyes bright with unshed tears and returning spirit. "Do your worst. Make me pay. I'm fresh out of things I care about. I've got absolutely nothing left to lose, so look out, Justin. I'm not going to live up to your idea of a society wife. I'm going to be myself, and I'm sorry if it destroys any of your old illusions."

He eyed her quietly. "Meaning what?"

"No affairs," she replied, picking the thought out of his mind. "Despite what you think of me, I'm not starved for a man."

"That much I'd believe," he said shortly. "My God, I get more warmth out of an ice cube than I ever got from you!"

She felt the impact of those words like daggers against her bare skin. She should have realized that he thought her frigid, but it had never really registered before.

"Maybe Tom Wheelor got more!" she threw at him.

His black eyes splintered with rage. He actually started toward her before he checked himself with the iron control that he kept on his temper.

Shelby saw that movement, and thanked God that he stopped when he did. She lifted her chin. "Good night, Justin. Thank you for a roof over my head and a place to live."

His eyelids flickered as she started up the staircase. Looking at her he recalled years of dreams, of remembered delight in just being with her, frustration at having to hold back only to lose her anyway. He still cared. He'd lied to protect his pride, but he cared so much. And he was losing her, all over again.

He wanted to tell her that he hadn't meant to accuse her of being frigid. He'd wanted her to distraction, and she hadn't wanted him. That had hurt far more than having her break their engagement, especially when he'd found out that Tom Wheelor was her lover. It had damned near killed him. And here she was throwing it in his teeth, hitting him in his most vulnerable spot. He'd always wondered if she found him revolting physically. That was what made him believe that she'd meant what she told him about not wanting him, about wanting Tom Wheelor instead—that reluctance in her to let him get close to her.

And she was different now. She wasn't the shy, introverted young woman he'd known six years ago. She was oddly reckless; high-spirited and uninhibited when she forgot herself. But he couldn't bend. He couldn't make himself bend enough to tell her what was in his heart, how much he still wanted her, because he didn't dare trust her again. She'd hurt him too badly. He watched her go up the staircase, his eyes black and soft and full of hunger. He didn't move until she was out of sight.

Chapter Four

Shelby had hoped beyond hope that Justin might still love her. That he might have married her not so much out of pity as out of love. But her wedding day had convinced her that what little emotion had been left in him after years of bitterness was all gone. He still blamed her for what he thought she'd done with Tom Wheelor, and he thought she was frigid.

She didn't know how to deal with her own fears and his anger. Her marriage was going to be as empty as her life had been. There would be no black-headed little babies to nurse, no soft, sweet loving in the darkness, no shared delight in making a life together. There would be only separate bedrooms and separate lives and Justin's hunger for vengeance.

The black depression that she'd taken to bed on her wedding night got worse. Justin tolerated her presence, but he was away more often than not. At meals, he spoke to her only when it was necessary, and he never touched her. He was like a polite host instead of a husband. And day by miserable day, Shelby began to feel a new recklessness. While Justin was away one weekend, she went on a white-water rafting race with Abby's friend Misty Davies. She tried her hand at skydiving. She joined a fencing class. She went back to the old, more reckless days of her adolescence. Justin had never really known her, she thought sometimes. He seemed surprised by the things she enjoyed and a time or two he acted as if her life-style bothered him. Well, what had he expected her to do, she fumed, stay at home and arrange flowers? Perhaps that was the image he had of her, that she was a pretty socialite with beauty and no brains.

She'd kept working after the wedding, but Barry Holman insisted that she take a few days off. It wasn't right, he said, for her to work through her honeymoon. She wanted to laugh at that, and tell him that her husband didn't want a honeymoon. Justin had come home from his latest trip and had gone straight to the feedlot office with an abrupt and coolly polite greeting. After a few bored hours, Shelby phoned the office, just to see how things were going. She liked her job. She missed working terribly. It was something to do; it helped keep her mind off her marriage and her own inadequacies.

When she called, the poor temporary secretary, Tammy Lester, answered the phone, obviously half out of her mind trying to cope with an impatient, frustrated Barry Holman. So Shelby dressed in a cool white and red summery dress and white high heels and went to work.

The old sedan she drove broke down halfway there and she had to have it towed in to the dealer car lot where she had her mechanical work done.

Once Shelby was at the dealership, as fate would have it, she noticed Abby's little sports car was there and up for sale. The sight of the car brought back memories. Shelby had driven one like it during six of the blackest months in her life, the time she'd spent in Switzerland after she'd given back Justin's ring. She'd loved that car, but she'd wrecked it accidentally. The wreck hadn't dampened her enthusiasm for fast cars, though. Now she wanted one—it appealed to the wild streak in her that had never totally disappeared. It wasn't a suicidal streak; she just loved a challenge. She liked sports cars and the exhilaration of driving in the fast lane.

Justin didn't know that Shelby had a wild streak, because he'd accepted the illusion of what she appeared to be rather than wondering what was beneath the surface. Well, he was in for a few shocks, she decided, starting now.

Because the dealer knew that Shelby had just married Justin, he didn't even ask for a cosigner on the note. He sold her the car outright, with payments she could afford on her own salary.

She parked the vehicle right outside the office, delighting in its new paint job. Abby had had it painted red with white racing stripes just before she traded it for something more sedate. The new colors suited Shelby very well. She sighed over it, delighted that she could afford it and even manage the payments by herself. All her life she'd depended on her father's money. There was something challenging and very satisfying about taking care of herself financially. She was sorry now that she'd panicked at being on her own and rushed into marrying Justin. She'd hoped for something more than a roof over her head, but that wasn't going to happen. Justin was taking care of her, just as he'd taken care of Abby, and if he had any lingering desire for her, it didn't show. After he'd accused her of being frigid, she'd kept out of his way altogether. If only she wasn't so repressed, she could have told him what the problem was and how frightened she was of intimacy. But it was hopeless. Justin would probably be as embarrassed as she was to talk about it, anyway. So things would just have to rock along as they had been, until one of them broke the silence.

When she got to the office, Barry Holman was pacing the floor while the temporary secretary cried. They both turned as Shelby put her purse in the top drawer of the desk and smiled.

"Can I help?" she asked.

The woman at her desk cried even harder. "He yells," she wailed, pointing at Barry Holman, who looked furiously angry from his blond head to his big feet.

"Only at incompetents!" he flashed back.

"Now, now," Shelby soothed. "I'm here. I'll take care of everything. Tammy, why don't you make Mr. Holman a cup of coffee while I straighten out whatever's fouled up, then I'll show you how to update the files and you can keep busy with that. Okay?"

Tammy smiled, her soft brown eyes quiet. "Okay."

She got up and Shelby sat down. Her dark brows lifted as Barry Holman glanced at her uncomfortably.

"It's your vacation," he said. "You shouldn't be here."

"Why not? Justin is working, why shouldn't I?"

He frowned. "Well…"

"Tell me what needs to be done, and then I'll show you my new car." She grinned. "It was Abby's, and they let me buy it without even a cosigner."

"Naturally, considering your husband's credit line," he mused. She gave him a strange look, but he ignored it, delighting in his good fortune. "Here, this is what's giving Tammy fits."

He produced two scribbled pages of notes on a legal pad that he wanted transcribed and put into English instead of abbreviations and scrawls, and fifty copies run off with different salutations on each.

"Simple, isn't it?" he said. He glared toward the back of the office. "She cried."

Shelby wanted to. It was an hour's work just to translate his handwriting. But she knew how to use the computer's word-processing program, and Tammy had three simplified tutorials spread out on the desk, none of which would explain the program to a person who'd never used a computer.

"She asked me what these were for." Barry Holman sighed, picking up one of the diskettes in its jacket. He looked up. "She thought they were negatives."

Shelby had to bite her lower lip. "She's never had any computer training," she reminded him.

"That's no excuse for not having a brain," he returned hotly.

"Mr. Holman!" Tammy exclaimed, glaring at him as she came back with three cups of black coffee on a tray. "That was unkind and unfair."

"Didn't they tell you at the temporary-services agency that computer experience was necessary to do this job?" he grumbled.

"I have computer experience," Tammy replied with

hauteur. "I play games on my brother's Atari all the time."

Mr. Holman looked as if *he* wanted to cry. He ground his teeth together, went back into his office and closed the door.

"I guess I told him." Tammy grinned wickedly.

There was a loud, feverish, furious, *"Damn!"* from the vicinity of Mr. Holman's office. Shelby and Tammy exchanged amused glances.

"They didn't tell me about the computer," Tammy confided. "They asked if I had office skills, and I do. I type over a hundred words a minute and take dictation at ninety. But I don't read Sanskrit," she whispered, pointing at the scribbling on the legal sheets.

Shelby burst out laughing. It felt so good to laugh, and she thanked God for this job, which was going to save her sanity. She shook her head and, putting the books aside, she began to explain the computer's operation to Tammy.

After work, she took the long route home. Mr. Holman had relaxed after lunch, and he was tolerating Tammy much better now. In fact, he hadn't even growled when Shelby had mentioned that it might be economical to have two secretaries in the office because of the backlog of filing and updating the computer's entries. He'd talked about taking on an associate, and if he hired Tammy full time, he could do it.

Shelby turned the small sports car onto the highway sharply, delighting in its rack-and-pinion steering and easy handling. She gunned it up and up and up, loving the speed, loving the freedom and the wind tearing through her long hair. She felt reckless. As she'd told Justin, she had nothing left to lose. She was going to enjoy her life from now on. Justin could just do his worst.

There was a slow car in front, and she didn't even brake. She surged around it and barely got back into her lane as a white car sped in the opposite direction. She thought it looked familiar, but she didn't look in the rearview mirror. It was going toward the feedlot. She passed the turnoff, increasing her speed. She wasn't ready to go home to her cell just yet.

Calhoun was muttering a prayer as he pulled up in front of the feedlot. That was Abby's old car, and it had been Shelby at the wheel. He'd barely recognized her in that split second, her face laughing with pleasure at the speed, her hair flying in the wind. She made Abby's friend Misty Davies look like a safe driver by comparison.

Justin looked up from his desk as Calhoun came in and closed the door behind him. "It's almost time to go home," he remarked, glancing at his Rolex. "I didn't think you were coming back today from Montana."

Calhoun grinned. "I missed Abby. Speaking of Abby,"

he added, perching himself lazily on the edge of his brother's desk, "a wild woman driving her sports car just came within an inch of running me down."

"Didn't Abby sell it?" Justin remarked.

"She certainly did. I insisted."

"I see." Justin smiled faintly. He leaned back with his cigarette smoking in his lean fingers. "I gather that some other fool's wife is driving it?"

"You could put it that way. She was doing eighty if she was doing a mile." His dark eyes narrowed. "Are you sure you want Shelby to have it?"

There was a shocked silence. "What do you mean, do I want Shelby to have it?" Justin sat up abruptly. "Are you telling me Shelby was driving that sports car?"

"I'm afraid so," Calhoun said quietly. "You didn't know?"

Justin's expression became grim. Shelby wasn't happy and he knew it. Her most recent behavior was already worrying him, although he was careful to keep his misgivings from Shelby. But purchasing a sports car was going too far. He was going to have to talk to her. He'd avoided confrontations, letting her settle in, keeping his distance while he tried to cope with the anguish of having Shelby in his house when she backed away the minute he came into the room. But this was too much.

He couldn't let her kill herself. He got up from the

desk without even looking at Calhoun, plucked his hat off the hat rack and started for the door. "Was she going toward the house?" he asked curtly.

"The opposite direction," Calhoun told him. His eyes narrowed. "Justin, what's going on between the two of you?"

The older man looked at him, black eyes glittering. "My private life is none of your business."

Calhoun folded his arms. "Abby says Shelby is running wild, and that you're apparently doing nothing to stop her. Are you that hell-bent on revenge?"

"You make it sound as if she's suicidal," Justin said coldly. "She's not."

"If she was happy, she wouldn't be like this," the younger man persisted. "You've got to stop trying to live in the past. It's time to forget what happened."

"That's damned easy for you to say." Justin's black eyes flashed. "She threw me over and slept with another man!"

Calhoun stared at him. "You don't have my track record, but you're no more a saint than I am, big brother. Suppose Shelby couldn't accept the women in your past?"

"It's different with men," the older man said irritably.

"Is it?"

"She was mine. I was so damned careful never to put

a foot wrong with her. I held back and gritted my teeth to keep from scaring her, and she flinched away from me every time I touched her. And all the while she was sleeping with that pasty-faced boy millionaire. How do you think I felt?" he blazed. "And then she told me that I was too poor to suit her expensive tastes, she wanted somebody rich."

"She didn't marry him, did she?" Calhoun returned. "She left for Europe and went wild, just as she's going wild now. She was in a wreck in Switzerland, Justin. In a sports car," he added, watching the horror grow in his brother's eyes, "just like the one she's driving now. She was grieving for you. Even her father realized that, at last."

Justin fumbled a cigarette into his mouth and lit it. "Nobody ever told me that."

"When would you ever listen to anything about her?" Calhoun replied. "It's only in the past few months that you've calmed down enough to talk about anything connected with the Jacobses."

"I wanted her," Justin ground out. "You can't imagine how I felt when she broke it off."

"Yes, I can," Calhoun replied. "I was there. I know what it was like for you. But you never even considered that Shelby might have had a reason. She tried to explain it once, to tell you why she broke off the engagement. You wouldn't even listen."

"What was there to listen to?" Justin asked impatiently. "She'd already told me the truth, in the beginning."

"I never believed it," Calhoun replied. "And neither would you have, if you hadn't been in love for the first time in your life and so damned uncertain about your own ability to keep Shelby. You were always worried about losing her to another man. Even to me. Remember?"

It was hard to argue with the truth. Justin knew he'd been possessive about Shelby. Hell, he still was. But how could he help it? She was a beautiful woman, and he was a plain, unworldly man. He'd never been able to understand why Shelby had stayed with him as long as she had.

"Even now," Calhoun continued quietly, "it seems to me that you're trying your best to make her leave you."

Justin smiled mockingly. "What do you expect me to do, tie her in the cellar?" he asked reasonably. "I can't make her stay if she doesn't want to. Hell—" he laughed coldly "—I can't even touch her. She flinched away from me the one time I tried to make love to her," he said bluntly, remembering. His eyes went blacker and he looked away. "I can't get near her. She's afraid of me that way."

"How interesting," Calhoun said, choosing his words,

"that such an experienced woman of the world could be afraid of sex. Isn't it?"

Justin frowned. "What do you mean?"

Calhoun didn't answer him. He was smiling a little when he started out the door, but Justin couldn't see the smile. "I've got to get home. See you, big brother." And before Justin could reply, he was gone.

Justin took a minute to get his temper under control. He went out the door behind Calhoun without a word to his secretary, his eyes narrow with concern. Calhoun had delayed him too long. Suppose Shelby wrecked that little car?

He went up and down the road, but he didn't see any sign of the sports car. Later, he went to the house, and almost went down on his knees with relief when he found it parked at the steps.

He had to force himself to behave normally when his hands were almost shaking from fear that he might find her in a ditch somewhere. He walked into the house, tossing his hat onto the hat rack, and went into the dining room, where Shelby was sitting in a chair halfway down the long cherry-wood table, talking to Maria about some new recipe.

She looked toward the doorway, but when she saw him, all the laughter and animation went out of her like a light that was suddenly turned off. She was wearing a red and white dress and her hair was down around her shoulders in a pretty, dark, waving tangle. The wind, he thought absently, tearing through her hair in the convertible.

"I've traded cars," she said defiantly. "How do you like it? It was Abby's. You don't even have to cosign with me, I can make the payments from my salary."

Justin glanced at Maria, who knew the look and made herself scarce. He sat down at the head of the table, lit a cigarette and leaned back in the chair to stare intently at Shelby. "The last thing in the world you need is a sports car. You already drive too damned fast."

She searched his dark eyes, reading the thinly veiled concern. "Somebody saw me in the car this afternoon," she guessed.

He nodded. "Calhoun."

"I thought it was him." She studied her hands in her lap, turning the thin gold band on her wedding finger. "I like speed," she said hotly.

"I don't like funerals," he shot back. "I don't intend having to go to yours. You'll take that sports car back tomorrow or I'll take it back for you."

"It's mine!" she cried. Her green eyes flashed angrily. "And I won't take it back!"

He took a long draw from his cigarette. In his reclining position, his white silk shirt was drawn taut over tanned muscles. His chest was thick with hair that peeked out through the unfastened top buttons of his shirt. His jacket was off, his sleeves rolled up. He looked devastatingly masculine, from his disheveled black hair to his sensuous mouth.

"I'm not going to argue about it, honey," he replied. Through a veil of smoke, his black eyes searched hers. "Calhoun told me you wrecked a car overseas."

She flushed. "That was an accident."

"You aren't going to have any accidents here," he said. "I won't let you kill yourself."

"For heaven's sake, Justin, I'm not suicidal!" she protested. She lifted her coffee cup to her lips and took a fortifying sip of the black liquid.

"I didn't say you were," he agreed. He moved his ashtray on the tablecloth, watching it spin around. "But you need a firmer hand than you've been getting."

"I'm not Abby," she said. Her finely etched features grew hard as she looked at him. "I don't need a guardian."

He looked back, black eyes searching, quiet. "And while we're on the subject, I don't like you working for Barry Holman."

She blinked. She felt suddenly as if control of her own life was being taken away from her. "Justin, I didn't ask how you liked it," she reminded him. "I told you before we married that I wanted to keep on working."

"There's more than enough to do around here," he said. He tapped an ash into the ashtray. "You can manage the house."

"Maria and Lopez do that very nicely, thank you," she replied. She stiffened. "I don't want to stay home and swirl around the house in silk lounge pajamas and throw parties, Justin, in case you wondered. I've had my fill of charity work and flower arranging and social warfare."

He was looking at the cigarette, not at her. "I thought you might miss those things. In the old days, you never had to lift a finger."

She studied her neat hands in her lap, pleating the thin silky fabric of the red and white dress. "My father saw me as a parlor decoration," she said tautly. "He would have been outraged if I'd tried to change my image."

He frowned slightly. "Were you afraid of him?"

"I was *owned* by him," she replied. She sighed, raising her eyes to Justin's. The curiosity there puzzled her, but at least they were talking for a change instead of arguing. "He wasn't the easiest man to live with, and he had terrible ways of getting even when Ty and I disobeyed."

"He kept you pretty close to home," he recalled. "Although he trusted you with me."

"Did he really?" she laughed hollowly. "Justin, you

were the second man I ever dated and the first I ever went out with alone. You look shocked. Did you think my father let me live the life of a playgirl? He was terrified that some fortune hunter might seduce me. I lived like a recluse while he was alive."

Justin wasn't sure he understood what he was hearing. His head tilted a little and his eyes narrowed. "Would you like to run that by me again?" he asked. "You hadn't been out with a man alone until you went with me?"

"That's it," she agreed. "I didn't get out of my father's sight until after I broke the engagement and went to Switzerland." She smiled sadly. "I guess the freedom was too much, because I ran wild. The sports car was just an outlet, a way of celebrating. I never meant to wreck it."

"How badly were you hurt?" he asked.

"I broke my leg and cracked two ribs," she said. "They said I was lucky."

He finished his cigarette and crushed it out. "I didn't realize you were that sheltered," he said quietly. He was only beginning to understand how innocent she'd been in those days. If she'd only dated one other man, then very likely her first taste of intimacy had been with him. He thought about that, and felt himself go taut. He'd expected her to have a little experience, even though he'd known she was virginal. But if she'd had none, it was easy to understand why his ardor would have frightened her so.

"I couldn't talk about things like that with you," she confessed. "I was young and hopelessly naive."

He stared at her narrowly, his black eyes glittering. "I frightened you the night we got engaged, didn't I?" he asked suddenly. "That was why you pulled back—not because I disgusted you."

She caught her breath audibly. "You never disgusted me!" she burst out, hurting for him. "Oh, Justin, no! You didn't think that?"

"We didn't know very much about each other, Shelby," he said, his voice deep and measured. "I suppose we both had false ideas. I saw you as a sophisticated, elegant society woman. And while I knew you were innocent, I thought you'd had some experience with men. If I'd had any idea of what you've just told me, I damned sure wouldn't have been that demanding with you."

She went red and averted her eyes. She couldn't find the right words. Amazing, that they were married and she was twenty-seven years old, and this kind of talk could still embarrass her.

"I was afraid you couldn't stop," she murmured evasively.

He sighed heavily and lifted his coffee cup to his lips, draining it. "So was I," he said unexpectedly. "It was touch and go for a few seconds, at that. I'd gone hungry for a long time."

"I didn't think men had to, these days," she said softly. "I mean, society is so permissive and all."

"Society may be permissive. I'm not," he said flatly. His black eyes flashed at her. "I never was, in the way you mean. A gentleman doesn't seduce virgins—or take advantage of women who don't know the score. That leaves party girls." He held the cup in his big, lean hands, smoothing over it with his thumb. "And just to be frank, honey, the type never appealed very much to me."

Her soft eyes searched over his hard features, lingering on his chiseled mouth.

"I guess you never lacked offers, all the same," she said, letting her gaze fall to her lap again.

"I'm rich." There was cool cynicism in the words. "Sure, I get offers." He studied her face calculatingly. "In fact, Shelby, I had one while I was in New Mexico last week, wedding ring and all."

Her teeth clenched. She didn't want him to see that it bothered her, but it was hard to hide. "Did you?"

He put the cup down. "You're as possessive about me as I am about you," he said then, surprising her gaze up to lock with his in a slow, electric exchange. "You don't like the thought of other women making eyes at me, do you, Shelby?"

She crossed her legs. "No," she said honestly.

He smiled mockingly as he lit another cigarette. "Well, if it's any comfort, I froze her out. I won't cheat on you, honey."

"I never thought you would," she replied. "Any more than I'd cheat on you."

"That would be the eighth wonder of the world," he remarked with deceptive softness, "considering your hang-ups. We've been married for almost two weeks, and you still look like a sacrificial lamb every time I come near you."

She drew in a slow, steadying breath. "Yes, I know," she said miserably. She smiled bitterly. "I'm aware of my own failings, Justin. I guess you won't believe it, but you can't possibly blame me any more than I blame myself for what I am."

He scowled. He hadn't meant to put her on the defensive. His pride was stung and he was striking out. But he didn't want to hurt her anymore. He'd done enough of that already.

"I didn't mean it like that," he said on a weary breath. "It's the way things happened, that's all." He looked his age for a minute, his expression bleak, his dark eyes haunted. "You savaged my pride, Shelby. It's taken a long time to put it behind me. I guess I haven't, just yet."

"I didn't get off scot-free, either," she murmured. Her thin shoulders slumped. "I've had my share of grief over what I did."

"Why?" he asked shortly.

She closed her eyes and winced. "I did it for your sake," she whispered.

He let out an angry breath. "Well, that's a new tack, at least." He ground out the half-finished cigarette and got to his feet. "I've got some paperwork to do before Maria gets supper on the table." He paused beside her chair, watching the way she stiffened as he got close to her. He reached down and caught a handful of her long hair, dragging her head back so that he could see her eyes. "Fear," he ground out, searching them. "That's all I ever see in your eyes when I come near you. Well, don't sweat it, honey. You won't be called on to make the supreme sacrifice. I'm not desperate!"

He let her go and moved past her with anger in every line of his powerful body, without another word or a backward glance.

Shelby felt the tears come and she didn't stop them. He didn't know why she was afraid, and she couldn't tell him. He just assumed that she withdrew because she didn't want him. Nothing was further from the truth.

She did, desperately. But she wanted him controlled and gentle, and she remembered how it had been when he wasn't.

She got up from the table and went up to her room to spend a few quiet minutes before they ate getting herself back together again. It was so hard to talk to him, to get around his growing impatience. Her rejection was doing terrible things to him, and even now she felt protective. She wanted to give him what he wanted, to erase those hard lines from his face. But she was so frightened of the demands he might make on her.

If only she could tell him. But her sheltered background made it too embarrassing to explain why she was the way she was. Until she could find a way to make him understand, it was going to put an even worse strain on their marriage.

Chapter Five

If Shelby had hoped to find Justin less angry over dinner, she was doomed to disappointment. He sat at the head of the table like a stone man, barely speaking through the meal. She couldn't talk to him. She didn't know what to say.

Afterward, he went out the door without a word and Shelby felt a sense of utter desperation. If only she could go to him and put her arms around him, explain how she felt, why she was the way she was. But would he believe her, with their past?

Misery wrapped around her like a blanket. She got her purse and went out to her car. If Justin thought she was going to sit around by herself for what was left of the evening, he could just think again.

She started the sports car, revved the engine, backed out and roared away. The wonderful thing about the little car was the delicious feel of its controlled speed. She loved the straight road, the sense of freedom she felt with the wind in her long hair, the exhilaration of being alone with her thoughts.

Justin hated her, but that was nothing new. He always had. She'd hurt him and he was never going to forgive her. She didn't know why she'd agreed to marry him; it was never going to work out. She'd been a fool to go through with it in the first place, so she had only herself to blame for her present misery.

She was so deep in thought that she didn't notice the stop sign until she was on it, and the loud baritone of a truck's horn made her blood freeze.

A huge transfer-trailer truck was barreling down the highway. Shelby's little car wasn't going to be fast enough to beat that mammoth vehicle across the intersection, and it was touch and go if she'd be able to stop at all.

With her heart in her throat, and the numb certainty of death stiffening her body, she hit the brake. The car went into a spin, the squeal of tires terrible in the later afternoon stillness, her face frozen with terror as she lost control and the sky went around and around and around…

The car spun into the deep ditch and leaned drunkenly sideways, but amazingly it didn't turn over. Shelby sat, shaken but unhurt, nausea bitter in her throat and the world spinning around her. There was the sound of another car screeching to a halt. A door opened. There was the sound of running feet and then, suddenly, a man's anguished shout.

"Shelby!" The man's face was familiar, but somehow unfamiliar. It was hoarse and choked and blackly furious. "Answer me, damn it, are you all right?"

She felt her seat belt being forced away from her with hands that were lean and brown and shaking. She felt those same hands running over her body, searching for blood or broken bones, exquisitely gentle.

"Are you all right?" Justin asked huskily. "Do you hurt anywhere? For God's sake, sweetheart, answer me!"

"I...I'm fine," she whispered numbly. "The door...?"

"It won't open, the frame's sprung. Easy does it, now." He carefully reached down to get her under the armpits and with formidable strength he lifted her clear of the car. When she was on the ground, swaying, he picked her up with exquisite tenderness and carried her up from the ditch. The truck driver had stopped down the road and was coming toward them, but Justin didn't seem to see him. His expression was rigid with control, but he couldn't stop his arms from trembling under her slender body.

That fact finally registered in Shelby's dazed mind.

She looked up then and saw his face, and her breath fluttered. He was flour-white, only his eyes alive and glittering blackly in that set, haunted face. He looked down at her, his arms convulsively dragging her against his chest.

"You little fool…!" he choked.

As long as she lived, she knew she'd never forget the horror she saw in his eyes. She reached up to hold him, her only thought to remove that look from his eyes.

"It's all right, Justin," she murmured softly. His reaction fascinated her. She'd never seen him shaken before. It made her feel protective, that tiny chink in his cool armor.

"I'm fine, Justin," she whispered. Her eyes searched his, amazed at the vulnerability there. She touched his mouth, her soft fingers caressing as they slid up into his thick, dark hair. "Darling, I'm all right, really I am!" She pulled his mouth down and put hers softly against it, loving the way he let her kiss him, even if it was only out of shock—which, in fact, it was. For several seconds she savored the newness of it, then something stirred in her slender body, and her mouth pushed upward, hungry for a harder, deeper contact than this. It had been years since they'd kissed, since they'd really kissed. She moaned softly and he seemed to come out of his trance. His arm contracted, and his hard mouth opened hungrily against hers on a wild, shattered groan.

His mouth hurt as it dragged against hers while he muttered something violent and unintelligible against her soft lips. He pulled back with evident reluctance as the truck driver came running down the highway toward them.

"Is she all right?" the man asked, panting from the long run he'd had. "My God, I was sure I'd hit her...!"

"She's all right," Justin answered tersely. "But that damned car won't be when I can lay my hands on my rifle."

The truck driver sighed with pure relief. "Damn, lady, you can sure handle yourself," he said with admiration. "If you'd lost your nerve and thrown up your hands, you'd be dead and I'd be a mental patient."

"I'm sorry." Shelby wept, her nerve broken from the combination of the near miss and the exquisite ardor of Justin's hard mouth. "I'm so sorry. I didn't even see you coming!"

The truck driver, a young man with red hair, just shook his head, barely able to get his breath. "Are you sure you're all right?"

"I'm fine," she said, forcing a trembling smile. "Thank you for stopping. It wasn't your fault."

"That wouldn't have made me feel any better," she was told. "Well, if you're sure, I'll be on my way." He looked at Justin, and almost offered to help, but the glitter in those black eyes wasn't encouraging.

"As my wife said, thanks for stopping," Justin said.

The younger man nodded, smiled and walked away with patent relief, wondering why a woman that pretty would marry such a desperado. He was glad she wasn't hurt. He wouldn't have relished having to face that wild-eyed husband unarmed.

Justin didn't say another word. He turned, carrying Shelby to the Thunderbird. He balanced her on his knee, opened the passenger door and put her inside very gently.

"What about my car?" she asked.

His black eyes met hers. "Damn your car," he said huskily. He slammed the door and went around to get in under the wheel. But he didn't start the car. He sat with his hands, white-knuckled, gripping the steering wheel for a long moment while Shelby waited for the explosion that she knew was about to come. Justin had been badly shaken and somebody was going to pay for it. Now that he was sure she was all right, she could imagine that he was loading both verbal barrels.

"Go ahead, give me hell," she said tearfully, searching in the glove compartment for a tissue. "I was driving too fast, and I wasn't watching. I deserve every lecture I get." She blew her nose. "How did you get here so fast?"

He still didn't speak. After a minute, he sat back in the bucket seat and fumbled a cigarette out of his pocket. He lit it with still-trembling hands, staring straight ahead.

"I followed you," he said curtly. "When I heard you gun the car out of the driveway, I was afraid you might try to take out your temper on the highway, so I tagged along." His head turned and his black eyes flashed at her. "My God, I paid for sins I haven't even committed when I saw you spin out."

She could imagine how it had been for him, having to watch. Even though he didn't love her, it would have been terrible.

"I'm sorry," she said inadequately, folding her arms across her breasts shakily.

His chest rose and fell with a huge, angry breath. "Are you, really?" he said. He was back in control now, and the cool smile on his face infuriated her. "Well, you can say goodbye to that damned sports car. Tomorrow, I'll go downtown with you and steer you toward something safe."

"What did you have in mind, a Sherman tank?" she asked with ice in her tone.

"A bicycle, if you keep this up," he corrected angrily.

"I told you once before, Shelby, your reckless days are over."

"You're not going to order me around!" she shot at him through trembling lips and clenched teeth. "I'm not your ward!"

"No," he agreed with a mocking smile. "You're my wife, aren't you? My saintly, untouched wife who can bear anyone's hands except mine."

It was too much. She burst into tears again, turning her face to the window, burying her eyes in the soggy tissue.

"Don't," he groaned. "For God's sake, stop it. I can't stand tears!"

"Then don't look, damn you," she whispered, stomping her foot.

He swore roughly, digging into his pocket for his freshly laundered linen handkerchief. He thrust it into her trembling hands, feeling as if someone had kicked him.

"You'll make yourself sick. Stop it. You're all right. A miss is as good as a mile, isn't it?" he asked, his voice softer now, deeper. He touched her hair hesitantly. It was all coming back into focus, little by little. He frowned, because now he remembered something that panic had knocked out of his mind. She'd touched his face and whispered something, and she'd put her mouth against his to comfort him. What had she said…?

"You called me darling," he said aloud.

She moved jerkily. "Did I? I must have been out of my mind, mustn't I?" She sniffed and mopped herself up. "Can we go home, Justin? I need something to drink."

"I could use a neat whiskey myself," he said heavily. His eyes searched over her wan, sad little face. "Are you sure you're all right?"

"I'm tough," she murmured.

"Tough," he agreed. "And reckless, stupid, impulsive—"

"You stop that!" she protested. Her pale green eyes glared at him, red-rimmed.

"You kissed me."

She went from white to rose red and averted her eyes. "You were upset."

"I've been upset before, but you never kissed me, Shelby." His dark eyes narrowed as he reached for the ignition switch. "Come to think of it, in all the years we've known each other, that's the very first move toward me you've ever made."

She leaned back against the seat, her arms folded. "Justin, my purse is still in the car," she murmured evasively.

He reached down to the floor, picked it up and put it in her lap. "You grabbed it before I lifted you clear," he said. "It came along for the ride."

"You aren't really going to shoot Abby's old car, are you?"

He reversed the car and then pulled in a perfect circle back the way he'd come. "It might get that gentle a treatment if it's lucky," he muttered.

"Justin! It wasn't the car's fault!"

"Sit back and relax now, Shelby. I'll have you home in a minute."

She ground her teeth together as he sped down the road at no less a speed than she'd been driving. "Pot," she muttered.

"Pardon?"

"Pot! The one that calls the kettle black! You're doing sixty!"

"It's a big car."

"What has that got to do with it?"

"Never mind." He smoked his cigarette, frowning thoughtfully. Things had been pretty clear in his mind until ten minutes ago. Now he began to wonder if he hadn't got things twisted. He'd assumed that Shelby found him repulsive all those years ago, that she still did. But her soft lips had been warm and eager, and for those few seconds she'd been absolutely ardent. Of course, she was frightened, he had to admit, and reaction did funny things to people. But if she was that concerned when he was upset, there had to be a little caring left in her.

He pulled up in front of the house and, despite her protests, carried her up to the door where he balanced her long enough to open it.

"No need to worry Maria…" he began, but no sooner had he got the words out than Maria came running down the hall. When she saw Shelby's white face, a stream of Spanish broke from her.

"I'm all right," Shelby told her. "The car went into the ditch, that's all."

Maria looked at Justin. That wasn't all, but she knew better than to make a fuss. "What do you want me to do, Señor Justin?" Maria asked.

"I'll get her upstairs. How about pouring me a neat whiskey and bringing up a brandy for Shelby?"

"*Sí, señor.*"

"Why can't I have a neat whiskey?" Shelby asked.

Justin's dark eyes searched hers and he pulled her just a little closer as he went easily up the staircase with his soft burden cradled against his chest. "You're just a baby."

"I'm twenty-seven," she reminded him.

He smiled gently. "I'm thirty-seven," he reminded her. "And that's a pretty formidable ten-year jump I've got on you, honey."

The careless endearment made her flush. She lowered her eyes to his shirt. He'd changed earlier, before they ate.

This one was Western cut and blue plaid. It suited him. It smelled of detergent and starch, smoke and cologne. She loved being in his arms. If only she could tell him that, and explain why she was afraid of him. But she couldn't.

He carried her into her room and put her on the bed, his eyes going hungrily over the way that damned red and white dress clung in all the right places. It wasn't low-cut, but it displayed her high breasts in the best possible way, and looking at them made him ache.

Shelby frowned at the expression on his face. "What's wrong?" she asked, fatigue in her soft voice.

He straightened. "Nothing. I'll have Maria bring up the brandy. You'd better have a hot bath and then I'll take you to the doctor. I want you examined, to make sure you haven't done any damage."

She sat up, her eyes like saucers. "Justin, I'm all right!"

"You're not a doctor and neither am I. You took a hell of a jolt and you were damned near in shock when I pulled you out of that car." His jaw set stubbornly. "You're going. Hurry up and get changed. Wear something—" he hesitated "—less sexy."

Her eyebrows arched. "I beg your pardon?"

He turned toward the door. "I'll phone the doctor while you take a bath."

She stared after him blankly. "I don't want to go to the doctor."

He just closed the door, ignoring what she did or didn't want. Taking control, as usual, she fumed. She wanted to throw things. She was all right, couldn't he see that? She burst into tears of frustrated temper and went into the bathroom. She felt as if her knees had been knocked out from under her.

After her bath, she dried her hair and put on a neat white blouse and gray skirt and brightened it with a gray and red scarf at her throat. She wondered why he wanted her to wear something less sexy, and then felt her heart skip at the realization that *he* must have found the red and white dress sexy. She smiled demurely. That was the first time since their marriage that he'd admitted to finding her attractive. If only she could be sure that he wouldn't lose control, it might have given her enough courage to do more than just kiss him.

She picked up the brandy snifter Maria had left with a teaspoon of brandy in it and sipped it quietly. She had kissed him, all right. He was going to worry that to death. But he'd been upset and she'd wanted so desperately to comfort him that her usual inhibitions hadn't built a wall between them. And the kiss had been delicious. Her mouth still tingled from the rough sweetness of his. And then she remembered why it had been so sweet. He'd let her make all the moves. He hadn't taken control away from her. She frowned.

A knock on the door interrupted her brooding. She opened it. Justin was already looking impatient.

"How do you feel?" he asked.

"I'm sore..." she began.

"The doctor's waiting. Let's go." He took the brandy snifter from her, put it on her dresser and escorted her out of the room.

The doctor he'd found was at the hospital emergency room. Shelby felt nervous and edgy, because she'd hardly been near a hospital since her wreck in Switzerland, except to Dr. Sims for her premarital examination. But this wasn't Dr. Sims. This was a nice young doctor named Hays, very personable and kindhearted, and obviously a little amused by Justin's irritated concern.

"You'll be stiff for a couple of days, but I'm sure your husband will be relieved to know that you've done no lasting damage," Dr. Hays said after he'd finished his examination and she'd answered the necessary questions. "Just one more thing—there's no possibility that you might be pregnant?" he asked quietly, made more curious by her blush and Justin's averted face. "An experience like this could be risky..."

"I'm not pregnant," she said huskily.

"Then you'll be fine. I'm going to give you some muscle relaxants in case you need them. You can take a non-aspirin analgesic for pain, and a little extra rest tomorrow might be beneficial. Of course, if you have any further problems, let me know."

Shelby thanked him and Justin muttered something before he escorted her out of the examination room and down the hall to pay the bill. By the time they were through and on their way back to the house, it was almost eight o'clock and dark outside.

Justin was quiet all the way home. Shelby knew why. It was the doctor's very natural question about pregnancy. It had embarrassed Justin and probably enraged him as well, because intimacy was such a bone of contention between them.

"You should have told him that we could get you in the *Guinness Book of World Records* if you got pregnant," he said through his teeth as he parked the car in the driveway and cut off the engine.

She turned her purse in her lap. Now that the tension was lifting, she only felt tired and sore. "What did you do with my car? It wasn't on the highway when we came past the intersection."

His black eyes shifted toward her and then away. "You don't want to talk about it, do you?"

"I'm frigid," she said dully. "Let's just leave it at that, unless you want a divorce."

"I want a wife," he said harshly. "I want kids." His jaw tautened as he lifted his cigarette to his mouth. "Oh, God, I want kids, Shelby," he said in a faintly vulnerable tone.

That was something they'd never talked about, except in the very early days of their association. She leaned her head back against her seat, nibbling her lower lip and stared down at her lap. "You probably won't believe it, but so do I, Justin."

He turned in his seat to look at her downcast face, his eyes dark and quiet. "How did you plan to get any without help?"

Her hands contracted on her purse. "I'm afraid," she said softly, because for once she was too tired to lie, to find excuses.

There was a long pause. "Well, childbirth isn't really the terror it used to be, from all I've heard," he said, getting the wrong end of the stick. "And there are drugs they can give you for pain."

She looked up at him, shocked. "What?"

It was incredible that he believed she was afraid to have a child. She just stared at him without moving.

"It doesn't have to be right away, either," he said doggedly, averting his gaze out the window, as if the subject embarrassed him. It probably did. Shelby remembered that he'd always found it difficult to talk about things like pregnancy and that he never did discuss intimate matters in mixed company. In his own way, he was as reticent as she was. It was one of the things she'd always loved about him.

She was trying to understand what he meant when he took another draw from the cigarette and put it out. There was a dull flush across his cheekbones and he wouldn't look at her.

"You could talk to the doctor about something to take," he said tersely. "Or I could use something. You don't have to get pregnant if you don't want to. I won't force you to have a child."

She went beet red and stared out her window, her hands trembling and cold as the intimacy of what he was saying finally got through to her. She cleared her throat. "I…could we go inside now?" she whispered. "I'm tired and I ache all over."

"It's hard for me to talk about it, too," he said quietly. "But I wanted you to know. To think it over. If that's why you won't let me touch you…"

"Oh, don't!" She buried her face in her hands.

He sighed roughly. "I'm sorry. I shouldn't have said anything." He got out and came around the car to help her out. "Did he give you any muscle relaxants or do I need to go to the drugstore for you?" he asked.

"He gave me some samples," she said. She walked

alongside him up the steps, ashamed of the way she'd changed the subject and shied away from the discussion. She wanted to tell him what was wrong. But talking to Justin that way was so embarrassing.

"You go on up and have an early night," he said, as remote as if he'd been talking to a total stranger. "I'll have Maria bring you up some hot chocolate. Do you want anything to eat?"

"No, thank you." She paused at the foot of the staircase and smoothed her hand over the banister. She didn't want to go. Her eyes lifted to his across the hall and she looked at him with hopeless longing and anguished shame. "I shouldn't have married you," she whispered huskily. "I never meant to make you unhappy."

His jaw went taut. "I never meant to make you unhappy, either, but that's what I've done."

She hesitated. "You never told me what you did with the sports car," she said after a minute. "Can't I have it back?"

"Sure," he said, lifting his chin and pursing his lips. "We can have it made into an ashtray or a piece of modern art."

Her eyebrows shot up. "What do you mean?"

He shrugged. "It's about five inches thick and four feet long by now. A bit big for an ashtray, I guess, but framed, it would make one hell of a wall decoration."

"What are you talking about? What did you do with it?"

"I gave it to Old Man Doyle."

She turned her head slightly as the words registered. "He owns a junkyard."

He smiled faintly. "Sure does. He has a brand-new crusher. You know, one of those big machines that you use to push old cars into scrap metal…"

She flushed. "You did that on purpose!"

"You're damned right I did," he said with a glittery challenge in his eyes. "If I'd taken it back to the car lot, I couldn't be sure that you wouldn't rush right down there and buy it again. This way," he added, pulling his hat low over his eyes, "I'm sure."

"I still owe for it! It was a lot of money!"

He smiled pleasantly. "I'm sure you can explain it to the insurance company. Atmospheric pressure? Termites…?"

She was stuck for a reply when he turned and went into the kitchen.

She went up the staircase, smoldering. It had been an upsetting day all around, and it wasn't improving. Her mind whirled with questions and problems.

At first, she hadn't wanted to take the muscle relaxants, but she got sore as the night wore on. Finally she gave in, downing them with a sip of cooling hot chocolate. She put on her gray satin pajamas and climbed under the covers. Minutes later, she was asleep.

But then the dreams started. Over and over again, she could see herself in the sports car, but in Switzerland. She'd been speeding around the Alps with skill and ease until she was almost at the bottom of a mountain. She'd hit a patch of ice and all her experience at the wheel hadn't been able to save her. The car, that time, had rolled. And rolled. And rolled.

She was pitching down the side of the white mountain, sky and snow combining in a terrible descent. She waited for the impact, waited, screaming…

Hands lifted her from the pillow, gently shaking her.

"It's all right," someone said. "It's all right. Wake up, Shelby, you're dreaming."

She snapped awake as if a switch had been thrown in her brain. Justin was holding her, his black eyes narrow with concern.

"The car…" she whispered. "It was pitching down the mountain."

"You were dreaming, little one," he said. He smoothed the dark tangle of her hair away from her flushed cheeks and her shoulders. "Only dreaming. You're safe now."

"I always was, with you," she said involuntarily, leaning her head on his shoulder. She sighed heavily, relaxed now, secure. Her cheek moved and he stiffened, and she realized that she was resting on bare skin, not a pajama top.

The light was on and he was sitting beside her on the bed, his dark hair tousled. She almost lost her nerve when she lifted her cheek away from his muscular upper arm, but she breathed easily when she saw that he was only bare from the waist up. He was wearing dark silk pajama trousers, but his muscular chest was completely bare. Thick black hair curled down to the low waistband of the pajamas, and the very sight of him was breathtaking.

Shelby felt her breath catch at all that masculinity so close to her. She knew without being told that he wasn't wearing anything under those trousers, and it made her feel threatened.

"Did you take those pills the doctor gave you?" he asked quietly.

"Yes. They made the aching stop, but now I'm having nightmares." She laughed jerkily. She pushed back her thick cloud of hair, glancing up at him apprehensively. "Did I wake you?"

"Not really." He sighed. "I don't sleep well these days. It doesn't take much to wake me. I heard you scream."

She didn't sleep well, either, and probably for the same reason. She locked her arms around her knees, curling up to rest her forehead there. "Today's accident brought back the wreck I had in Switzerland," she murmured drowsily. "I was concussed and I kept drifting in and out." She moved her forehead against the soft satin. "They told me I called for you night and day after they brought me to the hospital," she said without meaning to.

"Me, and not your lover?" he asked coldly.

"I've never had a lover, Justin," she said shyly.

"Sure. And I'm the king of Siam." He got to his feet, looking down at her half angrily. She was lovely in those satin pajamas. He'd never thought about what she wore to sleep in, but now he was sure he'd think of nothing else. The jacket was low-cut and he'd had a deliciously tempting glimpse of her firm breasts when she'd first come awake. They were small, he thought speculatively, but perfectly formed if their outline under that jacket was anything to go by. His eyes narrowed and he had to pull his gaze away, because he wanted to look at them with a hunger that made him go rigid.

He turned away. "If you're all right, I'll go back and try to sleep. I've got an early appointment in town at the bank."

She watched him go with a deep sadness. The distance between them grew all the time, and she was making him unhappier by the day. "Thank you for coming to see about me," she said dully.

He paused with his hand on the doorknob, his gaze concerned. "You'd die before you'd do it, I know," he said slowly. "But if you get frightened again, you can double up with me." He laughed coldly. "It's safe enough, in case you're worried. I won't risk my ego again with you."

He was gone before she could contradict him. She winced at the pain those words had revealed. She felt worse than ever, knowing how she'd hurt him.

And it was so unnecessary. All she had to do was tell him. For God's sake, she was twenty-seven years old! Yes, and sheltered to the point of obsession by her money-hungry father, who'd been afraid to lose her to a poor man. She'd never even been kissed intimately until the night they got engaged. She wondered if he knew that.

He probably didn't, she decided. She got out of bed and turned on the light, heading for the door. Maybe it was time she told him.

Chapter Six

It didn't occur to her until she was out in the hall, barefooted, at Justin's door, that three o'clock in the morning wasn't the best time to share intimate secrets with a man who'd gone starving for physical satisfaction since his marriage. She hesitated, nibbling her lower lip. The light was still on in his room, but it was pretty quiet in there.

She frowned, wondering what to do, and brushed back her unruly hair with a sigh.

"He's not in there," came a soft, deeply amused voice at her back.

She whirled to find Justin behind her, holding a jigger of whiskey. "What are you doing out here?" she asked.

"Watching you prowl the halls. What were you planning to do, go in there and rape me?"

She burst out laughing. It bubbled up from some un-known place, and her eyes twinkled up at him. "I don't know how," she confessed.

He actually smiled. She was pretty when she laughed. She was pretty any way at all. He lifted the whiskey rue-fully. "I thought it might help me sleep," he said.

"I'm afraid nothing's going to help me," she mur-mured. She shifted from one bare foot to the other, aware of his curious scrutiny and her own loud heartbeat.

"Do you want to sleep with me?" he asked.

She flushed. "That wasn't the only reason I came." She glanced up and then down again at his own bare, very big feet. "Did you know that nobody had ever kissed me intimately until you did?"

He blinked. "You came down the hall at three o'clock in the morning to tell me that?"

She shrugged. "It seemed pretty important at the time," she said. She looked up at him sadly, her pale green eyes searching his lean, craggy face, his sensuous mouth, the firm, hair-roughened muscles of his chest and stomach. "It's amazing," she murmured, her eyes fascinated by the bare expanse of brown muscle.

"What is?" He frowned, watching the way her eyes went over him. It was disturbing. Surely she knew that.

"That you don't have to chase women out of your room with a broom handle," she murmured absently.

His eyebrows arched. "Have you been into my brandy snifter?"

"I guess it sounds that way, doesn't it?" She raised her eyes to his. "Can I sleep with you, Justin? I'm still pretty shaky. If…" She cleared her throat and looked away. "If it won't bother you too much, I mean. I don't want to make things any worse for you than they already are."

"I'm not sure they could get worse," he said quietly. He searched her wide, soft eyes. "All right. Come on."

She followed him inside. She'd never been in his room before, although she'd been by it a number of times and had peeked in curiously.

The furniture was old. Antique, like that in the house she'd grown up in. She wondered if it went far back in his family, if he'd inherited it from his parents. She smoothed her hand over a long bedpost, admiring the slickly polished wood of the four-poster and the beige and brown striped sheets on the bed.

"I didn't think you liked colored sheets," she said conversationally. "Maria said you didn't."

"I don't," he said curtly. "Maria does. She swears that she lost all the white sheets and had to replace them."

"Well, these are nice," she murmured.

"Climb in."

He held the top sheet back and let her slide under it.

"I'll adjust the air-conditioning if it's too cool in here to suit you," he offered.

"No, it's fine," she said. "I hate a hot bedroom, even in winter."

He smiled faintly. "So do I." He turned off the light and came back to the bed. The mattress lowered as he sat down, obviously finishing off his whiskey.

"You, uh, you do sleep in pajama bottoms?" she asked, grateful for the darkness that spared her blushes.

He actually laughed. "Oh, my God."

"Well, you don't have to make fun of me," she muttered, fluffing the pillow before she laid her head on it.

"I always thought you were a sophisticated girl," he said pleasantly. "You know, the liberated sort with a string of men on your sleeve and the kind of sophistication that goes with champagne and diamonds."

"Boy, were you in for a shock," she murmured. "Until you came along, I'd only dated one man, and the most he did was to make a grab for me and get himself slapped. My father was obsessed with keeping me innocent until he could sell me to someone who'd make him even richer. But you don't know that, of course, you think he's a saint."

He switched on the light. His eyes were black and steady on hers, noticing the flush that covered her cheeks.

"Will you turn that off, please?" she asked tightly. "If I'm going to talk about such things, I can't look at you and do it."

"Prude," he accused.

She glared at him. "Look who's talking."

He smiled ruefully. He cut off the lights, too. She felt the mattress shift as he lay back on it and pulled the sheet up over his hips.

"All right. If you want to talk, go ahead."

"My father never wanted you to marry me, Justin, despite the show he put on for you," she said shortly. "He wanted me to marry Tom Wheelor's racing stables so that he could merge them with his and get out of debt."

"That's a hard pill to swallow, considering what I know about your father," he said, remembering that it was her father's money that had helped his family's feed-lot. He wondered if she'd ever found that out, and almost said so when he heard her sigh.

She shifted. "Nevertheless, it's true. He was all set to ruin you if I hadn't gone along with him when he cooked up that story about my marrying Tom."

"You admitted that you'd slept with Tom," he reminded her. His tone darkened. "And I know how little you wanted to sleep with me."

"It wasn't because I found you repulsive," she said.

"Wasn't it?"

Before she could say another word, he'd rolled over. One lean arm went across her body, dragging her against him. In the darkness, he sought her mouth with his and kissed her with rough abandon. Her hands went up against his hair-roughened chest, pushing at solid warm muscle, while his mouth demanded things that frightened her. His knee insinuated itself between both of hers and she stiffened and pushed harder, fighting him.

He let her go without another word and got up. His hand flicked the light switch. When he turned toward her, his eyes were blazing like forest fires, his face livid with barely controlled rage.

"Get out!" he said in a biting fury.

She knew that she couldn't say anything now that would calm him. If she tried to argue or smooth it over, she might unleash something physical that would scar her even more than his ardor had six years before.

She got out of the bed, her eyes apologetic and tearful, and did as he'd told her. She didn't look back. She closed the door gently and, still crying, made her way down the long staircase.

Justin's study was quiet. She turned on the light, went to the liquor cabinet, and with hands that shook, found a brandy snifter. She poured brandy into it and swished it around. She wanted to jump off the roof, but perhaps this would do instead.

The house was so quiet. So peaceful. But her mind was in turmoil. Why couldn't he understand that violent lovemaking frightened her? Why wouldn't he listen?

She'd pushed him away, that was why. She'd fought him. But if she hadn't, and he'd lost control... Her eyes closed on a shudder. She couldn't even bear the thought.

Her legs shook as she made her way to the sofa and sat down, her body bowed, her forehead resting on the rim of the glass. Tears blurred it. She sipped and sipped, until finally the sting of the liquor began to soothe her nerves.

When she realized that she was no longer alone, she didn't even look up.

"I know you hate me," she said numbly. "You didn't have to come all the way down here to say it."

Justin winced at the tears on her face, at the anguish in her soft voice. His pride was shattered all over again. But it hurt him to see her cry.

He poured himself another whiskey and sat down on the edge of the heavy coffee table in front of her. "I've been up there calling you names," he said after a minute. "Until it suddenly got through to me what you'd said, about never letting another man kiss you intimately."

"I'm a scarlet woman, though," she said bitterly. "I slept with Tom. I even told you so."

"You've just told me that your father lied about it." His black eyes narrowed. He took a sip of the whiskey and put the glass down. He knelt just in front of her, not touching her, his eyes on a level with hers. "I remembered something else, too. Just after you wrecked the car, you kissed me. You weren't afraid of me, and you weren't repulsed, either, Shelby. But you were making all the moves, weren't you?"

Her eyes lifted to his. So he'd made the connection. She sighed worriedly. "Yes," she said finally. "I wasn't afraid, you see."

"But up until then," he added, his shrewd eyes making lightning assessments, "I'd been pretty rough with you when we made love."

She flushed, avoiding his gaze. "Yes."

"And it wasn't revulsion at all. It was fear. Not of getting pregnant. But of intimacy itself."

"Give that man a cigar," she murmured with forced humor.

He sighed, watching her fondle the brandy snifter. He took it out of her hands and put it on the coffee table. "Get up."

Startled, she felt him lift her from the sofa. He put her to one side and stretched out on the cushions, moving toward the back. "Now sit down."

She did, hesitantly, because she didn't understand this approach.

He took one of her hands and drew it to his chest. "Think of me as a human sacrifice," he murmured dryly. "A stepping stone in the educational process."

Her lips parted on a sudden gasp as she realized what he was doing. Her eyes darted up to his, curious, shy. "But you...you don't like that," she said perceptively, because in the past he'd always made the moves, he'd never encouraged her to.

"I'm going to learn to like it," he said frankly. "If it takes this to get you close to me, I'm more than willing to give you the advantage, Shelby."

Tears stung her eyes. She bit her lower lip to stop its trembling. "Oh, Justin," she whispered shakily.

"Can you do it this way?" he asked softly, his eyes black and alive with tenderness. "If I let you, can you make love to me?"

The tears broke from her eyes and ran down her cheeks. "I wanted to tell you," she wept. "But I was too embarrassed."

"It's all right." He put his big hand over hers and traced the tiny blue veins in it. "I should have realized it a long time ago. I won't hurt you. I'll never hurt you."

She laughed through the tears. Amazing, that he should puzzle it out for himself. She smiled and bent hesitantly to his warm mouth and touched it with her lips.

Justin felt as if his heart were about to burst. God

only knew why he'd never understood before. Obviously Wheelor had hurt her, and she'd drawn away from any further intimacy. He hated knowing that the other man had been her first lover, but he couldn't stand by any longer and watch Shelby beat herself to death emotionally over it. They had to start someplace to build a life together, and this was the very best way.

He felt her soft, shy mouth with a sense of wonder. She still didn't know a lot about kissing, and he smiled under her searching lips. He'd been celibate for a long time, but in his younger days, his lack of looks hadn't kept him from getting some experience. He knew what to do with a woman, even if discussing such things in public made him uncomfortable.

He didn't touch her. As he'd promised, he lay there with his body keeping him on the rack and let her soft mouth toy with his.

"Come closer," he breathed against her lips. "You're as safe as you want to be."

"It isn't hurting you?" she asked worriedly.

"When it gets that bad, I'll tell you," he promised, lying through his teeth, because it was already that bad.

She smiled, moving so that her soft breasts rested fully on his chest, her legs chastely beside his and not over them. There was a fine tremor in his lips when she bent again, but he still hadn't tried to pull her down or to make the kiss more intimate.

Her hands moved into his thick hair, ruffling it, and her lips traced patterns on his face, loving its strength. He was so sweet to kiss. She laughed with pure delight at the new freedom to touch him as she'd wanted to for so many lonely years.

His eyes opened and he studied her curiously. "What was that all about?"

"If you knew," she said, "how long I've wanted to do this…"

His jaw clenched. "You might have told me."

"I couldn't." She touched his broad chest. "It's so intimate a thing to talk about." Impulsively, she leaned down and brushed her mouth over the hard muscle of his breastbone. "Justin, I've missed you so much."

His chest rose heavily under the tiny caress. "I've missed you, too," he said huskily. "God, Shelby, I can't…!" He clenched his teeth.

She looked up. "It isn't enough for you, is it?" she asked hesitantly. "I guess I seem pretty green."

His eyes darkened. "I want to touch you," he breathed. "I want to put you on your back and slide that jacket out of my way."

Her body trembled over his. "If you lost control, it

would be just the way it was upstairs," she ground out. "I get scared!"

"I swear to God I won't lose it," he said curtly. "Not if I have to run out into the night screaming."

She believed him. It was the most difficult thing she'd ever done, to trust him now. But she swallowed hard and moved gently alongside him and onto her back, watching him shift so that he was poised over her.

"Trust comes hard, doesn't it?" he asked softly.

"Yes." She searched his face quietly. "I could have died this afternoon. I keep thinking about it, and how insignificant things seem at the point of death. All I thought about was you, and what a sad memory I'd left you with."

"Is that what this is all about?" he asked with a smile.

"Not really." She studied his hard mouth. "I was hungry for you, when you let me kiss you. I wanted to know if I could stop being afraid. But upstairs, when you grabbed me, I just went to pieces."

"I'm not going to grab you this time." He bent, barely touching her mouth with his. He brushed it, bit at it, until her lips began slowly to follow his. He felt her breath quicken. And then his fingers began to trace patterns on the pajama jacket.

At first she stiffened, but his movements were very slow and undemanding, and his mouth was gentle. He lifted his head, feeling her begin to relax, and he smiled reassuringly. "Okay?" he whispered.

The tenderness was new. Her eyes smiled up at him. "Okay."

He looked down at her breasts and saw hard peaks forming where his fingers teased. He put his thumb over a hard tip and heard her gasp and felt her body shudder. He liked that reaction, so he did it again, and this time she arched a little.

"I like that," he said softly, holding her eyes. "Do it again."

She did, but only because she couldn't help it. "I feel… strange," she whispered. "Shuddery."

"So do I," he whispered back, and brushed his mouth lazily over her lips until they parted. "Do you want me to tell you what I'm going to do now?"

Her heartbeat went wild. "Yes," she said against his mouth.

He smiled. "I'm going to unbutton your jacket."

Her breath sighed out quickly against his lips as she felt his hard fingers flicking buttons out of buttonholes. Then the fabric was open down the middle and he was slowly easing it away. He drew it just to the curve of her breasts and looked into her eyes, registering the faint shyness there and the excitement that she couldn't hide.

"You're small," he whispered. His fingers drew along one smooth curve. "I like my women small."

She trembled at the way he said it, at the knowledge in his black eyes, at the experience in the fingers that traced up and over and then stopped short of that hard, aching peak. She shuddered when he did that. He did it again, and she gasped.

His nose brushed against hers. His breath mingled with her own, tasting smoky and warm. "Yes, you want it, don't you?" he mused softly. He traced her again and this time he didn't stop. His hand smoothed over her and down, taking the hard tip into his moist palm and pressing down over it.

She cried out. The sound seemed to shock her because she swallowed, moistening her lips with her tongue.

"You act," he whispered, moving the fabric aside sensually, "just like a virgin with her first man." He peeled the satin away from her breasts and looked down. His breath caught, because the creamy mounds and their hard mauve tips were shaped so exquisitely that they took his breath.

"Do you really not mind…that I'm small?" she heard herself whisper.

"Oh, God, no," he returned. His eyes held hers and his fingers traced her soft skin. "Will it shock you if I put my mouth on them?"

"Yes," she said, smiling.

He smiled back and bent his head toward her body. She arched up at the first touch of his lips on her breasts, thinking that in all her life, she'd never dreamed there could be such pleasure in being touched. Her hands tangled in his thick hair and held him against her while his light, brushing caresses made her tremble. She moaned and tears sprung to her eyes.

He felt her body tremble and understood why. It was the advantage he'd been waiting for. His lean, callused hands smoothed down her hips, over her flat belly. They caressed the satin away so expertly that she didn't mind, didn't care. His hands touched her as if she'd always belonged to him, and she loved the touch, the slow tenderness of his rough hands on her skin.

His mouth opened, moist, the suction on her breast making her draw up with pleasure. She felt her hands helplessly gripping his muscular arms, pulling at him. She was whispering something that she didn't understand, pleading with him for something she didn't even know about. She needed… something.

Her mouth bit at his shoulder. When he lifted his head and looked down at her, she could barely see him through a red haze. She thought he smiled as his mouth fastened on hers. Then she felt his tongue go into her mouth in slow, exquisite thrusts and her body went wild under his.

She pulled at him, her arms around his neck. She felt him against her, felt the hard, warm contours of his body and the heat of his rough skin against her soft skin. She realized dimly that his pajama trousers were gone, but the touch of him against her was so exquisite that she didn't really want him to stop.

"It's going to happen now," he whispered into her mouth as his knee eased between her long, trembling legs. "I won't hurt you. I won't rush you. You can still stop me in time, if you want to. We're going to do this with such tenderness that you won't be afraid of me. Now just lie still and trust me for another few…seconds…"

She was trembling and so was he, but she'd never wanted anything in her life the way she wanted to belong to him. This was Justin. He was her husband and she loved him more than her life. He'd been so patient, so tender, that she wanted to give him her body along with her heart.

"Justin," she whispered achingly, watching his face harden. She felt the first touch of him and jerked a little.

"Shh," he whispered back. He smiled at her, forcing himself to hold back. "I'm going to watch you," he breathed huskily. "I'll know the instant it happens if there's the first hint of pain."

It was incredibly intimate. The lights were on. But all she could see was his face. She could feel his breath, quick and hard on her face, she could see the pulse beating in his throat. But she wasn't afraid, not even of his weight on her body, crushing her down into the cushions. He was hers, and she was going to take him…

She felt the pain like a hot knife. She clutched at him and her eyes got as big as saucers. She cried out and tears ran down her face.

Justin's eyes darkened and the pupils grew and grew and she realized then that he was frozen like a statue over her. His lips parted. His breath blew out. He looked down at her incredulously. He moved again, and watched her clench her teeth even as he knew for certain why she was doing it.

"I'm sorry," she whispered. Her hands reached up. "Don't stop," she said. "It's all right, I think I can…bear it…!"

"My God!"

He drew back, struggling away from her to sit up with his back to her, bowed, his body shuddering wildly. "My God, Shelby!"

"Justin, you didn't…you didn't have to stop," she whispered, biting her lip. "It would have been all right."

He wasn't listening. His head was in his hands and he shivered. He reached for the whiskey glass that still had a swallow of liquid in it, and his hands shook so badly that he almost spilled it before he got it to his mouth.

He stood up and Shelby flushed and averted her shocked eyes from his blatant masculinity.

"I'm sorry," he said curtly. He reached for his pajama bottoms and got into them distractedly. Then he stood looking down at her until she went bloodred and tried to curl up.

But he wouldn't let her. He reached down unsteadily to pick her up. He cradled her in his arms and sat down in his armchair, holding her with marvelous tenderness, whispering endearments into her dark hair, holding her while the tears came.

When she stopped, he mopped her eyes with a tissue. Her cheek was against his broad, shuddering chest, nestled against the thick hair, and her breasts were lying soft against his stomach. She shivered at the intimacy of it, because she didn't have a stitch on.

"You're my wife," he whispered when he saw her embarrassment. "It's all right if I see you without your clothes."

She curled closer. "Yes, I guess it is. It's just…new."

"My God, yes, I know."

There was an unmistakable note in his voice. She looked up, giving him a sudden and total view of her pretty breasts. He had to drag his eyes back up to hers.

"My virgin bride," he whispered huskily. His fingers touched her breasts hesitantly, with something like reverence. "Oh, Shelby. Shelby!"

"I…Dr. Sims made me have some minor surgery, but he muttered about it when I wouldn't let him do a proper job," she said, hiding her eyes from him. "I guess it wasn't quite enough…" Her face went red.

"Why wouldn't you let him do it properly?"

"So that I could prove that I hadn't slept with Tom," she said simply.

"You little fool!" He tilted her eyes up to his. "If I hadn't stopped upstairs, or if I'd ever lost my head with you… God, it doesn't even bear thinking about!"

She bit her lip, staring at his broad chest with its thick pelt of hair. "Justin…it would have stopped hurting," she began shyly.

"Like hell it would." He leaned back with a rough sigh. "I hate to be the bearer of bad tidings, honey, but you're going to have to go back and have the rest of that surgery."

"But…"

He tilted her eyes up to his. "A little pain is one thing, but you've got one hell of a lot of proof there," he said curtly. He shifted restlessly, noting her embarrassment and feeling just a little of his own at trying to explain things to her. He drew her head against his chest and bent to brush his mouth softly over hers. "Put your clothes back on while I top off your brandy snifter. The feel of you is making me hurt."

He got up and put her down on the sofa with only a cursory glance. While she fumbled her way back into her pajamas, he poured brandy into her glass and whiskey into his, and then went searching for a cigarette.

She knew her face was flaming. She'd never imagined that intimacy was so…intimate. But along with the shyness was a kind of excitement that went along with her new discoveries of Justin. He didn't lose control and go wild and hurt her. He was slow and patient and considerate. That made her blush even more.

"Who told you that men go nuts and hurt women when they make love?" he asked conversationally. "Because you seemed to think that's what was going to happen upstairs."

She took the brandy snifter and watched him go back to the armchair, where he sat and pulled up an ashtray. "You did," she said hesitantly. "The night we got engaged, and you lost control."

His eyebrows shot up. "Did I lose it that badly?"

"I thought so." She studied the snifter. "I knew I had this problem, you see, and I'd already been told about the surgery I'd have to have before my first time." She shrugged. "I've been terrified of it ever since my fifteenth birthday, when the doctor examined me for a female dysfunction. Some girls have a little discomfort, but he told me it would be unbearable if I didn't have the surgery. Then when you came on so strong, and I didn't think I could stop you…"

"You didn't tell me any of this," he said quietly.

"How could I?" She sighed miserably. "Oh, Justin, I'm twenty-seven and as green as a preadolescent! I can't even talk about it now without blushing!"

"I thought you were repulsed by me," he said, his voice deep with remembered pain. "I never dreamed… And then you told me what you did about Wheelor, and my ego shattered." His broad shoulders rose and fell. "I've been a lot rougher with you than I ever would have been if I'd known the truth. It hurt so damned bad to think that you'd been with someone else, and when you flinched away, it made me sick."

"At least now you know why I flinched away," she said with a sigh.

He took a draw from the cigarette. "I want you damned bad," he said without preamble.

She lowered her eyes to the carpet. "I want you, too."

"Then let's do something about it. Go see Dr. Sims. Have the surgery. Let's have a real marriage. The kind where two people sleep together, share together, make babies together."

Her face flamed, but she looked up. "You really do want children, don't you?"

"I want them with you," he said simply. "I never wanted them with any other woman."

"Then I won't need to…to take anything."

He smiled slowly. "No."

She got up, nervous and shy all over again. "I guess it wouldn't be a good idea for us to sleep together?" she asked, without realizing how wistful she sounded.

He got up, drawing her eyes as he towered over her. "Maybe it wouldn't, but we're going to. Even if we can't make love, I can hold you."

Her breath sighed out. "Justin, I'm sorry for so many things."

"So am I, but we can't go back." He bent and brushed a gentle kiss across her mouth. "We'll take it one day at a time. I won't rush you again."

She smiled at him. "Thank you."

He smiled back, but he didn't say anything. She watched him put everything away before he came back to her, turning out the light. He still had his cigarette in hand as they went upstairs together.

"Are you all right?" he asked her when they were in bed, and she was curled up beside him. "I didn't hurt you badly?"

"No," she whispered in the concealing darkness.

"I didn't frighten you, either?" he persisted, as if it mattered.

"Not at all," she assured him, going closer. He was warm and muscular and she loved the feel of him against her. "Not once." She nuzzled her cheek against him. "You're very tender."

"That's how lovemaking should be," he said quietly. "But I'm rusty, Mrs. Ballenger. I've been celibate for quite a while."

She held her breath. "A few months, you mean?"

"Um, not quite." He brushed his mouth over her forehead. "For about six years, Shelby."

She caught her breath. "My gosh! I didn't dream…!"

"It's a good thing," he murmured. "I guess you'd have run from me screaming if you'd known, thinking that a man who'd gone hungry that long would be ravenous and uncontrollable."

"But you weren't."

"You needed tenderness, so that's what you got. You won't always get it, after we've had each other a few times," he said flatly. "I don't like it that way all the time."

The mind boggled at what he did like and she realized that he'd been curbing his instincts, holding back, to make things easier for her. "Justin…"

"Shhh." He kissed her mouth softly. "Go to sleep. You're arousing me."

"I'm sorry."

He kissed her again and rolled over onto his stomach with a long sigh. "Good night, baby doll."

"Good night, Justin."

But she didn't sleep for a long time. There were a thousand questions buzzing around in her mind, and only a few answers. At least she'd gotten one big hurdle out of the way, and Justin still wanted her. That was something. Even if he couldn't love her, he might grow to have some kind of affection for her again. He couldn't blame her totally about the past, since he knew she was still innocent. Or could he? It occurred to her then that he might still want vengeance for the bitterness and humiliation he'd suffered. That was a sobering thought, and it kept her awake for a very long time.

Chapter Seven

Justin could hardly believe what he saw when he woke up the next morning. He was so used to the dreams of Shelby ending at dawn. But here she was, with her long, dark hair on his pillow, her soft, elfin features relaxed in sleep, her mouth full and sweet and tempting.

He lay there, just watching her, for a long time. He'd been lonely without her. More lonely than he'd realized until they were speaking again. When they were dating, he'd dreamed of having Shelby in his bed, relaxed in sleep, and doing just this—watching her sleep. She couldn't know how precious she was to him, or that last night had been a revelation, a culmination of every longing he'd ever had, even though he hadn't been able to finish what he'd started. Just finding her virginal was a shock of pure delight.

He didn't even start to think about why she'd deceived him. He was too enraptured by the sight of her lovely face in sleep, by her dark head lying so trustingly on his pillow.

When she didn't stir, he smiled gently and bent to brush her lips with his.

He saw her long black eyelashes flutter and then lift. She sighed, saw him and smiled, a new softness in her pale green eyes.

"Good morning," she whispered.

"Good morning." He kissed her again. "Did you sleep well?"

"I've never slept so well in all my life. And you?"

"I could say the same." He pulled the sheet back over her, tucking it in. "You don't have to get up yet."

"Are you going to work this early?" she murmured with a sleepy glance at the clock.

"I have to fly up to Dallas, honey," he said, rising. "A new customer. I'll be home by dark."

"I don't have to be at work until nine," she said with a smug smile.

"I wish you'd give up that job," he said, frowning down at her.

"Justin, I like it," she protested, but not vehemently.

"I don't like having you so handy to Barry Holman," he murmured.

She stared at him. "Maybe he is a womanizer, but not with me," she told him. "He's a very nice man and he's good to me."

Justin turned away. It wouldn't do to have her know how jealous he was of her handsome boss. "I've got to get a shower."

She watched him rummage in his drawer for underwear and head toward the bathroom, her eyes hungry on his bare torso. It seemed so unreal, the intimacy that they'd shared the night before. She blushed just remembering it, but he was gone before he saw the scarlet flush on her cheeks.

She wondered if she should have told him about Tammy Lester and the way Mr. Holman seemed so interested in her. She might do that later.

But she dozed off while he was in the shower, and when she woke up again, he was dressed in a pale gray suit that clung lovingly to the powerful lines of his tall body, and he was straightening his red and gray striped tie in the mirror.

"Is Maria up this early to feed you?" she murmured sleepily.

"I'll have breakfast on the plane." He turned, digging into his pockets, and tossed a set of car keys on the bed beside her. "Take the T-bird to work. Your transportation problem will have to wait until tomorrow."

She sat up, holding the keys. "But how will you get to the airport?"

He cocked an eyebrow. "I wonder if my heart will take all this concern?" he asked.

Her soft eyes ran over him and then the night before came back with alarming clarity. She saw him the way he'd been downstairs with her, felt again the intimacy…

"My God, what a scarlet blush," he murmured, loving her reactions. "I suppose you'd get under the bed if I started reminiscing?"

"You bet I would," she said with her last bit of pride. Then she ruined it all by smiling and hiding her face in her hands. "Oh, Justin," she whispered, remembering.

He sat down on the bed beside her, drawing her forehead against his chest. He smelled of cologne, and just being close to him made her weak and giddy.

"Do you feel like going to work?" he asked then, tilting her eyes up to his. "You don't have to."

"I know." She sighed gently. "But I'm only sore. I was more scared than hurt in the first place."

"You weren't the only one," he murmured. "I've got five new gray hairs this morning, thanks to you."

She reached up and touched his neatly combed hair at the temple, where silver hairs were threaded through the black ones. "I'm sorry. I was running away, I guess. You seem to hate me from time to time."

"Sometimes I thought I did," he confessed, and he didn't smile. "Six years is a long time to brood. I believed you, about Wheelor." He slid his hand under her nape. The fingers contracted suddenly, not hard enough to hurt, but hard enough to pin her forehead to his jacket. "Why?" he asked in a deceptively soft voice. "Why lie to me about it? Wasn't breaking the engagement enough, without ripping my pride to shreds, as well?"

And there it was, she thought, the bitterness seeping through. He was never going to get over what she'd done, and the fact of her innocence physically didn't seem to make much difference. It certainly wasn't going to stop him from blaming her for the past, even if he wanted her desperately. He'd always wanted her, but that wasn't enough anymore. Her eyes went misty with sadness. He'd told her last night that he'd been six years without a woman. That showed how bitter he was, that he didn't even want women anymore. But he wanted her, and she could imagine that it made him forget the past when he was close to her. Years of celibacy would probably make a man forget a lot when he was in the throes of passion.

Her world crumbled. She closed her eyes with a small sigh.

"I told you why last night," she said. "It was Dad's idea."

"And I told you before, your father liked me. He did everything in the world to help me. That night he and Wheelor came to see me, he even cried, Shelby."

Her eyes lifted to his. "It all goes back to trust, and I know how little of that you have for me," she said. "Not that it's all your fault, Justin. I didn't help things by deliberately lying to you in the beginning. But you don't trust me at all."

His jaw tautened. "I can't," he said. He let go of her all at once and got to his feet, moving away. "I want you, you know that. But I can't let you close. A woman who'll betray a man once will do it twice."

"I'm still a virgin," she reminded him uncomfortably.

"That isn't what I meant. You lied to me. You sold me out." He took a deep breath and pulled out a cigarette. "I'm not even sure you wouldn't do it now, with that slick boss of yours." He glanced at her set face, his eyes glittering. "It's easy to see how little encouragement he'd need from you, and he's good-looking, isn't he, honey? There's nothing plain about him."

"You aren't plain," she muttered.

"How perceptive of you to know I was talking about myself," he snapped. "Stay out of trouble while I'm gone, and don't put your foot down on my accelerator."

"I won't touch your precious car, if you'd rather," she shot back, her green eyes flashing. "I'll take a cab, and let all of Jacobsville see me do it!"

He glared at her and she glared back. And all at once, he started to grin, then to smile, and finally laughter burst from his set lips and glittered in his black eyes.

"Hellcat," he murmured.

"Savage," she threw right back.

He tossed the cigarette into the big ashtray on his dresser and moved toward her purposefully. She threw off the covers and headed for the other side of the bed, but he was too quick. Before she was halfway over, he had her flat on her back and had pinned her with the length of his big, hard-muscled body.

"That's it, struggle," he encouraged with a groan. "My God, can you feel what's happening to me?"

She could. She stopped, her cheeks like red flags.

"Well, the world won't end," he said with soft amusement. "You know how I feel when I'm aroused, and last night we didn't have several layers of clothes between us."

"Stop!" She buried her face in his throat, clinging, trembling with embarrassment and excitement.

"You baby," he chided, but the words were tender. He rolled over onto his back, pulling her over with him, his dark eyes searching her pale ones as she poised over his chest. He looked down at the deep cleavage of her pajama jacket and the faint swell of her breasts above it where they were pressed against him. "Is this better?" he murmured.

"You're a horrible man, and I don't think I want to live with you anymore," she said, pouting.

"Yes, you do." He coaxed her mouth down to his by pulling a strand of her long, silky hair. "Kiss me."

"You'll rumple your suit," she said.

"I've got a lot of other suits, but I want to be kissed. Come on, I've got a plane to catch."

She gave in to the gentle teasing. All the arguing was forgotten the minute her soft mouth touched his hard one. She felt his hand sliding into her hair, pulling gently, and her lips parted to the soft, intense searching of his warm mouth.

"After you see the doctor, we'll have to wait a couple of days before we can finish what we started last night," he whispered into her mouth. "So don't start worrying about that and getting nervous all over again, okay?" His dark eyes searched hers. "I won't rush you, Shelby. This time, it's going to be exactly the way you want it."

She kissed his eyes, gently closing the eyelids, lingering on the thick lashes in a rage of tenderness. She wanted to whisper that she loved him more than her own life, that everything she'd done that had hurt him had been, in the beginning, only to protect him. But he didn't trust her yet, and she was going to have to bring him around before she could share her deepest secrets with him.

"Will you believe me when I say that I'm not afraid of you anymore?" she whispered against his lips.

"Honey, that's pretty hard to miss, considering the position we're in," he whispered back.

"What positi…Justin!"

He laughed as he flipped her onto her back and slid over her, nibbling warmly at her lips. "This position," he whispered. "Kiss me goodbye and I'll go."

"I've already done…that…several times," she whispered, the words punctuated with soft, clinging kisses.

"Do it several more and I'll work on getting my legs to support me," he murmured dryly. "My knees are pretty weak right now."

"So are mine." She linked her arms around his neck and bit his lower lip. "You're mine now," she said quietly, her eyes holding his. "Don't you go off and flirt with other women."

Her possessiveness made him ache. He slid his hands under her back and lifted her up, taking his time as he bent hungrily to her open mouth. He kissed her with growing insistence until his own body forced him to either stop or go on.

He rolled away reluctantly and got to his feet, taut with pride as he looked down at his handiwork. She was sprawled in delicious abandon on the sheets, her hair like a halo around her, her mouth soft and red and swollen from his kisses, her eyes dreamy with desire.

"If I had a photograph of you that looked the way you look now," he said huskily, "I'd walk around bent double every time I looked at it. I've never seen a woman as beautiful as you are."

"I'm not even pretty," she chided, smiling. "But I'm glad you like me the way I am. I like you, too."

He drew in a slow breath. "I'd better get out of here while I can. It helps to remember your condition."

She averted her eyes to the sheets, feeling nervous.

"You'd really have let me go on, wouldn't you?" he asked, his voice deep with feeling. "Even knowing how bad it was going to hurt you, you wouldn't have stopped me."

"I wanted you to know," she whispered.

"It took a lot of courage." He frowned, watching her. "Did it hurt you, when I accused you of being frigid?"

"A little," she said, trying to spare him.

He sighed angrily. "A lot, I imagine. Try to remember that I didn't know the truth, and don't hate me for it. There are a lot of things you don't know about me, either, Shelby." He turned then, retrieving his cigarette from the ashtray. "I'd better get a move on," he said after a cursory glance at the thin gold watch on his wrist. "No speeding," he cautioned from the door.

The remark intrigued her, but she knew he wasn't going to tell her any more than he wanted her to know. "All right. Have a good trip."

"I'll do my best."

He didn't say goodbye. He gave her one last glance and closed the door behind him. Shelby watched him leave with mixed emotions. Sometimes she wished she could read his mind, because that was the only way she was ever going to know how he really felt about her. She wondered if he knew himself.

She got up and dressed and drove the Thunderbird to the office, taking a minute to make an appointment that afternoon with Dr. Sims. By the time she got home, she was worn out, from the combination of an unexpectedly long day trying to keep peace between an irritable Mr. Holman and a venomous Tammy Lester, and having the rest of the surgery done—which was embarrassing as well as uncomfortable, because she had to tell Dr. Sims why she needed it.

But a cup of fresh coffee and a nice supper soothed her. She went upstairs to her own room, wishing she had the right to go straight to Justin's. But he hadn't said anything about the sleeping arrangements, so apparently he'd thought of last night as a temporary thing because of what had happened.

She went to sleep early. She didn't hear the car come in, or Justin's footsteps heading toward his own bedroom expectantly. She didn't hear the muffled curse when he found his bed empty, or the shocked silence when he found Shelby asleep in her own.

He closed the door firmly and went to his room, dreams going black in his eyes. He'd expected her to be waiting up, or at least sleeping in his bed. But she hadn't, and he didn't know if she'd just been uncertain about what to do or if she was putting a wall between them because of the argument they'd had that morning.

Shelby, blissfully unaware of what had happened after she was asleep, went down to breakfast the next morning full of hope. Only to find a cold, taciturn Justin at the table looking at her as if she'd just tried to shoot him.

She stopped suddenly in the doorway. Her long denim skirt swung around her calves, her hands going nervously to the blue cotton blouse and scarf she was wearing with it.

"Good morning," she said, faltering.

"Hell, no, it isn't," he said.

Her eyebrows arched. "It isn't?"

He lifted his coffee cup and sipped the rich black liquid. "I'll have one of the boys drive you to work," he said. "May I have the keys to the Thunderbird?"

She reached into her skirt pocket and put them beside him on the table, but he caught her hand before she could move away.

He looked up, his expression brooding. "Why did you go back to your own room?"

She sighed and then smiled. "Because I didn't know if you still wanted me to sleep with you," she said sadly. "You were half mad when you left, and you didn't say anything." Her shoulders lifted and fell. "I didn't want to impose."

"My God, honey, we're married," he said huskily. "You couldn't impose on me if you tried."

She stared down at the big, lean hand holding hers. Its warm strength made her tingle. "You've been very remote since we've been married."

"I think you're beginning to understand why, though, aren't you?" he asked softly.

She looked down into his dark, quiet eyes. She nodded. "You…want me."

"That's part of it," he agreed without elaborating. "Did you see Dr. Sims?"

Her blush gave him the answer even before she nodded.

He drew her down in the chair beside him. "I'll drive

you to work," he said and pushed a platter of eggs toward her.

She smiled, but she didn't let him see her do it.

Justin had calmed down by the time they got to Jacobsville, but Barry Holman set him off again immediately when they reached the office. The handsome blond lawyer was outside on the street, looking all around, and to an onlooker, it might have appeared as if he was waiting impatiently for Shelby. To Justin, unfortunately, that's exactly what it looked like.

Holman's head lifted when Justin pulled the Thunderbird up at the curb, and his face lit up. He smiled with exaggerated pleasure and rushed to meet Shelby with a cursory nod to Justin, whose expression turned murderous.

"Thank God you're here," Barry enthused, opening the door for her. "I was afraid you were going to be late. How pretty you look this morning!" He knew about day-before-yesterday's mishap, of course, but Shelby was shocked by his attentiveness and was already beginning to wonder what ailed him as he helped her onto the sidewalk. "I'll take good care of her, Justin," he said, adding fuel to the fire, grinning at her smoldering husband.

Justin didn't answer him or speak to Shelby. He slammed the car door, his eyes glittering in Shelby's direction, and roared away down the street.

"What's wrong?" Shelby asked, mentally nervous about Justin's unexpected anger. Mr. Holman had certainly given Justin a bad impression of their working relationship.

"That woman has got to go," he said without preamble, waving his hands. "She's locked herself in my office and she won't let me in. I've called the fire department, though," he added with a smug glitter in his eyes. "They'll break the door down and get her out, and then she can leave. Permanently."

Shelby put a hand to her head. "Mr. Holman, why is Tammy locked in your office?"

He cleared his throat. "It was the book."

"What book?"

"The book I threw at her," he said irritably.

"You threw a book at Tammy!" she gasped.

"Well, it was a dictionary." He shifted with his hands in his pockets. "We had a slight disagreement over the spelling of a legal term, which I should know, Shelby," he added angrily, "after all, I'm a lawyer. I know how to spell legal terms; they teach us that in law school."

Shelby, who'd sampled some of Mr. Holman's expertise at spelling legal terms, didn't say a word.

He shifted again. "Well, I said some things. Then she said some things. Then I sort of tossed the book her way. That was when she locked herself in my office."

"Just because of the book," she probed.

He stared down at the pavement. "Uh, yes. That. And the broken glass."

Her eyes gaped. "Broken glass?"

"The window, you know." He moved sheepishly toward the curb, having spotted what he was searching for earlier. He picked up the torn dictionary with a faint grin. "Here it is! I knew it had to be out here somewhere."

Shelby was torn between laughter and tears when the fire truck came blaring down the street with its siren going and pulled to a screeching half at the curb.

"You didn't tell them why you needed them to come here, by any chance?" Shelby asked as she watched the firemen, because they'd come in a pumper truck and were very obviously unwinding a long, flat hose.

"No, come to think of it, I didn't. Hi, Jake!" Mr. Holman called to the fire chief with a big grin. "Good of you to come. Uh, there's not exactly a fire, though. I'm more in need of a different kind of help."

Jake, a big, burly man with a red face, came closer. "No fire? Well, what do you need us to do, Barry?" he asked, gesturing to the men to roll up the hose again.

"I need you to break down my office door with an ax," Mr. Holman said.

"Why?"

"I lost my key," Mr. Holman improvised.

"Then wouldn't a locksmith do you more good?" Jake continued. He was beginning to give Shelby's boss a strange kind of look.

Mr. Holman frowned thoughtfully. "Oh, no, I don't think so. It wouldn't make nearly the impression that an ax would."

Jake was looking puzzled.

"One of our…employees…has locked herself in the office and won't come out," Shelby explained.

"Well, my gosh, Barry, an ax banging the door down would scare her slam to death!" Jake said.

"Yes," Mr. Holman smiled thoughtfully. "It sure as hell would."

Just as Jake started to speak, Tammy Lester came out of the building, looking explosive, and went right up to Barry Holman and hit him as hard as she could.

"I quit," she said furiously, almost trembling with rage. "Sorry, Shelby, but you're back to being a one-woman office. I can't take one more day of Mr. God's Gift to Womanhood! And you can't spell, Mr. Big-Shot Attorney!"

"I can spell better than you can, you escapee from a high-school remedial spelling course!" he yelled after her. "And don't expect that I'll come running, begging you to come back! There must be hundreds of stupid women who can't spell in this town who need work!"

Jake was gaping at the normally calm attorney. So was Shelby. She was having a hard time trying not to laugh. That would only complicate things, of course. She eased past the fire chief and quickly went into the office to escape what was about to happen.

And sure enough, she'd barely gotten inside the carpeted office when Jake let Mr. Holman have it with both barrels. There was something about false alarms and potential arrests...at that point, Shelby closed the door and went to her computer.

She worried about the way Justin had reacted to Mr. Holman waiting on the street for her. It didn't look good, and Justin was already wildly jealous of the man. That didn't make a lot of sense, but then Shelby didn't know a lot about men. She assumed that it was only a surface jealousy, because Barry Holman was handsome and a womanizer and Justin was possessive and very territorial. She never once thought that it might be anything more than that.

Because it disturbed her, she phoned the house to explain to Justin what had happened. But Maria told her that he hadn't come back yet. She tried again at lunch, but he was out with a client. So she went back to work and forgot all about it, while Mr. Holman sputtered and muttered about Tammy for the rest of the day and finally closed the office an hour early because he wasn't getting any work done.

"Don't worry about making up the time," he told Shelby quietly. "We've got court next month, and you may have to put in some overtime getting out briefs and helping me with research." He glowered at the door. "I was going to let Miss Lester help with that, since she does seem to have a feel for legwork. But now that she's quit for such a stupid reason, you'll have to do it."

"Most secretaries would get nervous if their bosses threw books at them," Shelby pointed out.

"I didn't hit her, did I?" he asked mockingly. "I hit the window. That reminds me, you'd better call Jack Harper and get him over here tomorrow to put in another windowpane." He looked uncomfortable. "And, uh, you don't need to go into details about how it got broken. Do you?"

"I'll tell him an eagle flew through it," she agreed.

He glared and stomped off toward his car.

Shelby started toward where she usually parked her car when it dawned on her that she didn't have a car.

"Oh, Mr. Holman," she called without thinking, "could you drop me off at the feedlot? I haven't been able to get Justin, and he won't be here for another hour to pick me up."

"Sure. Come on."

He helped her into the black Mercedes and shot off down the road toward the Ballenger feedlot. "What happened to your new car?" he asked. "Engine trouble?"

She smiled wistfully. She hadn't told him about the sports car, even though he knew she had been driving Justin's car the day before. "Justin gave it to Mr. Doyle."

"He runs a junkyard," Mr. Holman reminded her.

"That's right, he does, and he has a brand-new car crusher." She sighed. "Justin said if I liked, he could have my sports car made into a nice wall decoration. It's about five inches thick…"

"What did he do that for?" the lawyer asked.

"He thinks I'm reckless," Shelby said. "I think he's planning to buy me something sedate. Like a Sherman tank."

Mr. Holman smiled. "I hope I didn't get you into any trouble this morning," he said belatedly as he turned off on the long road that led to the feedlot. "I wasn't thinking. I was glad to see you because I knew that you could talk her out of the office if the firemen didn't work."

"Tammy's really a nice woman," she said.

He glowered. "She's a pain."

"If you'd give her half a chance, she might surprise you. She's very efficient."

He shifted against the seat. "I did notice that you're pretty rushed. I didn't mean to rob you of her help."

She glanced at him. "You might consider asking Tammy to come back. Maybe she's sorry, too."

He pursed his lips. "Maybe she is. I suppose I could

drop by her dad's house and just mention that she could come to work tomorrow."

"It might be a better idea to call first," Shelby said, remembering Tammy's temper.

"I'll do that." He pulled up at the feedlot office and grinned. "Thanks for being so understanding."

"My pleasure. No, don't get out. I can open the door all by myself." She laughed. She got out, smiling at him, and waved him away.

Behind her, Justin stood watching, a cigarette smoking in his lean fingers, his height emphasized by the jeans and chambray shirt and boots he wore around the feedlot. His hat was pulled low over his black eyes and he looked dangerous.

Shelby turned and saw him and stopped suddenly. "Uh, hi."

He lifted the cigarette to his mouth. "You're an hour early."

"We had a problem at the office." She flushed, and that made it worse. "I need a ride to the house."

"Calhoun's going that way," he returned. "He can drop you off."

He went inside the building, leaving her standing in the sun with the sound of the cattle lowing and moving in the sprawling complex ringing in her ears.

Calhoun came out in a beige suit, scowling. "Justin

is sitting behind his desk with his feet crossed, not doing a damned thing, and he dragged me out of a meeting to run you home," he said, stunned. "Not that I mind, Shelby. I'm just curious. Is he at you again?"

"When isn't he?" she said curtly. "Mr. Holman brought me out here. I guess Justin thinks I seduced him on the highway!"

"Shhh!" Calhoun put his finger to his lips and pulled her toward his white Jaguar. "Don't make him any worse than he already is. His secretary's already threatened to walk out!"

"He has that effect on so many people," she said with venom in her tone. "Overbearing, unfeeling, insensitive, insufferable…!"

"Now, now," he soothed. "You'll just work yourself into a lather, and it won't solve anything. He's only jealous. You're a woman. You ought to know exactly what to do about that."

She flushed and averted her face as he helped her into the front seat and got in beside her.

He glanced in her direction curiously, noting her scarlet blush. It amazed him how much alike Justin and Shelby were; both old-fashioned and full of hang-ups.

He started the car and cleared his throat. "Do you mind if I say something pretty personal, Shelby? Since we're related these days and all?"

She couldn't look at him. "That depends on what it is."

"Yes, I can imagine. You react just like Justin does," he mused. He pulled out onto the road and pressed down on the accelerator. "Well, it's this. My brother isn't exactly a lily, but in recent years he's been a hermit. He hasn't dated anybody. He's sort of rusty with women, is what I'm driving at."

"I could tell you what he is, if you weren't his brother," she muttered, clutching her purse.

"Shelby," he said patiently, "the best way to get a man's attention, and knock the fire off his temper, is just to hug him as hard as you can and let nature take care of the details."

She went scarlet. She knew that Calhoun was pretty much like her boss, a man who knew women well. But if she couldn't talk to Justin about intimacy, she certainly couldn't talk to Calhoun about it.

"He wouldn't like it," she said in a husky voice.

"He'd like it," he returned. He reached over and patted her shoulder gently. "He's so crazy about you that he can't see straight. You take my word for it, honey, he'll fold up like an accordion if you use the right approach. And that's all I'll say. How are you and the sports car getting along?"

She gaped at him. He didn't know? "Justin didn't tell you?"

"Justin doesn't talk much when he's at the office," he said pleasantly. "Mostly he works, and when he doesn't, he broods."

"I had a near-miss in the car, actually," she mumbled. "I spun out and almost hit a truck." She felt his stunned glance. "Justin took the car away and had it crushed."

"Good for Justin," he said unexpectedly. "That car was dangerous." He stared at her. "And you know better than most how dangerous."

She cleared her throat. "Switzerland was years ago."

"All the same, Justin was right. He wouldn't want to have to bury you so shortly after your wedding, you know."

"Wouldn't he?" she asked bitterly. "I think he hates me."

"I wish I could convince you what a joke that statement is." He pulled up in front of the house and smiled at her. "I dare you. Play up to him and see what happens. He's as unknowledgeable about women as you are about men, so keep that in mind. And don't, for God's sake, mention that I said so," he said under his breath. "The one time Justin and I really got into it, we both had to have stitches. Okay?"

"Okay." She opened the door and glanced back shyly. "You're a nice man."

"Of course I am," he said. "Ask Abby if you don't believe it." He grinned with the smugness of a man who knows how much he's loved. "See you."

"Tell Abby hello and give her my love."

He laughed and waved as he went down the road. Shelby thought about what he'd said and wondered if she might be able to get up enough nerve to take his advice.

If Calhoun was right, and Justin was as backward as she was, it might really be interesting to see what would happen. Then she remembered his ardor and wondered if Calhoun actually knew his brother at all. The Justin Shelby experienced on the sofa wasn't a man who didn't know what to do with women. Justin was pretty tight-lipped with everyone, and Calhoun might not know exactly how well informed his big brother was.

But the thought of tempting Justin was delicious, and now she had no more reason to be afraid of him. She knew that he could be tender and that he wouldn't lose control too soon. And now, thank goodness, there would be no more painful barrier to inhibit her. She smiled thoughtfully as she went up the steps, already making exciting plans for the night ahead.

Chapter Eight

It was well after dark when Justin finally came home from the feedlot, looking worn and in a black temper. He spared a glance at the dining room, where Shelby was eating her lonely meal, and went upstairs without even a hello.

She sighed, wondering if there was worse to come. She finished her dessert and was sipping coffee when he came back downstairs. He'd obviously just showered, because his hair was still damp around the temples. He was wearing a clean gray and blue plaid western shirt with gray denim slacks, and his temper hadn't improved.

He sat at the head of the table and began to fill a plate with lukewarm beef and gravy and buttered new potatoes.

"Maria could warm it up for you in the microwave," Shelby ventured.

"If I want Maria to do anything, I'll ask her," he said.

So it was going to be that kind of evening. She put her napkin aside and straightened the skirt of the red and white dress she'd worn deliberately because Justin had thought it sexy.

She wasn't quite sure how to reach him. He looked so unapproachable, just as he had in the earliest days of their relationship. She studied his hard face quietly. "Justin, if you're still angry about this afternoon, Mr. Holman closed the office an hour early, and I was already on the street when I realized I didn't have a car," she said. "He was kind enough to drop me off at the feedlot on his way home. He comes right by it, you know."

He looked up, black eyes glittering. "And you know how I feel about your damned boss."

She glowered at him. "Yes, I know, but I didn't think that you'd mind him giving me a ride home. He's a perfect gentleman when he's around me," she said shortly. "I've told you that until I'm blue in the face, Justin!"

"You might have phoned me," he returned. "I'd have come after you."

"I didn't even know if you were at the feedlot," she said. She put her fork down gently. "I didn't know if you'd come, either, after the way you roared off this morning without even saying goodbye."

He pushed his plate away, hardly touched. "He was waiting for you, pacing back and forth," he replied icily. "And then he practically carried you to the sidewalk. I damned near got out of the car and went for him then, Shelby. I don't like other men touching you."

If he expected her to be irritated by that flat statement, he was disappointed. The admission made her pulse skip. She stared at him, wondering if he even realized what he was admitting. She sighed wistfully, and smiled at him. "I'm glad."

He frowned. "What?"

"I'm glad you don't like other men touching me." She picked up her coffee and sipped it. "I don't like other women touching you, either."

He shifted in the chair. "We weren't talking about that."

She smiled, because he seemed to have forgotten what they *had* been talking about. She pushed back her long, dark hair and her eyes sparkled as they searched his. "Calhoun said you dragged him out of a meeting and made him drive me to the house."

He reached for a cigarette and looked uncomfortable. "I was pretty hot."

She wondered if it was his jealousy of her boss, or

frustration. Calhoun had intrigued her by what he'd said about the way Justin would react if she made advances. She wanted to find out herself.

But thinking about it and doing it were entirely different things. Sitting there, looking at the taciturn, stern man across from her, she couldn't really imagine going over to him and sitting in his lap. It would have been lovely, though, to feel welcome if she reached out to him.

She colored delicately from her own thoughts and put her coffee cup down. "What about a car for me?" she asked.

"I forgot," he murmured. "We'll go tomorrow."

"All right."

He ignored the fresh apple pie in a saucer beside him and finished his coffee. "I got a new movie in the mail today," he remarked. "A black-and-white war movie, made in the early forties. I thought I might watch it."

"You'll enjoy that, I know."

He eyed her warily. "You could watch it with me. If you wanted to," he added carelessly, so she wouldn't know how badly he wanted her to.

But she sensed it. She smiled. "If I wouldn't be in your way, I'd like to. I like war movies."

"Do you?" He smiled slowly. "How about science-fiction?"

Her eyes lit up. "Oh, yes!"

He actually laughed. "I've got quite a collection of old ones, and a good many new releases."

"All we need now is some popcorn," she remarked.

"Maria!" he called.

The housekeeper came to the doorway. "*Sí*, Señor Justin?"

He threw a request at her in rapid-fire Spanish, and Maria grinned and answered in kind. She laughed, made another remark, which caused Justin's cheeks to go a ruddy shade, and went back to the kitchen with a wink in Shelby's direction.

"What did she say?" Shelby asked, because her Spanish was sketchy at best and she didn't have Justin's facility for languages.

"That she'd make the popcorn and bring it in," he replied shortly. "Well, come on, if you're coming."

He got up and went out of the room, leaving her to follow.

The living room was cozy with only the end table lamp on. Shelby curled up on the sofa, barefooted, with the bowl of popcorn between herself and Justin. Maria stuck her head in long enough to say that she and Lopez were going to her sister's for the evening, and then the house was quiet except for the loud excitement of bombs going off and machine-gun fire as the Allies and the Axis fought it out all over again on the screen.

When they got down to the inevitable unpopped kernels in the bottom of the bowl, Justin moved it and took off his boots before he lit a cigarette, propping his long legs on the coffee table. As the movie ran on, Shelby found herself moving helplessly closer to him. Her hand slid hesitantly across to his free one, where it lay on the sofa. She started to touch it and then stopped, shy and uncertain.

He glimpsed the movement and turned his head. "Do you have to have permission to touch me, Shelby?" he asked, his tone deep and slow and gentle.

"I don't know," she replied. "Do I?"

"No." He watched her with patient amusement until she moved her hand toward his again and touched it, tingling at the warm strength of his fingers as they wound through hers and contracted.

She smiled shyly and turned her attention back to the movie again. She didn't see it or hear it, though, because Justin's thumb was rubbing gently against her moist palm. She felt the movement like a brand, burning her blood, making her hungry. Her lips parted as she remembered the last time they'd been on this sofa together, and what they'd done. She remembered the leather cool against her back, the weight of Justin's body over hers in an intimacy that could still color her cheeks scarlet.

"Do you like mysteries?" she asked, for something to say during a lull in the battle scene.

"Sure," he said easily. "I've got a few Hitchcock thrillers, and a copy of *Arsenic and Old Lace* with Cary Grant."

"I love that one," she mused. "I laughed myself sick the first time I saw it."

"How about John Wayne westerns?" he asked with a sly glance.

She laughed. "I've seen *Hondo* so many times, I can even growl along with the character's dog."

"So have I." He studied her for a long moment, admiring the way she looked in the red and white dress, liking the length of her dark hair. "We always did have a lot in common, Shelby. Especially guitar." He rubbed his thumb over the tips of her fingers. "Do you ever play?"

She shook her head. "Not anymore. I...lost the taste for it."

"So did I," he confessed, because after they'd broken it off, he couldn't bear the memories the guitar brought back. "Maybe we could practice together again sometimes."

"That would be nice." She smiled at him. He smiled back. And the television set seemed a long way off as the smiles faded and the look became long and intensely arousing.

His fingers contracted roughly on hers and he drew

in a steadying breath. "Come here, sweetheart," he said softly.

She tingled all over at the way he said the endearment, because he hardly ever used one at all. He made her feel young and vulnerable. She slid closer with subdued eagerness and curled up against him with her head going to rest naturally on his hard shoulder.

"Don't go to sleep," he murmured dryly.

"I'm not sleepy," she said with a sigh. She smiled and nuzzled her cheek closer. "You smell spicy."

"You smell like a gardenia," he murmured. "It's a scent I never connected with anyone but you."

"It's the perfume I used," she said.

He took his hand away from hers and paused to put out his cigarette. Then he lifted her and turned her across him, so that she was lying in his lap with her head on his chest.

"If you'd rather watch something else, I don't mind," he said softly, knowing full well that the movie was the last thing on both their minds.

She couldn't have cared less what was on the screen, because all she'd seen since the beginning of the movie was Justin's hard profile. But she didn't say that.

"This is fine," she assured him.

"Okay."

He smoothed her long hair, holding her slender hand to his broad chest while he tried to pretend an interest in the movie. He was aware of Shelby now, of the scent of her, of the softness of her breasts pressed against his hard chest, of her warm hand touching him.

Her caressing fingers made his heartbeat quicken. He felt the first stirrings of desire in his powerful body and when he looked down and saw the hunger echoing in her soft eyes, he lost all efforts at pretence. Unhurriedly, he unsnapped the pearly buttons of his shirt and slowly drew Shelby's hand against thick hair and hard, warm muscle, coaxing her to touch him. While her fingers worked on his body, his mouth began to trace patterns on her forehead, her closed eyelids, her nose, her cheeks, her chin and throat.

She felt her breathing quicken as he drew her closer. His nose brushed against hers. His mouth began to search for her lips, and when he found them, the touch was explosive.

She heard his breath sigh out heavily as his mouth became demanding, intimate. His fingers slid into the thick fall of hair at her nape and arched her throat so that her mouth pushed against his, answering his hungry ardor.

Her heart went wild. Her quick, unsteady breathing suddenly matched his. She dug her nails helplessly into his hard chest, and he groaned against her lips.

"Sorry," she faltered.

He took her lower lip between his teeth and traced it

with his tongue. "I liked it," he whispered, and his mouth opened hers, very slowly, while he stretched his length alongside hers. He sighed, and she felt the touch of his body from head to toe while the kiss grew warmer and slower and more intense. "Kiss me hard, Shelby," he breathed huskily.

She reached up, her inhibitions wearing away under the deep caresses. Her fingers slid into his thick black hair and savored its coolness as her mouth began to answer his.

The movie blared away, the battle scenes loud in the stillness, but neither of them heard. The kisses grew longer, drugging, aching as Justin's hands worked at buttons and snaps. Shelby felt his bare chest against her breasts without a protest. It was delicious, the touch of skin against skin, just as it had been a few nights earlier. But this time, the old fears were greatly diminished, because now she knew that what he did wasn't going to hurt her. She knew how gentle he could be, how patient.

She felt his hands sliding the dress away, tenderly smoothing it down her long, trembling limbs. She caught her breath and in the dim light of the lamp, he smiled at her softly.

"It's all right," he whispered. "I won't go too fast. You can still stop me, if you want to."

That gave her back the choice, and made everything

all right. She began to relax, letting her hands slide hungrily over his hard, hair-roughened muscles. It was heaven to touch him this way, to be given the freedom to learn him with her hands. She looked up into his dark eyes with the discoveries lying vulnerable in her soft eyes, and he smiled down at her.

"Oh, Justin," she whispered huskily. "It's so sweet!"

He bent and lowered his mouth onto hers, feeling the words sigh against his lips. He slid his hands gently over her, feeling the ripple of her skin under them. She was like satin to the touch, and he'd gone hungry for what seemed forever.

In the back of his mind, he knew there was no chance that he was going to be able to stop, but she didn't seem to be worried about that. She pulled him down to her and her mouth was suddenly as ardent as his, as uninhibited.

Still kissing her, he managed to get out of his own clothes, and then she was against him, trembling, while he slowed his pace and began to arouse her all over again with exquisite patience until he felt the passion shaking her slender body.

"Now," he whispered when she was crying with her need. He eased down, turning her face up to his with a caressing hand. "No. Don't turn away. I want to see."

She colored feverishly, but she looked up at him at the instant his body took possession of hers.

His lips parted. It was the most profound experience of his life. All the long years of loving her, needing her, and it was finally going to happen. She was his. There were no more barriers. He felt her accept him totally and his breath caught.

She stiffened just a little at the newness, the stark intimacy, but he slowed and hesitated.

"It's all right," he whispered tenderly, and bent to kiss her, coaxing her to relax, to let it happen. "Yes. Like that." He laughed jerkily at the ease of it, at the exquisite sense of oneness. "Oh, Shelby!"

Her face was bloodred, but she didn't look away. His face was taut with victory, his eyes glittering blackly with it. She reached up, her trembling hands going to his cheeks to bring his head down so that she could reach his mouth.

"Love…me," she whispered, her voice breaking as he moved and she felt the first sweet piercing pleasure. "Justin…love me!"

The words broke his control. He couldn't believe what he was hearing, much less what he was feeling. He went under in a wave of white heat, crying out as the force of the pleasure took his restraint and left him helpless in the drive for fulfillment.

Somewhere in the back of her mind, Shelby knew that she should be frightened by his lack of control. But his movements were causing a kind of silvery tension that made her body sing with pleasure. Ecstasy was just out of her reach, and she stretched toward it with her last thread of strength just as Justin caught her hips and pulled.

She felt the world go spinning down under her, and she cried out his name again and again and again…

He laughed. She felt his lips at her temples, on her cheeks, her mouth, in kisses that were as tender as they were comforting.

"The first time," he breathed, laughing again as his mouth covered hers, trembling. "My God, the first time!"

She opened her eyes, still shaking from the sudden descent from a kind of pleasure she'd never dreamed existed. She gazed up at him, fascinated by the way he looked. He seemed years younger. His hair was damp, his face sweaty, his eyes glittering with exultant pleasure. He was shuddering, his body heavy over hers, damp.

"Justin?" she whispered, disoriented.

"Are you all right, sweetheart?" he asked softly. "I didn't hurt you?"

"No." She blushed and lowered her eyes to the pulse in his throat.

"Look at me, you coward."

She forced her gaze up to his and he bent and brushed his mouth over her closed eyes.

"I...I never realized..." She couldn't find the words. She clung to him, hiding her face against his damp throat.

He turned, holding her warmly against him on the long leather sofa, sighing with exquisite pleasure at the way she held him. "So many lonely nights, Shelby," he whispered. "So many dreams. But even the dreams weren't this sweet." He pulled her closer. "Kiss me, honey."

She lifted her face to his, obediently putting her swollen lips against his. He trembled and eased her gently onto her back, so that they were completely joined. He looked into her eyes with a dark, soft question in his. She didn't answer him. She lifted her body against him, and he saw the words in her eyes. He bent, sighing unsteadily, and his mouth opened over her parted lips. He moved down, and she clung, and the world went again into shared oblivion.

He carried her upstairs a long time later, cradling her in his arms like the most precious kind of treasure. He put her into his bed and climbed in beside her, turning off the lights. He curled her against his tired body and sighed with haunted pleasure. She was asleep only seconds before he was.

* * *

Shelby felt a kiss brush her lips. "Justin," she whispered softly and opened her eyes.

He was sitting on the bed beside her, dressed in jeans and a chambray shirt, smiling. "I have to go to work," he whispered.

"No," she moaned, reaching up.

He eased the covers away and brought her across him, touching her soft breasts with exquisite tenderness while he kissed her. "We made love," he whispered.

"Several times," she whispered back, and then spoiled her new image by flushing furiously.

He nibbled her lips. "I didn't use anything," he said quietly, searching her eyes.

The blush got worse. "Neither did I."

He touched her lips with one lean finger. "I know. Is it going to matter, if you get pregnant?" he whispered.

"No," she moaned. "I want a child with you."

He caught his breath and bent to kiss her with aching tenderness, pleased beyond words at the way she said it, at the need he felt in himself, in her. "Did you sleep?"

"I'm still asleep," she whispered at his lips. "I dreamed it all, and I don't want to wake up."

"It wasn't a dream." He kissed her. "Have I hurt you?"

"Oh, no," she whispered quickly. "Not at all!"

His dark eyes sketched her face adoringly. "You'll

sleep with me from now on," he said. "No more walls, no more looking back. We start here, now, together."

"Yes," she whispered, sighing, her heart in her eyes. "Don't go to work."

"I have to. So do you." He glowered down at her. "But no more rides with the boss, got that?"

"I'll call you. I promise." She reached up and kissed his cheek. "You can't possibly be jealous after last night."

His lean hand smoothed her breast. "Don't kid yourself," he said softly. "I'll be ten times as possessive now that I've made love to you. You're mine."

"I always have been, Justin," she said quietly, wondering at the way he was looking at her, at the heat of possession in his black eyes. Surely he was sure of her now?

He searched her eyes and then let his gaze run hungrily over her slender body. "Exquisite," he breathed. "All of you. I've never felt anything half as profound in my life as what I felt with you. I feel...whole."

Her heart skipped a beat, because that was how she felt. But she loved him, and he only wanted her. Or was it possible that he was finally beginning to feel something for her?

"I feel that way, too," she said.

He smiled. "But you were a virgin, honey," he mused, brushing his mouth over her nose. "I wasn't."

She glared at him. "So I noticed."

That glare made him feel all man and a yard wide. He bent and nipped her mouth with his teeth, softly arousing. "It was a long time ago, and it has nothing to do with you. For the past six years, I haven't even kissed another woman, and that's gospel. You don't have a damned thing to be jealous of."

She hugged him fiercely, her head against his bare chest. "I'm sorry."

"There's nothing to apologize for," he replied. He kissed her forehead with breathless tenderness. "I've got to go," he groaned. "I don't want to, but Calhoun's going to be out of the office all day, and I have to be there."

"I know." She rubbed her cheek against him. "Will you drop me off at work?"

"Of course. What do you fancy for breakfast?"

She looked up at him with the answer sparkling in her eyes. He laughed with pure delight, stood up with her in his arms and tossed her into the center of the bed, watching her scramble under the sheet with indulgent amusement.

"Not now," he murmured dryly at the blatant invitation in her eyes, even through her shyness. "Get dressed before all this stoic control melts."

"Spoilsport," she said, sighing.

"I don't want to overdo it," he said with sudden

seriousness. "You're still new to this. I don't want to hurt you."

Her eyes softened. "And I was afraid of you." She shook her head.

"I can understand why. But you won't need to be, ever again." He turned away, stretching hugely. "God knows how I'll keep my mind on work, but there's always tonight," he added from the doorway with a slow grin. "What do you want for breakfast?" he repeated.

She smiled shyly. "Eggs and bacon."

"It'll be waiting."

He went out and she got up and got dressed, feeling as if her feet weren't even touching the floor when she walked.

He was at the table waiting when she got there. She'd put on a simple gray skirt with a pale blue blouse for work, and her hair was in a neat French twist. It was a sedate outfit, which was what she meant it to be. Since she knew how possessive Justin was, she didn't want to spoil their delicate new relationship by making it look as if she was taking special pains with her appearance to go to work.

He looked up when she came into the dining room, and he smiled at the image she projected.

"Very businesslike," he said with approval. He leaned back in his chair, the action pulling the shirt taut over his hard-muscled chest. He looked devastating that way, with the light shining on his black hair and emphasizing his deep tan. He wasn't a handsome man, but Shelby thought he was the most attractive man she'd ever seen.

"I'm glad you approve," she said, smiling at him.

He got up and seated her next to him, pausing to drop a warm, slow kiss on her mouth. His eyes searched hers, warm and soft and darkly glowing. "Pretty creature," he whispered. "Eat your eggs before I make a meal out of you."

She laughed with pure delight and dragged her eyes down to her plate. She could hardly believe the way things had changed in the past few days. Her eyes adored him. He was hers, now. For the first time, she felt really married. Finally they were on their way to a lasting relationship.

The following days emphasized it. She thought about Justin all day at work, and when they got home at night, there were no more arguments, no more barriers. He kissed her coming and going, and every night he made love to her and she slept in his arms. It was as close to heaven as she'd ever been, like a waking dream that never seemed to sour or end. They spent time together, riding, playing the guitar, watching movies on the VCR. It was a new beginning, and Shelby could almost believe that what they had was perfect.

But even as they drew close physically, even as they spent more time together, still Shelby could feel the emotional distance between them. Justin shared none of his deepest feelings with her. He never spoke of love, even when they were the most intimate. He didn't talk about the past or the future. It seemed to her as if he was doing his best to take it one day at a time, without bothering about tomorrow.

His reticence worried her. She was as much in love with him now as she had been in the very beginning, but Justin was adept at hiding what he felt. He had a poker face that she'd never been able to see through. He wanted her. That was obvious and delightful. But if there was more than desire in him, Shelby never saw it.

She kept on with her job, even though she knew that Justin wanted her to give it up. He was only fractionally less jealous of her boss, but he didn't make any more harsh remarks. Meanwhile, Barry Holman had talked Tammy Lester into coming back to work, and things were developing very nicely between them. Shelby expected a breakthrough any day, because they were already exchanging heated looks.

And there was another development at home, too. Over four weeks had passed since Shelby and Justin had been intimate for the first time, and there were growing signs that their intimacy might bear fruit. She hadn't mentioned her suspicions to him, but she was almost sure that she was pregnant. The thought made her delightfully happy. Having a child with Justin would make her happiness complete, and he'd said himself that he wanted children. It would be the final balm, to heal the breach that existed between them. And when the baby came, Justin might begin to care about her as well as the child.

She was curled up on the sofa when he came into the room, scowling. He'd just been on the phone and he looked preoccupied.

"Is something wrong?" she asked gently, sitting up straight. He looked very somber for a change.

He glanced at her and grimaced. "I've got to fly up to Wyoming for a few days. I've been asked to appear in court as a character witness for a friend of mine who's being sued." He sighed. "I don't want to go, but he'd do it for me. I think he's getting a raw deal."

He sat down beside her, drawing her close, while he smoked his cigarette and explained that the rancher was being accused of selling contaminated beef to a packing plant.

"You're sure he didn't do it?"

"I'm sure," he replied. He kissed her absently. "I wish I could take you with me, but I'm going to stay with Quinn Sutton. He's not much of a woman's man."

"I see. He's a grizzled old hermit," she teased.

He chuckled. "Actually, he's about my age and jaded. He lost his wife to another man about ten years ago and he never got over it. She had a child, a little boy. She left the boy behind and Quinn's raised him. I don't know what the boy will do if his dad goes to jail." He shook his head. "Hell of a mess."

"I hope he doesn't have to go to jail," she said. Her pale green eyes searched his face. "I'll miss you, Justin."

He wrapped her up tight and kissed her hungrily. "No less than I'll miss you, honey," he whispered. "I'll phone you every night. Maybe it won't take too long."

"It had better not. If you leave me alone at night too long, I'll run away with some sexy man," she teased, knowing there wasn't a sexier man alive than her husband.

But Justin, still unsure of her even after the weeks of exquisite pleasure, didn't realize what she meant. He held her, his chin on her hair, and stared quietly over her head, wondering if she was already beginning to tire of him. She was a beautiful woman, and he wasn't a handsome man. She seemed to enjoy sleeping with him, but he wanted much more than her slender body in the darkness. He wanted her to love him.

"Don't speed while I'm gone," he cautioned quietly.

She laughed softly. The small American car he'd

bought her wasn't a speeding kind of automobile. He'd made sure of that first, but apparently he wasn't going to trust her completely.

"I won't," she promised. "And Maria and Lopez will be here at night, so you don't have to worry about me. I'll be fine. I'll just be lonely," she added, sitting up. Her eyes searched his. "Justin, you're worried. What about?"

He shifted. "Just business, honey," he said evasively. His eyes narrowed as they searched hers. "You aren't getting tired of marriage already, are you?"

She actually gasped. "What?"

"You heard me. I can't give you all that your father could. I just hope it's enough."

She reached up, bringing his face down to hers. "Oh, Justin, you're all I want!"

She kissed him, feeling the ripple run through his powerful body at the touch of her mouth against his. It still amazed her, that wild reaction she got when she kissed or touched him. He never said anything about it, but he seemed to love having her make the first move, having her reach out to him. She didn't do it often, because she was still the least bit shy with him. But it was getting easier. His response was encouraging.

He lifted her, turned her, and his mouth grew hungry. The passion between them never seemed to wane. If anything, it was even stronger now than it had been at the beginning. She held nothing back, and her lack of inhibition keyed a similar lack in him. He was still tender, but occasionally his ardor grew demanding and fierce, and at those times she knew a fulfillment that surpassed her wildest dreams.

"When do you have to go?" she whispered, trembling because his hands were under her soft blouse, touching her.

"Tomorrow."

"So soon?"

He lifted her, getting to his feet in one smooth, graceful motion. "We've got all night," he whispered over her mouth before he took it. "God, I want you! I want you all the time…"

She moaned under his hard mouth, loving his touch, needing the ardent sweetness of his arms. She clung to him as he opened the door and carried her slowly upstairs. If only she could tell him how much she loved him, share the delightful secret that she was hoarding. She wanted to. In fact, she started to. But as she opened her mouth to tell him, his lips began to probe hers tenderly. And as always, the spark of desire knocked every thought out of her mind except Justin, and the exquisite pleasure of loving him in the darkness.

He was gone when she woke up the next morning. She barely remembered feeling his mouth brush hers, hearing his whispered goodbye. But she'd been so tired, and she hadn't fully awakened. When she did, she wished then that she'd made him listen. She had an odd feeling that she should have tried harder, a premonition that their harmony was about to be disrupted. But perhaps it was only her condition and her uncertainty about Justin's feelings for her. Surely they were so close now that nothing could rebuild the old wall that had kept them apart for six years.

Chapter Nine

Court was in session, and there was more work than ever in the small office for Shelby and Tammy. Mr. Holman was working on two divorce cases, a land settlement, a suit for damages resulting from a highway car crash, and he was defending a local man who'd been charged with manslaughter. No sooner did Tammy get through researching one case than she had to start on the next. The land settlement involved complicated research in the county clerk's office, looking up plats and deeds. One of the divorces involved allegations of child abuse, and that required a deposition from an emergency-room physician who'd treated the child—Mr. Holman did that, of course, with the court stenographer. But

Tammy had to get the medical records and take down potential testimony from a psychologist and check into the husband's criminal record. The car crash meant more delving into police records and interviewing potential witnesses, and the manslaughter charge looked like a full-time job in itself.

Shelby didn't envy the young woman her paralegal status. Tammy had been taking courses at night at a nearby junior college, and now it was paying off. Mr. Holman had already raised her salary and she was coping with things Shelby couldn't begin to understand. It was a good thing, Shelby thought, that she hadn't wanted that training herself. With her almost positive pregnancy, she wouldn't be able to work for many more months. She knew Justin was going to insist that she stay home the last month or so of her pregnancy. Secretly, she wanted that, too. She wanted the time to plan things for the baby, to get furniture and fix up a room for a nursery. She smiled, thinking about the look on Justin's face when she told him the news.

"I said," Mr. Holman interrupted her thoughts gently, "I'm afraid you're going to have to put in some overtime this week—you and Tammy. Civil court's in full swing, and superior court convenes next week. We don't have a lot of time to get our cases in order."

"I don't mind," Shelby assured him. "Justin's out of town, so I've got nothing to do in the evenings."

"His loss, my gain." The blond lawyer grinned. "Thanks, Shelby. I don't know what I'd do without you. I've got to run to the courthouse and then I'll be at Carson's Café for lunch. Back about one."

"Okay, boss."

He started out the door and collided with Tammy, who was rushing in. He caught her upper arms to steady her and she rested her hands on his chest to support herself. They looked at each other and froze there, a tableau that Shelby found oddly touching.

"You okay?" Barry Holman asked the young woman.

Tammy's full lips parted. "Yes," she breathed. She didn't look up, and she was blushing.

His hands contracted for a minute, then he let her go. "Be careful," he said softly, and smiled. "I don't want to lose you."

"Yes, sir," Tammy murmured huskily.

He let his glance drop to her mouth for one long instant, then he was gone, frowning and impatient all over again.

Shelby had to smother a grin. From fighting tooth and nail, the two of them had become shy and reserved and uncomfortable with each other. Tammy actually seemed to vibrate when the boss came into a room, and her face lit up like a neon sign.

"I, uh, have some notes to type," Tammy said, faltering.

Shelby smiled. "I'll go out and get us some lunch. What would you like?"

"Tuna-fish salad and crackers, and iced tea. Here. And thanks a million! I'll go tomorrow." Tammy grinned.

"That's a deal. I won't be long. Hold the fort."

Shelby went around the corner to the drugstore and found Abby bent over a greeting-card display.

"What are you looking for?" she asked her sister-in-law conspiratorially.

Abby chuckled, her blue-gray eyes lighting up. "A card for my gorgeous husband. His birthday is week after next," she reminded Shelby.

"How could I forget, when we're having the party for him?" Shelby replied. "Which reminds me, I was supposed to call you two days ago to go over the arrangements. I got busy…" She flushed. What had happened was that Justin had wrestled her down on the carpet when she'd picked up the phone to call Abby, and nothing had gotten done for the rest of the night.

"I gather that things are going well over at your place," Abby mused, watching the scarlet blush. "Calhoun says Justin sits around dreaming at the feedlot instead of working, and that he's got a photograph of you on his desk that he just stares at all the time."

Shelby laughed delightedly. "Does he, really?"

"You newlyweds." Abby smiled. "I'm glad it's working out for you. I knew it would. You two were always equal halves of a whole—even Tyler mentioned it that night you and Justin danced together at the square dance."

Shelby blushed. "I never dreamed it would work out like this, though," she confessed. "I've never been so happy."

"I imagine Justin feels the same." She studied Shelby's face curiously. "Why are you still working? Don't you want to stay at home?"

"Well, I didn't think it would be right to just walk off and leave Mr. Holman," Shelby confessed. "Tammy Lester's working out very well and sooner or later I'll go home. It's just that I wanted to try my wings. I've never been independent before. It's fun."

"So is marriage." Abby grinned. "I'm having a ball just being a housewife, as traitorous as that sounds coming from a modern woman. Was that Tammy I saw in the window this morning?" she added. "The shade was pulled down, but it was dark and there was a light behind her. She was leaning over Mr. Holman. She sure does look like you," she added. "Maybe not in person, but your silhouettes are really similar."

"It's probably because we both have long hair and we're tall and slender," Shelby said. "But she's stuck on the boss, and just between us, I think it's mutual. They started out hating each other. Now they're at the throat-clearing, foot-shuffling stage."

"Guess what comes next," Abby said wickedly.

Shelby laughed softly, averting her eyes. "Well, they'll get to that stage before much longer, I suppose. Calhoun doesn't know about the surprise party, does he?" she asked to divert the younger woman.

"Heavens, no, and he wouldn't drag it out of me at gunpoint, I promise. Justin phoned the other night and said he'd invited a couple of people who wouldn't be on my list. I don't guess he mentioned that to you?"

Shelby frowned. "Well…no. Who do you suppose he's invited?" Her green eyes flashed. "Surely he wouldn't invite any of his old flames…?" she mused to herself.

"I wouldn't worry too much about that," Abby murmured, because Justin had once confessed to her that he'd never been in Calhoun's league as a ladykiller. But Shelby didn't need to know that, and it was Justin's place to tell her when and if he wanted to.

"Then who?" she persisted.

"We'll have to wait and see. You might ask him when he gets back. Pity about Mr. Sutton, isn't it?" Abby sighed. "I met him and his son at one of those cattle conventions Calhoun and I went to month before last. He's not much to look at, very reserved, but bristling with masculinity, if you know what I mean. He looked right through me, and there was a woman who came on to him…" Abby shivered. "I used to think Justin was kind of remote when I first went to live with the Ballengers, but Mr. Sutton makes Justin look like an extrovert. He hates women."

"His loss," Shelby said with a faint grin. "Of course, he obviously has never encountered women of our caliber."

Abby burst out laughing. "Shame on you."

Shelby laughed, too. "Call me when you have time and we'll get those arrangements for the party finished. I've got to run. Tammy's at the office by herself."

"Okay. I'll just go through these cards again. Have a nice lunch."

"See you."

Shelby puzzled over what Abby had said all the way back to the office. She couldn't help but wonder whom Justin had invited that he hadn't told her about. She'd have to ask him.

He'd flown to Wyoming on Wednesday, and although he'd hoped to be back two days later, there had been complications and the hearing had been held over until Monday. He wasn't going to get back for the weekend.

"Oh, Justin," she moaned. "And I have to work late next week. We've got court."

"Quit that damned job," he said shortly. "A woman's place is at home, having children and keeping things straight."

A cold, deep voice in the background laughed and made a curt remark that Justin replied to.

"What was that?" Shelby asked curiously.

"Mr. Sutton thinks women are best when floured and salted and fried in lard," he mused.

"You can tell Mr. Sutton that men have to be marinated first," she shot back.

There was a murmur of voices and a deeply appealing laugh in the background. "Shame on you," Justin murmured. "I've got to go. This turkey goes to bed at nine, so I'll be left up in the dark if I don't hang up. Be good, sweetheart. I'll see you Monday evening."

"You can pick me up at work if I'm not here, okay?" she asked softly.

"Okay. Good night."

"Good night, Justin," she said softly and kissed the receiver before she put it back in the cradle. She missed him already until it was almost unbearable. She wanted him to come home so badly.

The next two days passed all too slowly, but Monday was hectic and she didn't have time to look forward to seeing her husband. It was one tangle after another. The phone never stopped and Tammy had to run to the courthouse twice to take information to Mr. Holman in court.

By the end of the day, Shelby wondered if she was ever going to get to go home. Mr. Holman came in needing letters typed and a new brief prepared. It was pages long, and even with the computer, it took Shelby a long time.

Meanwhile, Tammy was flitting around the office following orders while Mr. Holman got more and more impatient. Shelby knew there was going to be trouble from the way Tammy began gnawing on her lower lip and glaring toward the boss's office. At nine o'clock, he came to the doorway and made a sarcastic remark about a property-line measurement that Tammy had written incorrectly and the younger girl exploded.

"You expect miracles!" she told the angry blond man. "I'm working overtime, I haven't had supper, I've had to get down on my hands and knees to get some of this stuff for you, and you're yelling at me! I hate you!"

"You cream puff!" he threw back. "If you think this is hard work, try practicing law, honey!"

He gave her a smug smile and went back into his office.

"Oh, no, you don't, big shot," Tammy muttered. She followed him in, slamming the door.

There were raised voices. A chair scraped and something fell. Then there was a long, poignant silence that grew and grew. Shelby, sitting at her computer, smiled to herself. It looked as if that next step in the boss's courtship had just been taken.

But to the man sitting across the street in the black Thunderbird, the two figures so closely silhouetted in the window, against the thin shade, didn't look like Barry Holman and Tammy. They looked to him like Barry Holman and Shelby. From her height to her long hair, it looked like Shelby in that man's arms.

Justin felt his heart stop dead in his chest. He'd come straight from the airport into town, desperate to see Shelby again, so hungry for the sight of her that he'd taken a chance on her still being in the office. Only to find…this.

He thought the wounding would never stop. It was killing him to see Shelby in that man's arms. It couldn't be—but, then, it had to be. She'd teased him about finding another man if he stayed away too long. She wasn't a virgin anymore; she was a sensual woman now. Perhaps the hunger had gotten to her. It wasn't rational, but then, neither was jealousy, and he was eaten up with it. He wanted to go in there and kill that man. He wanted to throw Shelby out of his house, out of his life. He'd trusted her, and she'd betrayed him, again.

He didn't want to believe it, but what else could he believe? That was Shelby in that window, Shelby with her boss. He knew the sight of her too well to mistake her for anybody else, and who else could there be, because there was only one woman at the office and Shelby was the woman!

He started the car and pulled out onto the street, his dark eyes black with hurt, seeing the end of his dreams. She'd been fire in his arms, loving him, holding him, giving him everything he'd ever wanted. But she'd betrayed him in the past, and he'd forgotten that in their new closeness. He'd forgotten what she'd done to him before. She hadn't slept with Wheelor, but she'd still betrayed him— she'd thrown him over. And now history was repeating itself, and he didn't know what he was going to do. He drove home without even knowing how to get there, sick at heart and already grieving for Shelby all over again. How could she do that to him? How could she!

At the office, Shelby finally finished her chores and wondered whether or not to knock on Barry Holman's door. She decided against it. If they were in a clinch, it would be cruel to interrupt them.

She phoned the house and asked if Justin was there, but Maria said that he hadn't arrived yet. So she went out, leaving a note on her desk, got into her car and drove home. So much for Justin's promise to come and pick her up. But maybe he hadn't gotten home yet. She smiled, comforting herself with that thought.

She pulled into the driveway and left the car at the front steps, eager to see if he'd come in. She darted down the hall to his study, and there he was.

"Hello!" She laughed.

But the man whose black, cold eyes sought hers across the room didn't remotely resemble the tender lover who'd left for Wyoming last Wednesday. He was smoking a cigarette, and he looked as indifferent to her as a stranger might.

"You're late," he remarked.

"I…we had court," she said, faltering. "I told you I'd be working late."

"So you did." He took another draw from the cigarette. "You look worried. Is anything wrong?"

"I thought you might be glad to see me," she said with a hesitant smile.

He smiled back, but it wasn't pleasant. He was dying inside, but he wasn't about to let her see it. "Did you?" he asked carelessly. "I suppose you don't remember what you did to me six years ago. I'm sorry to disappoint you if you expected me to have fallen under your spell again. I haven't. What we had those few weeks was a small recompense for the anguish you gave me in the past. But I didn't realize you expected to build a future on it." He laughed coldly. "Sorry, honey. Once was enough. But don't think I can't live without you. You're like wine—I don't need to get drunk on you to enjoy the occasional sip."

She couldn't believe what she was hearing. She knew her face had gone quite pale. She was almost surely pregnant and Justin was telling her that he didn't want her anymore.

"I thought…you realized that I hadn't slept with Tom."

"Sure I did," he admitted. "But you broke the engagement all the same, didn't you, and told the whole damned world that I wasn't rich enough to suit you." His eyes glittered coldly. "Now it's my turn. I'm rich and I don't want you anymore, honey. Try that on for size."

She turned and ran, a sob breaking in her throat as she went helter-skelter up the staircase and into her old room. She locked the door and threw herself on the bed, crying helplessly. It was like a nightmare.

Several minutes passed. She'd thought, hoped, that Justin hadn't meant it. She'd listened and waited, hoping against hope that he might come after her, that he might reconsider what he'd said. But there were no footsteps on the staircase and she was finally forced to the conclusion that he wasn't going to follow her.

It didn't seem to bother him, either, that she'd gone to bed in her old room. She heard his footsteps much later going down the hall toward the bedroom they'd shared. The door closed and stayed closed.

Shelby didn't know what had gone wrong. When Justin had left for Wyoming, everything had been perfect for them. His emotional distance had disturbed her, but she'd been sure that he was beginning to feel something for her. Now, he was a stranger. The revenge she hadn't thought he wanted was now evident. He looked at her as if he couldn't care less about her, and what he'd said had cut her to the bone.

She finally slept, wondering how she was going to manage to go on. Exhausted, tears streaking her pale cheeks, she faced the loss of everything she'd ever loved. And Justin was first on that list.

Down the hall, the man who'd just returned from Wyoming was lying awake, too, missing the familiar sound of Shelby's breathing, the feel of her soft body against his in the darkness. He felt guilty and sick at the way he'd spoken to her, at the tears and hurt he'd caused. But he was hurting, too. He'd thought that Shelby loved him, and all along she'd only married him because she'd lost her home and security. She was playing him for a fool all over again, keeping a man in the background. The fact that it was her handsome boss only made it worse. Now he knew why she'd fought him about giving up her job. She was in love with her playboy boss, that was why she'd refused to come home. And now he'd seen proof of her disloyalty. He could hardly bear the pain. He didn't know how he was going to go on living with her after what he'd seen.

Just for a minute, he considered the possibility of confronting her with the truth. But what good would that do? He'd confronted her with Tom Wheelor, and she'd lied. She'd lied at the time, and she'd lied since. He'd been lured into a false sense of security. He'd really begun to trust her again. What a good thing that he'd gone into town unannounced tonight to bring her home. Now she couldn't fool him again. He'd seen the real Shelby, and he was disgusted with her. He knew she'd been a virgin when she'd married him, but now that he'd gotten her over the hurdle of her first time, probably she was enjoying a totally new relationship with her boss.

That was the last straw. With an angry sigh, he closed his eyes and forced himself to put her out of his mind.

The next morning, he went downstairs with a carefully schooled expression, determined not to let Shelby know that he was cut to the bone emotionally. He'd die before he'd show it.

Shelby was up early, too, drinking black coffee and nibbling halfheartedly at toast. She looked up when he came into the dining room, her eyes swollen from crying all night, her expression one of hopeful uncertainty.

"You didn't mean what you said last night, did you?" she asked. Her green eyes searched his. "Did you, Justin?"

He moved past her and sat down casually at the head of the table, pouring coffee into his cup from the carafe before he answered her. "I meant every word of it, Shelby," he replied. He helped himself to bacon, eggs and biscuits, as nonchalantly as if she were a business associate. "Have some eggs."

She couldn't bear the sight of them, much less the taste. Her appetite had long since gone, and she was already in danger of losing the tiny bites of toast she'd taken. She shook her head.

His dark eyes narrowed as he studied her. She looked worn. Her long hair was luxurious, but her face was pale and pinched, even with makeup.

"I'm not very hungry," she added.

"Suit yourself." He didn't show his own lack of appetite. He was quiet long enough to clean his plate, but he could feel Shelby's eyes and they made him uncomfortable.

"What kind of relationship do you have in mind for us now?" she asked with the shreds of her pride drawn around her.

He pushed his plate aside and sipped his coffee. "You're my wife," he said coolly. "You'll live in my house and I'll take care of you. But we'll have separate rooms, and separate lives, from now on."

Her eyes closed on a wave of sorrow and shame. And what about the baby I'm carrying, she wanted to ask. What about our child?

"Surely sleeping alone won't bother you now," he chided. "Since you've already satisfied your curiosity."

"It won't bother me," she said huskily. She couldn't finish her coffee. The smell of it made her stomach churn. She got to her feet very slowly. "I'll be late if I don't leave now."

His eyes flashed. "God forbid that you should be late for…work," he said.

She was too sick to notice the hesitation or the venom in his tone. She got out while she could, forcing herself not to show weakness. That was the one thing she couldn't afford at the moment.

She went to work and was violently sick in the bathroom the minute she got there. She mopped her face with wet paper towels and sat quietly at her desk until she got the nausea under control. It was going to take time to reconcile herself to Justin's new coldness. It was like having a glimpse of heaven and then being forced back to reality again. She didn't know why he'd taken this way to get back at her. It was going to be almost impossible for her to stay with him, but she had nowhere else to go. Not yet, at any rate. And certainly not until she was over the first phases of morning sickness and able to move around better than this.

When the boss and Tammy got to the office, she had the nausea under control temporarily. But the late hours were difficult for her, and her appetite was well and truly gone. As the days dragged by, just to put one foot in front of the other was an ordeal.

Abby came over one evening and they worked out the details for Calhoun's birthday party. Abby noticed the atmosphere and almost said something, but Shelby looked so bad that she bit her tongue and kept quiet. Obviously, something had gone wrong.

"You haven't forgotten Calhoun's party?" Shelby asked Justin as they had an increasingly rare meal together before the party.

He looked up from food he didn't even taste, his eyes quiet and somehow haunted for an instant before he blinked and removed the expression. She looked bad. Her color was terrible and she seemed weak and lackluster. He knew it was because of his coldness, but he couldn't help it any more than he could help his feelings of betrayal and hurt.

"I haven't forgotten," he replied. He leaned back in his chair and studied her. "You don't look well."

"It's been a long week, Justin," she said dully. "And a little unexpected. You don't need to worry," she said with a faint laugh. "I'm all right. I'm just fine, in fact. I've got a roof over my head and food to eat, and a job. I've got everything you promised me when we got married. I don't have a complaint."

She put her fork down and got up, swaying a little. She caught the back of the chair, praying that the sudden blackness would relent before she went down. It did, and she turned away from Justin's quick movement toward her.

"Are you all right?" The words were torn from him. He hated the way she looked. She made him feel cold with guilt. Amazing, when she'd hurt him, not the reverse.

"I told you. I'm fine." She left the room with her head high, and went upstairs without another word. They spent no time at all together now. If they had a meal at the same time, it was unusual. Afterward, he always went to his study and she went to her room. Maria noticed, but she and Lopez kept silent. With Justin in his present mood, it was safer that way.

The night of the party, Shelby rested before she dressed. She'd found a dark emerald velvet dress that she'd worn the year before. It had been a little too small when she and Justin married, but the weight loss made it just the right size. It was floor length, sleeveless, with an A-line skirt and a rounded neckline. She pinned up her hair and complemented the dress with a dainty emerald necklace that had been her grandmother's. She looked frail even with makeup, and she wished that things were different between her and Justin. Abby would surely have mentioned her brief happiness to Calhoun. When Calhoun came tonight and was able to see the distance between his brother and sister-in-law, he was bound to mention it to Justin. Shelby didn't think she could bear another confrontation.

She touched her stomach, wondering how much longer she should wait before she saw the doctor. They could tell at six weeks, she knew, and it was almost that. But the problem was going to be how to keep it from Justin in a small community like Jacobsville. Perhaps she could go up to Houston and have herself tested at a clinic.

Music was playing downstairs. She dabbed on a tiny bit of perfume and went downstairs, carefully holding onto the banister. She felt wobbly. The past week had been a terrible strain, due to overwork and Justin's unexplained cold attitude.

She spotted Abby and Calhoun when she got to the first landing. They were arm in arm, looking so happy that they broke her heart. Calhoun was big and blond and Abby was slender and dark. They made a handsome contrast, Calhoun in dark evening clothes and Abby in a pale blue silk that matched her eyes.

Shelby didn't see Justin until she got downstairs. He was dressed in a dinner jacket, and he looked very elegant. Shelby wondered if he planned to put on an act for their guests, or if he was going to be himself. She didn't dare look at him too closely. He might see the hurt and longing in her eyes.

She turned toward the door, where Lopez in his white jacket was just opening it to admit the newest guest. Shelby stopped dead at the sight of the man who stood nervously just inside the hall, shifting his feet as he searched the room for a familiar face.

Shelby's eyes flashed. She couldn't believe that Justin had had the audacity to invite him. It was Calhoun's birthday, and she knew Justin wouldn't expect her to make a scene.

But that didn't even register as she moved out into the hall, ignoring Justin, and picked up a very expensive antique vase on the way.

"Hello, Tom," she greeted Tom Wheelor with icy politeness. "How nice to see you again."

And without a break in her stride, she lifted the vase and threw it straight at Wheelor's balding head.

Chapter Ten

Shelby watched, fascinated, as the antique vase whizzed past Tom's left ear and crashed into the hat stand in the corner, knocking Justin's battered black Stetson to the floor.

"Shelby?" Tom asked, moving back a step.

She reached out for the flower arrangement Maria had painstakingly created for the hall table.

"Shelby, don't!" Tom whirled, his hands over his head, and ran out the front door.

Shelby took off after him, blind to the shocked looks from the other guests, including her wide-eyed husband.

"Insect," she raged. "Weak-kneed money man!" She let him get halfway down the stairs before she heaved the flower arrangement in its delft bowl. It connected.

Tom almost lost his balance as he caught onto the balustrade with shards of pottery shattering around him.

He struggled the rest of the way down the steps and ran for his car. Shelby watched him go with fury in her eyes. He'd been responsible, indirectly, for all her heartaches. How could he have the gall to come tonight, of all nights, and at Justin's invitation? Did Tom really think she'd forgotten his part in her anguish? She'd even told him at the time just what she thought of him.

She turned and went back up the steps. She didn't even look at Justin.

"Good evening," she greeted the guests, as if nothing at all had happened. "Happy birthday, Calhoun! We're so glad Abby let us throw this party for you." She went close and kissed his tanned cheek.

"Thanks, Shelby," Calhoun murmured.

"Shall we go in to dinner?" Shelby nodded to the others, mostly friends of Justin's and Calhoun's whom she barely knew. She took Justin's arm as if she feared his touch would burn her. She didn't look at him or speak to him.

"What the hell was that all about?" he asked when they were temporarily out of earshot of the others, heading into the elegantly arranged dining room.

She ignored his question. "How dare you invite that man here?" she asked instead. "How dare you bring him

into our home, after the way he let my father use him
to break us up?"

"I wanted to see if there were any embers left from the
fire," he said with a cool smile.

"Embers?" She took a sharp breath. "You're lucky I
didn't kill him. I'm sorry I didn't!"

"Temper, temper."

"You can go to hell, Justin, dear," she said with a
smile as icy as his. "And take your moods and your taste
for revenge and your cold heart with you."

His black eyes narrowed. "Still sticking to your story
that your father made you break it off with me?"

"Why can't you believe me?"

"Very simple," he replied as the others filed into the
room. "It was your father's money that pulled the feed-
lot out of bankruptcy. He footed the whole damned bill."
His eyes registered her shock. "Surprised? It's hardly the
act of a man who wanted to break us up, wouldn't you
agree?"

Shelby knew her heart was going to beat her to death.
She grabbed the back of a chair and almost went down,
to Justin's surprise.

"Here, sit down, for God's sake," he muttered, easing
her into her place. "Are you all right?"

"No, I'm not." She laughed shakily.

Abby, noticing Shelby's sudden pallor, sat quickly

across from her. "Can I get you anything?" she whispered, glancing at the others.

"I'll be fine, if Justin will get away from me," she breathed, looking up at him with quiet rage.

He straightened, searching her furious eyes for a long moment. "My pleasure, Mrs. Ballenger," he said coldly, and turned his attention to their guests.

Shelby never knew afterward how she got through that dinner. She sat like a statue, answering questions, smiling, being the perfect hostess. But when she escaped upstairs to repair her makeup, Abby was two steps behind.

"What's happened?" her sister-in-law asked without preamble.

"For one thing, I'm pregnant," Shelby said stiffly.

Abby's breath sighed out, and her eyes softened. "Oh, Shelby! Does Justin know?"

"He doesn't, and you're not to tell him." Shelby sat down in her wing chair, easing her head back. "He's on the rampage again about the past. Just for a little while, things were going so well. Then he came back from Wyoming a stranger. He's been ice-cold ever since. How can I possibly tell him about the baby when he's acting like that?"

"It might soften his mood," Abby suggested.

"I don't need pity." She put her face in her hands with

a tiny shudder. "It's never going to work, Abby. He can't leave the past alone. I don't know what to do. I can't live like this anymore."

The tears slid past her hands and Abby bent, hugging her, saying all the right things, while she wanted nothing more than to go downstairs and hit Justin in the knee with a stick.

"What are you going to do?" Abby asked when the tears diminished and Shelby was wiping her red-rimmed green eyes with a tissue.

"I'm going to cut my losses, of course," Shelby said wearily. "I'm going to Houston tomorrow. I have a cousin there who'll let me stay with her until I can figure out where I'm going. I'll phone her later. I just need a little time to think. I can't do it here."

"What about your job?" Abby persisted, grasping at straws to keep Shelby from doing something stupid.

"Tammy and Mr. Holman are getting along very well," Shelby said. "As a matter of fact, I think they're very likely going to get married in the not-too-distant future. Tammy will take care of everything. I'll phone her tonight, too."

"You can't walk out on Justin like this, without trying to talk to him," Abby said softly, choosing her words. "I don't know what's gone wrong, but I do know how Justin feels about you. Shelby, you didn't see him that night Calhoun took you home from the square dance. But he was heartbroken that he'd made you cry. He cares deeply about you."

"He has a wonderful way of expressing affection," Shelby said. "First he tells me that we'll live separate lives, then he brings that…that *man* here!"

"I think he got the idea that you weren't carrying a torch for dear Tom." Abby chuckled.

"Tom and my father were two of a kind, both out to increase their already substantial fortunes," Shelby said. She stared down at the crumpled wet tissue. "But what hurts the most is that my father funded Justin and Calhoun's feedlot, and I didn't know it until Justin told me tonight." She sighed. "No wonder he wouldn't believe what I said about Dad trying to break us up. My father surely fixed things for me. Justin will never believe me again."

"He might listen if he knew about the baby."

"He's not going to," Shelby said doggedly. "It's my baby, not his. He can go to hell."

Abby's breath sighed out. Shelby looked bad, and talking wasn't going to solve anything. "Let's not discuss this now. You need to get some sleep and give this more thought when you're not so tired. Why don't you go to bed? I'll play hostess for you. I'll tell Justin you've got an upset stomach or a headache."

"He's the only headache I've got," Shelby said wearily.

Abby stood up, about to leave, when the door opened and Justin came in. He looked odd. Drawn and quiet and frankly puzzled.

"There's a woman here. A Miss Lester," he added. "She says she works with you."

"She's our paralegal," Shelby said dully. She wouldn't look at him. "What does she want?"

"She's coming up the staircase now. You can ask her." He shifted uncomfortably. "How long has she worked with you?"

"Several weeks," Shelby said. She looked up as Tammy came sheepishly into the room, looking bright-eyed and radiant. "Hi," she said with a smile. "What are you doing here?"

"I couldn't wait until tomorrow to show you my ring. Look!" She extended her left hand, where a huge diamond sparkled. "He gave it to me tonight."

Shelby laughed and got to her feet unsteadily to hug the younger woman. "I'm so happy for you. I had a feeling this was coming the other night, when the two of you went into his office and there was such silence!"

Tammy grinned. "Yes. Well, we seem to have started a good deal of gossip in town, outlined as we were against the window shade." She flushed. "Neither of us were thinking about being observed. But since we're engaged, it will be all right."

Justin had gone white. Abby saw his face and frowned but Shelby hadn't noticed. She was still talking to Tammy.

"Where's the boss?" she asked.

"Outside in the car, waiting impatiently. We're on our way to his parents' house to break the news. He wouldn't come in because of the party, but I just had to tell you! Isn't it great?" Tammy laughed.

"It certainly is. Congratulations!"

"Thank you. I'd better run." She hugged Shelby again. "See you bright and early tomorrow, okay?"

Shelby wanted to tell her that she wasn't going to be there Monday, but she couldn't, in front of Justin. Her plans to leave had to be kept secret.

"Yes," she agreed. "See you tomorrow. Tell the boss how happy I am for him, too," she added with a laugh.

"Okay. And I'm sorry for interrupting," Tammy added with a shy glance at Justin and Abby. "But I couldn't help it! Good night."

She left. Shelby sat down heavily. "Thank goodness," she told Abby with a breathless laugh. "Now the office can get back to normal again. It's been incredible working there for the past few weeks."

"She looks like you," Justin said curtly.

"Yes, she does," Abby agreed. She looked at Justin. Suddenly she knew that Justin had seen Barry Holman and Tammy in that window shade, silhouetted, and he'd thought it was Shelby. Maybe if she got out, they could talk about it and settle their differences.

"I'd better get back downstairs. Sure you're okay now?" she asked Shelby.

"I'm fine," Shelby assured her. "Thanks, Abby."

"I'll make your excuses."

Justin watched her go, searching for the right words to undo the damage he'd done. Shelby looked so wounded, so fragile. He could have shot himself for that frailty. He'd caused it by jumping to conclusions, by not listening to her. He hadn't trusted her, and now he wondered if he could ever repair the damage.

"Shelby…" he began slowly.

"I don't feel well," she said without preamble. "I'd like to lie down."

"You've lost weight," he remarked.

"Have I really?" She laughed, and it had a hollow sound. "Please go away, Justin. I don't have a single thing to say to you. I don't even want to have to look at you after what you did to me. Inviting that man here…!"

"I had to know!"

She looked up at him as she got to her feet. Her eyes blazed angrily. "I told you the truth. You wouldn't listen. You never have. You prefer your own interpretation, so go ahead and enjoy it. I don't care what you think anymore."

He stiffened. His pride was going to take a few knocks before this was over, and he knew he deserved it, after the way he'd treated her.

"Why did your father break us up?"

"He wanted me to marry Tom," she said, turning away from him. "He didn't want a poor son-in-law. On the other hand, he didn't like to make enemies, not in a small community, so he let me be the scapegoat. You played right into his hands when you went into business for yourself. That gave him leverage, and he used it."

"Then why did he lend me the money?" he asked curtly. "For God's sake, it was that loan that eventually caused his downfall. It took me years to pay it back, but it wasn't in time to do him any good."

She stared at the bed, with her back to Justin. "It was a long time ago. You may find the past comforting, but I don't. I had great hopes for the present until you decided to start evening old scores. Now I just feel tired and I want to go to bed."

He opened his mouth, but the words wouldn't come. He didn't know what to say. "I…saw you. At least, I thought it was you. In the window of your office when I came to pick you up the night I got home from Wyoming," he confessed hesitantly.

She turned. Her eyes widened. "You thought you saw me kissing him?"

His broad shoulders lifted and fell. "You and Tammy have similar profiles, and you'd never told me there was anyone in the office with you."

Her chin lifted. "Thank you," she choked huskily, "for your sterling opinion of my character and morals. Thank you for believing that I could never betray you with another man."

His cheeks went ruddy. "You'd betrayed me once!" he shot at her. "You left me for another man."

"I never did," she said firmly. "Never! My father threatened to ruin you and made me say what I did. He promised to save you, but I never realized that he did it with his own money."

"You dated Tom Wheelor," he added.

"No; it broke my father's heart that I refused to marry Tom," she said with a cold laugh. "Life without you was the purest hell I ever knew. I tried to tell you, but you wouldn't listen. You *still* won't listen." Tears clouded her eyes. "Well, I'm tired of talking to you, Justin. You're too bitter and too much in love with the past to ever give up your grudges. I can't live like this anymore. You've hurt me more than you'll ever know, even though I have to admit that my own cowardice helped things along. But what I did, I did to protect you, because I loved you too much to let you lose everything. All I ever wanted was you. But you only ever wanted me one way, and now that you've—how did you put it?—satisfied your desire for me, even that's gone, isn't it?"

His teeth ground together on a wave of pain. "Oh, God, Shelby," he whispered huskily.

"Well, don't lose any sleep over it, Justin. Maybe we were doomed from the beginning. Without trust, we don't have anything." She brushed the loose strands of hair away from her face. "I thought there was a chance for us, before you went to Wyoming. But if you still can't trust me, then we don't even have a common ground to build on. I'm so tired, Justin," she said then, sitting on the edge of her bed. "I'm so tired of fighting. I just want to go to sleep."

He ran his hand through his thick black hair, watching her. "Of course," he said quietly. "Tomorrow we'll talk."

She wasn't going to be here tomorrow, but she wasn't about to tell him that. "Yes. Tomorrow."

He wanted to hold her. To talk to her. To confess that his coldness had been out of jealousy, because he didn't think such a lovely woman could ever really love him. He'd never thought it, and his own uncertainty about his attraction for a woman like Shelby was the biggest part of the problem. But she did look worn, and it would be cruel to make her evening any harder than he already had.

"Get some rest. If you need me, just sing out."

"You're the last person on earth I need, Justin," she said quietly.

He drew in a slow breath. "My God, I know that. I always was." His black eyes slid over her hungrily. "It never seemed to make any difference, though. I couldn't stop wanting you. I never will."

He went out the door without looking back, and Shelby lay down on the coverlet and cried for all the happy years she'd never have with him, for the child she was carrying that he didn't even know about. She cried for all of them, and fell asleep in her evening gown, lying on top of the covers.

Justin found her that way the next morning. He didn't wake her. She looked so fragile, with her black hair haloed around her sleeping face. She was pale and he felt the guilt all the way to his soul. He'd hurt her. She was the most precious thing in his world, and he'd done nothing but hurt her.

He took off her shoes and pulled the quilted coverlet over her, his black eyes adoring on her face. "I'd fight the world for you, little one," he said softly. "What an irony it is that I can't seem to stop hurting you."

She didn't hear him. He reached down and touched her cheek gently, tracing it up to her eyebrows. His dark eyes softened, became tender.

"I love you," he breathed huskily. "Oh, God, I love you so! Why can't I tell you?" He bent and brushed his mouth with exquisite tenderness over her lips, a light touch that wouldn't awaken her. He stood up again, sighing heavily as he studied her sleeping face. "You said that I didn't trust you. Maybe the truth is more that I don't trust myself. You need someone gentler than I am. Someone less abrasive and set in his ways. I always knew it, but I couldn't find the strength to give you up." He lifted her slender hand in his and savored its softness. He smiled wistfully. "It would serve me right if I lost you. But I don't think I could stay alive if I did."

He put her hand on the coverlet and after one last glance at her sleeping face, he turned and went out of the room. Perhaps later they could talk, and he would tell her all these things when she was awake and listening. If he kept holding back, he stood a very real chance of losing her.

Shelby woke an hour after he left and her mind registered her evening-gown-clad person along with the coverlet that had been put over her. She wondered if she'd done that, or if Maria had covered her. Well, it didn't matter. She had things to do and not much time to do them in.

She tried to phone Tammy, but Tammy must have left for the office. Well, she'd call her from Cousin Carey's house in Houston. She did phone Cousin Carey and ask if she could visit for a day or two, and an invitation was extended with flattering immediacy. She and Carey had known each other since grammar school and were friends as well as relatives. She promised to see her cousin later in the day, hung up and got a reservation on the midday flight out of the Jacobsville airport that was Houston-bound.

She packed a suitcase, taking only what she had to have, and prayed that her morning sickness would hold off until she could get away.

She sneaked downstairs, called a cab and was almost out the door when Maria came into the hall to announce breakfast and found Shelby with a suitcase and a cab waiting.

"*Señora!*" Maria exclaimed helplessly.

"I'm only going away for a couple of days," Shelby said, faltering. "Abby knows where I'll be. You mustn't tell Justin. Promise me!"

Maria grimaced, but she finally agreed. She watched Shelby climb into the cab and drive away. She'd promised not to tell Justin. She hadn't promised not to call Abby. She picked up the phone and quickly dialed Abby's number.

Justin was on the telephone when Abby came into his office, dressed in jeans and a plaid shirt, her hair uncombed and no makeup on. She closed the door and sat down in the visitor's chair, watching the expressions that crossed her former guardian's face as he abruptly ended the telephone conversation and hung up.

"What's wrong?" he asked, because she looked worried.

"Everything!" she muttered, frowning. "I was half asleep when Maria called. Shelby made her promise not to call you, so she called me instead. I've broken speed records getting here. And now that I have—" she sighed "—I don't know how to say this to you."

He'd stiffened at the mention of Shelby's name. He'd had a premonition about her. He knew how badly he'd hurt her, and she'd mentioned last night that she couldn't take any more.

"She's left me, hasn't she, Abby?" he asked quietly.

"Yes, she has. The question is, what are you going to do about it?"

He lit a cigarette with steady hands while his world collapsed around his ears. He stared at the desk. "I'm going to let her go," he said after a minute. "I've hurt her enough."

Abby's breath stuck in her throat. "Justin!"

He looked up, the pain in his eyes making them even blacker. "You don't know how I've treated her," he said. "I was jealous and scared to death of losing her…" He broke off to run his hand roughly through his hair. "What have I got to offer her? How do I keep her?"

"You might try telling her that you love her," Abby said simply. "That's all she ever wanted."

His jaw clenched. "She wouldn't listen, after last night."

"You saw Barry Holman and Tammy, didn't you?" Abby asked.

He stared at her blankly. "Yes."

"And instead of telling Shelby, and letting her explain, you went off the deep end."

He smiled faintly. "Bingo."

"Oh, Justin." She shook her head. "She's on her way to Houston."

"Maybe she'll find someone there who can give her what she needs," he said, feeling bitter that he'd ruined all his chances.

Abby was getting nowhere and if Justin didn't go after Shelby, things were going to fall apart. She bit her lower lip. She didn't want to steal Shelby's thunder, but Justin was being difficult.

"Justin…how do you feel about babies?" she asked.

He was only half listening, his heart lying like lead in his chest. "I like babies," he said absently.

"Good. Then why don't you go after Shelby and get yours back?"

At first Abby didn't think he'd heard her. His eyes swung around and he stared at her. "I beg your pardon?" he asked.

"I said, Shelby's pregnant. If you really want a baby, you'd better get to the airport before she carries yours off to Houston with her."

"What the hell are you talking about?" he exploded.

"Now, Justin…!"

But he was on his feet and the chair was on the floor. He grabbed onto the desk for support. His eyes were wild and there was a tremor in the lean hand holding his cigarette. "A baby? Shelby's pregnant, and she didn't tell me?"

Abby was uncertain about what to do, so she rushed out of the office and found Calhoun.

"Come on." She pulled at his big hand. "I need you."

He grinned. "Now, honey, this isn't the place…"

"Justin's in shock."

That wiped the smile off his face. He followed her into Justin's office. The older man was right where Abby had left him, still white in the face and looking as if he'd been stabbed.

"You need to take him to the airport," Abby instructed.

"Airport, hell, he needs a doctor. What did you do to him?" he asked in a half whisper.

"I told him Shelby was pregnant."

Calhoun whistled through his teeth.

"And that she was on her way to Houston."

"I can drive," Justin said unsteadily. He started toward the door, but his eyes were dilated and his hand shook as he tried to put out the cigarette, knocking the glowing tip onto the desk.

Calhoun got it into the ashtray and took his brother firmly by the arm. "Don't you worry, big brother, I'll get you there on time." He glanced at Abby. "Which terminal?"

She grimaced. "Jacobsville airport only has one terminal."

"You're a big help," Calhoun muttered. "Anyway, I think there are only a couple of flights to Houston during off-peak hours."

"She's pregnant," Justin said huskily. "She didn't tell me. She knew and she couldn't tell me. It's all my fault. I failed her."

"Everything will be all right," Abby said reassuringly.

"God, I hope so." Justin glanced at her. "Thanks, honey."

"Don't tell Shelby I told you," Abby returned. "It's her place to tell you, but I was afraid you'd let her go if I didn't."

He only nodded, and finally he moved away from

Calhoun and went out the door. But he didn't argue when Calhoun gestured toward the Jaguar and got in under the wheel.

"What if the plane's already gone?" Justin asked, smoking like a furnace all the way to the airport.

"Then we'll get you a ticket to Houston." He grinned. "I'm going to be an uncle. Imagine that." He glanced at his taciturn brother. "And here I thought you and Shelby were living chastely."

"Shut up," Justin said, hiding embarrassment in bad temper.

"Whatever you say, big brother." He whistled to himself as he swung the car onto the highway and gunned the accelerator.

They reached the airport in record time. Justin was out the door almost before Calhoun stopped the car, half running to get into the terminal. They found the flight to Houston and Justin went to the ticket counter only to be told that the plane was scheduled to take off in less than five minutes.

Justin outdistanced Calhoun on his way to the concourse, his eyes fixed on the distant gate, his heart bursting with fear that she was going to get away before he got there. He broke into a run as the gate numbers got bigger, determined to make it in time.

Only another minute, he told himself, and he'd have

her in sight. Then he could talk to her, he could make her understand how much he loved her.

He pushed past a group of departing passengers from the concourse and made it to the empty ticket counter just in time to watch the clerk pull down the Houston sign and replace it with one for another city.

"The Houston flight," Justin asked curtly. "Where is it?"

"It left about two minutes ago," the clerk said pleasantly. "It's taxiing out to the runway now."

Justin felt his heart stop. He moved around the desk to the window and looked out. Planes were taking off, and one of them had Shelby on it. Shelby and his baby.

He stood there, frozen, his heart shattering. It was his own fault. He'd driven her to this. But he didn't know how in hell he was going to live with it. He could only imagine the anguish that had caused her to run away.

Calhoun touched his shoulder gently. "How about something to eat? Then we'll get you a seat on the next plane."

"I don't even know where to look for her, do you realize that?" he asked huskily. "My God, Cal, I don't know where she's gone!"

"It will be all right," Calhoun said firmly. "We'll find her. I swear we will."

Justin turned away from the window. "Food be

damned, I want a drink." He strode off toward the flashing Restaurant and Lounge sign down the concourse.

Calhoun followed, wondering how he was going to keep his big brother sober after his devastating letdown. Justin was shattered and Calhoun didn't quite know what to do for him. He'd said that they'd find Shelby, but he had no better idea of how to go about it than Justin did. It wasn't going to be easy to find one lone pregnant woman in a city the size of Houston. Especially if she didn't want to be found.

He stood out in the corridor, watching Justin go into the lounge and sit at a window table. He gave the waitress an order, and Calhoun sighed heavily. Well, maybe it would be a good idea if he went to the ticket desk and found out when the next plane left for Houston so he could get Justin a seat.

He was on his way down the concourse when a familiar face caught his eye. He stopped in the middle of the aisle and stared. He wasn't dreaming. That gray-clad woman with the small suitcase was Shelby, and she was coming straight toward him.

Chapter Eleven

Shelby felt the ground shake under her at the sight of Calhoun barring her path. She'd been certain Maria wouldn't say anything, but now she wasn't sure. Unless, of course, Calhoun was here to meet a client.

"Uh, hi, Calhoun," she said with a shaky smile.

He sighed. "Hi, yourself, Shelby." He noted the small suitcase she was carrying. "Going somewhere?"

She shifted restlessly. "Yes," she murmured. She stared at his suit instead of his face. "I'm leaving your brother."

"I know. Maria called Abby. Justin knows, too."

Shelby felt her face going pale, but a quick look around didn't produce Justin, and she sighed with relief. "He isn't with you, then?"

He took her arm gently. "I think it might help things along if you had a look at him. Come on, now, he won't bite."

"That's what you think," she muttered. "Where is he?"

"In there." He pulled her just inside the lounge entrance and nodded toward the corner, where Justin sat bareheaded and stooped with a bottle of whiskey and a shot glass in front of him. He was staring at the bottle obliviously while a forgotten cigarette sent up spirals of smoke from his free hand.

Shelby frowned. Justin didn't drink, as a rule. She remembered Abby saying something about him getting drunk the night of the square dance, but she knew it was a rare thing for him. He liked to be in control all the time. He didn't like having his mind fogged.

"What's he doing?" Shelby asked.

"Getting drunk, I imagine." Calhoun took the suitcase from her and looked down at her pale, fragile features. "Now, Shelby, would you say that he looks like a happy man?"

She grimaced. "No."

"Does he look like a man who's overjoyed that his wife has gone off and left him?"

She shook her head. In fact, he looked exactly the opposite. He looked defeated. Her pale green eyes ran over him lovingly, a soft sadness in their depths.

"I had to drive him here because he was shaking too bad to handle a car," he said quietly, nodding at her shocked expression. "He won't like remembering that, and when he's back together, I'm going to catch hell for having seen him in this condition. But I wanted you to know just how upset he is. That man loves you, honey. For years, you've been the only star in his sky. He's been alone all that time, and despite the fact that he's given you hell, I know he'd die for you. If you don't love him, the kindest thing you can do is to get out. But if you care about him, don't run away. Get in there and talk to him."

"I love him," she said simply. "But he believes bad things about me. He won't listen…"

"If you tell him how you feel, he'll listen. Believe it."

She looked up at him, weakening. "It's so hard…"

"Isn't life?" He bent and kissed her cheek gently. "Go on. Get it over. I'll sit in the concourse over there and look like a passenger and drink coffee. I'll look after your suitcase, too."

She smiled softly. "Thanks, Calhoun."

"My pleasure. Now go on."

She hesitated, but only for a minute. Calhoun was right. She was going to have to face Justin.

She walked nervously toward the table where he was sitting. As she got closer, she could see the paleness of his skin, the new lines that cut into his face.

"Justin?" she said hesitantly when she reached him.

He glanced up. Something flashed in his eyes as they went over her, tracing her body reverently. "You aren't here," he said quietly. "You left."

She bit her lip. He sounded as if he was talking to a ghost. "Not yet," she said gently. She eased into the chair beside his and stared at his lean hands. "I'm sorry to just run out like that. But I'd had all I could take."

"I know that," he said, his voice soft, tender. "I'm not blaming you. I never gave you a chance." He lifted the shot glass to his lips, but her fingers touched the back of his hand, coaxing him to put it down. He laughed hollowly. "I hate liquor, did I ever tell you? But it isn't every day a man loses everything he loves."

Tears moistened her eyes. She caught his hand and held it in both of hers, her face lifted, her expression open, loving. "You never said that you loved me, Justin," she whispered. "But I never stopped loving you. I never will. All I ever wanted was you."

His fingers contracted convulsively around hers. His black eyes glittered over her face. "Didn't you know, even without the words?" He breathed roughly. "My God, I'd have walked through fire if you'd asked me to. You were my world. I loved you…"

Her head nuzzled against his shoulder and she hated the crowded room, because she wanted nothing more in life than to throw her arms around him and hold him and kiss him and tell him all the things she'd never said before.

His arm went around her, holding her, and he drew in a shaky breath. "My God," he whispered at her forehead. "I thought you married me because you were alone and frightened."

"And I thought you married me because you felt sorry for me," she replied, letting the tears run freely down her face. "And all along, I loved you so."

His lean fingers brushed away the tears. He searched her misty eyes. "We've got to get out of here," he whispered. "I have to make you understand what I feel. I can't lose you now. Oh, God, Shelby, I'll die without you," he said huskily, and it was in his eyes, blazing out of them like black fire.

The tears came again. She got up, taking his hand. He went with her, holding her against him, even while he settled the tab, as if he couldn't bear to release her even that long.

Calhoun saw them come out of the lounge. He grinned knowingly and picked up Shelby's suitcase. "I'll drop you two off at the house," he offered. "Then I've got a meeting to get to."

They barely heard him. Justin looked completely oblivious, and Shelby was so close to him that she seemed a part of him.

He put them in the back seat and drove off, smiling smugly at his role in this reunion. Not that they seemed to notice him. They were too busy looking at each other.

He let them out at the front steps of the Ballenger house, setting the bag on the steps beside them. "I phoned Abby while you two were in the lounge. She said how about coming over to our place for supper? Maria's going to her sister's tonight, and Shelby sure isn't up to cooking."

"That would be nice," Justin said quietly. He clapped his brother on the shoulder. "Thanks."

"You'd do the same for me," Calhoun replied. He grinned. "In fact, you did, or have you already forgotten? See you at six. Goodbye, Shelby."

"Thanks, Calhoun," she said, smiling at him.

Justin picked up the suitcase and helped her into the house. Maria came running, a stream of Spanish echoing from her lips. Justin abruptly swung her up by the waist and planted a heartfelt kiss on her tanned cheek. She giggled when he put her down.

"Señor!" she chided. She was dressed up. "Lopez and I are leaving now, but I had to wait and make sure everything was all right. *Señor*, what about a meal this evening?"

"Calhoun's invited us over to eat with him and Abby," Shelby told her, and hugged her. "Thank you for calling Abby. I'll never forget what you did for us."

Maria grinned. "You would have found a way, *señora*." She laughed. "I only helped a little bit. Lopez and I must hurry. We will be back tomorrow, *señor*. I will cook you a magnificent breakfast!"

"We'll look forward to that. Godspeed."

Maria smiled and went down the hall into the kitchen, where Lopez was waiting.

Justin led Shelby into the living room, where Maria had a tray of coffee and small cakes waiting for them. After she sat down, he poured the coffee. But before he handed her the cup, he bent and kissed her with exquisite tenderness.

"I love you," he whispered softly, searching her eyes. "I always did, even if I couldn't find the right way to tell you."

She kissed him back. "That was all you ever had to say," she replied. "I loved you, too, Justin. But you never seemed to believe that I could."

He gave her coffee to her and sat down close beside her to sip his. "I was a poor man in those days, and I've never been much to look at," he confessed. "You came from a wealthy background, you were beautiful and pursued." He laughed. "I never felt like serious competition for men like Wheelor."

"Money and looks never counted for much with me," she said firmly. "You had qualities much more important." Her eyes searched his quietly. "But the important thing was that I loved you," she said. "Love doesn't depend on surface things or possessions."

He looked at her with undisguised hunger. "No. I don't suppose it does. I was unsure of you."

She smiled. "And now?"

"And now." He laughed softly. His free hand touched her face. The smile faded. "I've made you unhappy. I've hurt you and scorned you, all because I didn't trust you. But if I'd known how you felt, there wouldn't have been any doubts. None. Can you believe that, and forgive me for the way I've treated you?"

"I love you," she said simply. "Nothing else matters." She reached up and kissed him hungrily. "I understand why you thought what you did, Justin. It was my father's mischief-making, not anything either of us did that caused such heartache. But now it's enough that you love me. It's everything."

He put down his cup and hers and drew her across his lap, holding her hungrily. "I'd take back the whole six years, if I could," he whispered huskily. "I'd do anything to make it up to you."

"Justin…you've already made it up to me," she said with soft hesitation. She took his lean hand and pressed it slowly, gently, to her still-flat abdomen. She held it there and searched his eyes. "I'm carrying your baby."

He knew. But hearing it from her made it profound

and infinitely touching. He caressed the softness gently and, bending, brought her mouth under his to kiss her with exquisite caring.

"Shelby," he whispered. He kissed her again. "Shelby. You and a baby…"

"You aren't sorry?" she whispered, softly teasing.

He smiled at her with pride and love in his dark eyes. "I'm not sorry about anything. Are we having a son or a daughter?"

"I don't care, as long as we have a healthy baby." She reached up to hold him. "And I'm quitting my job, in case I haven't mentioned it. I think Tammy and the boss are going to be very happy without me."

"I'm going to be very happy with you, if this is what you really want," he said. He traced her lips with a long finger. "I won't cheat you of outside interests, if you want them. I won't insist that you be only a wife and mother."

"I won't be," she assured him, "although that's going to be my most important job for a little while. Then I may take courses or do some volunteer work. But right now, the baby is my main concern."

He laughed softly. "How long?" he whispered.

"I think I'm just at six weeks," she whispered back. "I'm going to the doctor next week to make sure."

"The first time we made love," he breathed, holding her eyes. "Wasn't it?"

She hid her face against him, laughing with shy embarrassment. "Yes."

"I'm good," he murmured dryly.

She pressed closer. "You're very good," she whispered and lifted her face.

He bent, easing his mouth down onto hers, caressing it. She relaxed against him, loving his touch, loving the strength of his body so close to hers. She sighed, and the sound went into his mouth, kindling a new and overwhelming desire.

Her hands slid around to the back of his head and he drew her hips against his, turning her, while his mouth became more and more demanding.

He wanted her. She knew the signs now, in ways she hadn't before. And she moaned, because he loved her and she loved him, and this time would be different than the other times. It would be the most poignant time of their lives.

"Do you want me?" he whispered against her lips. "Because I want you. Right here."

"The first time…was right here," she breathed, jerking a little when his hand eased between them to work at the pearly buttons down the front of her gray dress.

"It's handy." He chuckled, the sound rich and deep with love. "But there's always the carpet."

Her eyes searched his. "How kinky."

"Not at all. It's thick and soft…and there's no one to see us. And just to make sure…"

He got up, still smiling, and went to close and lock the door. He took off his shirt, watching the way her eyes went to the thick curling hair that arrowed down to the belt of his jeans. He liked the way she looked at him. Her eyes grew dark and soft and faintly sensuous.

He drew her up from the sofa, putting her hands on his chest, smoothing them over the warm, pulsating muscle. "Is it dangerous for the baby?" he asked softly.

She shook her head and pressed her lips against him. "Not if you're gentle. And when have you ever hurt me?"

"No regrets, Shelby?" he asked, hesitating.

She reached up to put her mouth against his. "Not even one."

His hands caught her hips and pulled them into his, moving her body with his so that she felt the force of his need. Her body reacted to it in a now familiar way and she reached up to get closer, signaling her hunger in subtle ways.

She kissed him until her lips grew swollen and tender, until her body began to feel the familiar hot shakiness that he aroused so easily in her.

He eased her down onto the carpet, sliding alongside her easily. He had her dress unbuttoned and her undergarments out of the way with lazy skill, and then she felt his mouth, and all her inhibitions went out the window.

She held his mouth against her, drowning in its moist caresses, loving the way he was with her. There had never been any fear of intimacy since their first time. Her body knew what kind of pleasure lay ahead, and now it reacted with delight, not apprehension.

For long, lazy minutes, he aroused her, not satisfied until she was trembling from head to toe and completely at his mercy. Only then did he undress himself, feasting on her soft curves and creamy skin while he discarded the rest of his clothing and lay back down beside her.

She looked up with misty eyes as he arched above her, catching his weight on his powerful arms, and she felt the exquisite tracing of his skin on hers as he eased down over her.

Her breath jerked at the first touch of him, and he laughed wickedly.

"It shouldn't shock you anymore," he whispered at her lips as he moved even closer. "You're an old married woman now."

"It isn't shock, it's...pleasure!" She clutched at him as he began to move. She buried her mouth against his shoulder, moaning again as his body merged so gently with hers. "Justin!"

"I love you," he whispered softly. "I've never really shown you how much, but now I'm going to. Lie still for me, little one. Let me take you straight into the sun." He eased his mouth over hers, and began to speak to her in husky whispers, in fluent Spanish. Love words. Descriptive words that he punctuated with slow caresses and tender tracings that made her weep with new pleasure. There was no holding back this time, no hidden worry, no barrier. He adjusted his movements to the needs of her body, taking his time, treating her with exquisite tenderness. And somewhere in the slow fire of it, she heard her voice cry out as she followed him into the whirlwind of fulfillment.

She couldn't stop trembling afterward. She clung to his shoulders, trying to keep her breathing steady, her heartbeat from shaking her. But he seemed just as affected, which made it less inhibiting.

"It's all right." He soothed her with his hands, kissing her face gently with lips that adored her. "It's all right. It's just the shock of coming down from such a height, sweetheart," he breathed. "I feel it, too."

"It's never been like this before," she whispered brokenly.

"But we never made love like this before," he whispered back. He lifted his head to search her dazed eyes. "Not this completely."

She touched his mouth with trembling fingers, lost in him, totally his. "I don't want to stop."

"Neither do I," he whispered softly. "We don't have to. We're alone in the house, with nothing else to do. We'll go upstairs and see if we can top what we've just had together."

He got up slowly, picked her up and started for the door.

"Justin, our clothes," she whispered, glancing back at the very evident turmoil of their garments leaving a visible trail.

He balanced her on his leg and unlocked the door. He opened it and started up the long staircase with her cradled against his damp, hair-roughened chest. "They'll still be there when we get back," he promised.

"But we don't have any clothes on," she protested.

He looked down at the pretty pink body in his arms with pure pride of possession. "I noticed."

"But Maria and Lopez…"

"…won't be back tonight." He put his mouth over hers. After a few seconds of it, she began to cling to him, loving the feel of him against her soft bareness. Loving, she thought while she could, was the most incredible pleasure. She kissed him back, all thought of arguing gone from her whirling mind.

It was longer the second time. He drew it out, his voice soft and slow, speaking partly in Spanish as he taught her new words and coached her in their enunciation. And all the while, he touched her, adored her with his hands and his eyes, whispered all she meant to him, how pleased he was about the baby they'd made. They reached heights they'd never scaled, and it was almost dark when they awoke in each other's arms.

"We slept," she murmured.

"No wonder." He grinned down at her, laughing when she blushed.

"I'm thirsty," she whispered.

"So am I." He got up, stretching lazily while her eyes adored his blatant nudity. "How about something cold and icy? And something to nibble on?"

"That would be lovely." She moved against the sheets, her eyes sultry. "Don't be long."

He chuckled. "I'll be back before you miss me."

He looked around for something to put on. His clothes were downstairs. Finally he went into the bathroom and came out with a huge colored beach towel with a giant frog on it. It was her bedroom he'd carried her to, and there was a noticeable shortage of male clothing.

"Damned flashy thing," he muttered, glaring playfully at her as he wrapped it around his hips. "You couldn't buy a plain one, I don't suppose?"

"I like frogs," she murmured.

He arched an eyebrow and, ignoring Shelby's giggles, went downstairs.

He filled two glasses with ice and sweetened tea from the refrigerator, made ham sandwiches, and put it all on a tray. He went out of the kitchen into the hall and paused at the foot of the staircase to adjust his slipping towel when the front door suddenly opened and Calhoun walked in.

He stopped dead, staring at his taciturn, very dignified brother standing in the hall with a giant frog towel wrapped around his lean hips. Justin was carrying a tray full of food and drink and he looked...strange.

"I thought you and Shelby were coming to supper," Calhoun began.

"Supper?" Justin echoed.

"Supper. It's almost seven. You didn't call and your phone seems to be off the hook. We were afraid something might have happened, so I came over to see about you."

Justin blinked. He'd taken the phone off the hook when he'd carried Shelby upstairs. He looked down at his towel. "Nothing's wrong. I was, uh, just taking a bath," he improvised, a little embarrassed at being caught in such a compromising situation even in his own home.

Calhoun noticed the open door of the living room and the trail of clothing. "In the living room?" he asked. "And since when do you wear dresses?"

Justin glared at him, his lips in a thin line. "I was sorting clothes at the same time. Then I got hungry."

"You were invited to supper."

"I got hungry first. I was going to have a bite to eat before I started getting ready." His complexion had gone ruddy by now.

Calhoun was grinning from ear to ear. "In the shower?"

"I was going to eat first," Justin said stubbornly.

"Where's Shelby?" Calhoun asked curiously.

Justin cleared his throat. "Upstairs. She was tired."

Just then, a plaintive voice came from upstairs. "Justin, are you ever coming back?" Shelby moaned. "I'm lonely."

Justin's face went scarlet. "I'll be right there!" he called tersely. He glared harder at Calhoun. "She's taking a shower, too."

Calhoun had to stifle laughter. He grinned knowingly at his older brother and turned on his heel. "When you finish your snack in the shower and get through sorting clothes, come on over and we'll feed you." He glanced at the towel. "Better put on some pants first, though, we wouldn't want to shock Abby. Honest to God, Justin, a frog?"

"It was the only damned thing I could find, and what's it to you?" Justin demanded hotly.

"Oh, I think it suits you," Calhoun replied. "I like frogs."

"We forgot the time," Justin said stiffly. "We'll be there in about thirty minutes, if it's convenient."

"No rush." Calhoun grinned wickedly. "If you think the living-room carpet is a good place, you ought to try it in a whirlpool bath," he murmured, and got out quick, because Justin looked torn between shock and homicide.

Justin carried the tray upstairs, his dignity bruised, and put it on the bedside table.

"Ice tea! I'm parched." Shelby laughed and picked up her glass to drink thirstily. "I heard voices."

"Calhoun came to see where we were," Justin muttered. "We were invited to supper, remember?"

"I didn't think about it," Shelby confessed.

"Neither did I. We can go in a half hour. Still want a snack first?"

"Maybe we'd better wait. We can always have them for a bedtime snack. I'll wrap them up and put them in the refrigerator when I've dressed." She looked at her husband lovingly. "Calhoun and Abby are married, too," she reminded him. "It's not so shocking to be caught spending the afternoon in bed with your wife, is it?"

He shifted. "No. But it's uncomfortable," he confessed

with a wry glance. "Six years of celibacy makes a man secretive, I guess."

"Six years." She reached up and kissed him very tenderly. "I thought I'd made you too bitter to sleep with anyone else. But it wasn't that at all, was it, Justin?" she asked quietly.

He touched her fingers to his lips. "I didn't want anyone else," he said with a sigh. "I loved you too much. It was you or nobody."

She had to bite her lip to stem the tears. "That's how I felt. I tried so hard to protect you," she whispered.

"I was doing the same thing for you, when we got married. I suppose both of us went overboard, though."

"But no more." She smiled. "Now we'll use our protective instincts on our baby."

"That sounds like a good idea." He bent and kissed her. "We'd better get dressed and go see the in-laws, little mama," he murmured. "Before they come back."

"It was nice of Abby to invite us."

"Yes. I hope you feel up to what's coming," he added. "Knowing Calhoun, it's going to be a trying supper."

She laughed, hiding her face against him. "I love you."

"I love you, too, honey." He got up, frog and all. "Shelby, would you have told me about the baby if Calhoun hadn't gotten me to the airport on time?"

She nodded. "It was your right. I wasn't really leaving you, Justin, I just needed a little time to think things through. I'd have come back. I'm not equipped to live without you any more." She stared at him hungrily. "Were you coming after me?"

"Of course." He chuckled. "I figured I'd spend several months searching the city for you, but that wouldn't have stopped me. I felt bad about what I'd said and done. But it was because I loved you that I'd have gone looking for you, honey, not out of guilt."

"Yes. Now I know." She sighed lazily, so much in love with him that she felt near to bursting with it. "I could eat a horse."

"I'll phone Abby to cook one. Get up and get your clothes on, woman. I'm starving."

"Don't look at me. Not eating was your idea."

She got out of bed and he swung her up against him, his eyes full of tenderness. "It sure was. I take these spells from time to time." He bent and kissed her. "Will you mind?"

She linked her arms around his neck and held him closer. "I won't mind at all."

Outside the night sky grew even darker, and a few miles down the road, Abby was starting to reheat the meat and vegetables in her Irish stew one last time. She'd tried to tell Calhoun that champagne didn't really go with such a simple dish, but he was too busy chilling it to listen. So Abby just laughed, and got down her best champagne flutes. Maybe he was right at that. It did seem like a good night for a celebration.

* * * * *